"The tension never lets up, building page by page to a nail-biting, hair-raising finale. The author is a master of sheer fright."

—*Florida Times-Union*

"Suspense that's almost discomfiting in its intensity. The characters are so fully dimensioned that they lift the book from the thriller genre to the rarefied atmosphere of the mainstream novel."

—*Durham Morning Herald*

"An eerie atmosphere . . . suspense is taut to the very end. Not a book to be read when one is alone at night."

—*The Buffalo News*

"Sinister and spine-tingling . . . page-turning excitement!"

—*The Spectator*

"The writing is elegantly spare and powerful, far better than you expect from a thriller. The characters are convincingly drawn, and the story is not only spine-tingling—it gives you an almost lethal shock."

—*San Francisco Chronicle*

DEAN R. KOONTZ

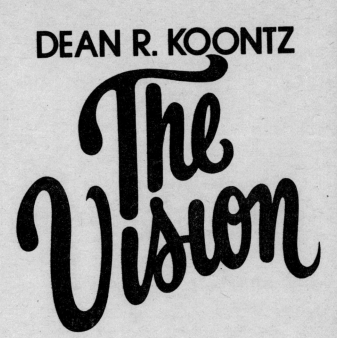

The Vision

BERKLEY BOOKS, NEW YORK

This book is for
Claire M. Smith
with love
and gratitude

This Berkley book contains the complete
text of the original edition.
It has been completely reset in a typeface
designed for easy reading and was printed
from new film.

THE VISION

A Berkley Book / published by arrangement with
G. P. Putnam's Sons

PRINTING HISTORY
Putnam's edition / November 1977
Berkley edition / March 1986

ISBN: 0-425-09860-5

A BERKLEY BOOK ® TM 757,375
Berkley Books are published by The Berkley Publishing Group,
200 Madison Avenue, New York, NY 10016.
The name "BERKLEY" and the "B" logo
are trademarks belonging to Berkley Publishing Corporation.

PRINTED IN THE UNITED STATES OF AMERICA

20   19   18   17   16   15   14   13   12

Monday,
December 21

1

"GLOVES OF BLOOD."

The woman raised her hands and stared at them, stared *through* them.

Her voice was soft but tense. "Blood on his hands." Her own hands were clean and pale.

Her husband leaned forward from the back seat of the patrol car. "Mary?"

She didn't respond.

"Mary, can you hear me?"

"Yes."

"Whose blood do you see?"

"I'm not sure."

"The victim's blood?"

"No. In fact . . . it's his own."

"The killer's?"

"Yes."

"He has his own blood on his hands?"

"That's right," she said.

"He's hurt himself?"

"But not badly."

"How?"

"I don't know."

"Try to get inside of him."

"I am already."

"Get deeper."

"I'm not a mind reader."

"I know that, darling. But you're the next best thing."

The perspiration on Mary Bergen's face was like the ceramic glaze on the plaster countenance of an altar saint. Her smooth skin gleamed in the green light from the instrument panel. Her dark eyes also shone, but they were unfocused, blank.

Suddenly she leaned forward and shuddered.

In the driver's seat Chief of Police Harley Barnes shifted uneasily. He flexed his big hands on the steering wheel.

"He's sucking the wound," she said. "Sucking his own blood."

After thirty years of police work, Barnes didn't expect to be surprised or frightened. Now, in a single evening, he had been surprised more than once and had felt his heartbeat accelerate with fear.

The tree-shrouded streets were as familiar to him as the contours of his own face. However, tonight, cloaked in a rainstorm, they seemed menacing. The tires hissed on the slick pavement. The windshield wipers thumped, an eerie metronome.

The woman beside Barnes was distraught, but her appearance was less disturbing than the changes she had wrought inside the patrol car. The humid air became clearer when she entered her trance. He was certain he was not imagining that. The ordinary sounds of the storm and the car were overlaid with the soft humming of ghost frequencies. He sensed an indescribable power radiating from her. He was a practical man, not at all superstitious. But he could not deny what he felt so strongly.

She bent as far toward the dashboard as her seat belt would allow. She hugged herself and groaned as if she were having labor pains.

Max Bergen reached out from the rear seat, touched her.

She murmured and relaxed slightly.

His hand looked enormous on her slender shoulder. He was tall, angular, hard-muscled, hard-faced, forty years old, ten years older than his wife. His eyes were his most arresting feature; they were gray, cold, humorless.

Chief Barnes had never seen him smile. Clearly, Bergen harbored powerful and complex feelings for Mary, but he gave no indication that he felt anything but contempt for the rest of the world.

The woman said, "Turn at the next corner."

Barnes braked gently. "Left or right?"

"Right," she said.

Well-kept, thirty-year-old stucco houses and bungalows, most of them California-Spanish in style, lay on both sides of the street. Yellow lights glowed vaguely behind drapes that had been drawn against the chill of the damp December night. The road was much darker than the one they had left. Sodium vapor lamps stood only at the corners, and purple-black, rain-pooled shadows filled the long blocks between them.

After he made the turn, Barnes drove no faster than ten miles an hour. From the woman's attitude, he gathered that the chase would end nearby.

Mary sat up straight. Her voice was louder and clearer than it had been since she began to use her strange talent, her clairvoyance. "I get an impression . . . of a . . . a fence. Yes . . . I see it now . . . he's cut his hand . . . on a fence."

Max stroked her hair. "And it's not a serious wound?"

"No . . . just a cut . . . his thumb . . . deep . . . but not disabling." She raised one thin hand, forgot what she meant to do with it, let it flutter back into her lap.

"But if he's bleeding from a deep cut, won't he give up tonight?" Max asked.

"No," she said.

"You're sure?"

"He'll go on."

"The bastard's killed five women so far," Barnes said. "Some of them fought like hell, scratched him and cut him and even tore out his hair. He doesn't give up easily."

Ignoring the policeman, Max soothed his wife, caressed her face with one hand and prompted her with another question. "What kind of fence do you see?"

"Chain-link," she said. "Sharp and unfinished at the top."

"Is it high?"

"Five feet."

"What does it surround?"

"A yard."

"Storage yard?"

"No. Behind a house."

"Can you see the house?"

"Yes."

"What's it like?"

"It's a two-story."

"Stucco?"

"Yes."

"What about the roof?"

"Spanish tile."

"Any unique features?"

"I can't quite see . . ."

"A veranda?"

"No."

"A courtyard maybe?"

"No. But I see . . . a winding tile walkway."

"Front or back?"

"Out front of the house."

"Any trees?"

"Matched magnolias . . . on either side of the walk."

"Anything else?"

"A few small palms . . . farther back."

Harley Barnes squinted through the rain-dappled windshield. He was searching for a pair of magnolias.

Initially he had been skeptical. In fact, he'd been certain the Bergens were frauds. He played his role in the charade because the *mayor* was a believer. The mayor brought them to town and insisted the police cooperate with them.

Barnes had read about psychic detectives, of course, and most especially about that famous Dutch clairvoyant, Peter Hurkos. But using ESP to track down a psychopathic killer, to catch him in the act? He didn't put much faith in that.

Or do I? he wondered. This woman was so lovely, charming, earnest, so convincing that perhaps she'd made a believer of him. If she hasn't, he thought, why am I looking for magnolia trees?

She made a sound like an animal caught in a sawtoothed trap for a long time. Not a screech of agony, but a nearly inaudible mewl.

When an animal made that noise, it meant, "This still hurts, but I'm resigned to it now."

Many years ago, as a boy in Minnesota, Barnes had hunted and trapped. It was that same pitiful, stifled moan of the wounded prey that caused him to give up his sport.

Until tonight, he had never heard precisely the same sound issue from a human being. Apparently, as she used her talent to zero in on the killer, she suffered from contact with his deranged mind.

Barnes shivered.

"Mary," her husband said. "What's the matter?"

"I see him . . . at the back door of the house. His hand on the door . . . and blood . . . his blood on a white door frame. He's talking to himself."

"What's he saying?"

"I don't . . ."

"Mary?"

"He's saying filthy things about the woman."

"The woman in the house—the one he's after tonight?"

"Yes."

"He knows her?"

"No. She's a stranger . . . random target. But he's been . . . watching her . . . watching her for several days . . . knows her habits and routines."

With those last few words she slumped against the door. She took several deep breaths. She was forced to relax periodically to regroup her energies if she were to maintain the psychic thread. For some clairvoyants, Barnes knew, the visions came without strain, virtually without effort; but apparently not for this one.

Phantom voices whispered and crackled, came and went in staccato bursts on the police radio.

The wind carried fine sheets of rain across the roadway.

The wettest rainy season in years, Barnes thought. Twenty years ago it would have seemed normal. But California had steadily become a drought state. This much rain was unnatural now. Like everything else that's happening tonight, he thought.

Waiting for Mary to speak, he slowed to less than five miles an hour.

Matched magnolia trees flanking a winding tile walk . . .

He found it taxing to see what lay in the headlights directly in front of him, and extremely difficult to discern the landscaping on either side. They might already have passed the magnolias.

Brief as it was, Mary Bergen's hesitation elicited Dan Goldman's first words in more than an hour. "We haven't much time left, Mrs. Bergen."

Goldman was a reliable young officer, the chief's most trusted subordinate. He was sitting beside Max Bergen, behind Barnes, his eyes fixed on the woman.

Goldman believed in psychic powers. He was impressionable. And as Barnes could see in the rearview mirror, the events of the evening had left a haunted look on his broad, plain face.

"We don't have much time," Goldman said again. "If this madman's already at the woman's back door—"

Abruptly, Mary turned to him. Her voice was freighted with concern. "Don't get out of this car tonight—not until the man is caught."

"What do you mean?" Goldman asked.

"If you try to help capture him, you'll be hurt."

"He'll kill me?"

She shuddered convulsively. New beads of sweat popped out at her hairline.

Barnes felt perspiration trickle down his face, too.

She said to Goldman, "He'll stab you . . . with the same knife he's used on all the women . . . hurt you badly . . . but not kill you." Closing her eyes, speaking between clenched teeth, she said, *"Stay in the car!"*

"Harley?" Goldman asked worriedly.

"It'll be all right," Barnes assured him.

"You'd better listen to her," Max told Goldman. "Don't leave the car."

"If I need you," Barnes told Goldman, "you'll come with me. No one will be hurt." He was concerned that the woman was undermining his authority. He glanced at her. "We need a number for the house you've described, a street address."

"Don't press," her husband said sharply. With everyone but Mary he had a voice like two rough steel bars scraped against each other. "It won't do any good whatsoever to press her. It'll only interfere."

"It's okay, Max," she said.

"But I've told them before," he said.

She faced front once more. "I see . . . the rear door of the house. It's open."

"Where's the man, the killer?" Max asked.

"He's standing in a dark room . . . small . . . the laundry room . . . that's what it is . . . the laundry room behind the kitchen."

"What's he doing?"

"He's opening another door . . . to the kitchen . . . no one in there . . . a dim light on over the gas range . . . a few dirty dishes on the table . . . he's standing . . . just standing there and listening . . . left hand in a fist to stop the thumb from bleeding . . . listening . . . Benny Goodman music on a stereo in the living room . . ." Touching Barnes' arm, a new and urgent tone in her voice, she said, "Just two blocks from here. On the right. The second house . . . no, the third from the corner."

"You're positive?"

"For God's sake, *hurry!*"

Am I about to make a fool of myself? Barnes wondered. If I take her seriously and she's wrong, I'll be the punch line of bad jokes for the rest of my career.

Nevertheless, he switched on the siren and tramped the accelerator to the floor. The tires spun on the pavement. With a squeal of rubber, the car surged forward.

Breathlessly she said, "I still see . . . he's crossing the kitchen . . . moving slowly . . ."

If she's faking all this, Barnes thought, she's a hell of a good actress.

The Ford raced along the poorly lit street. Rain snapped against the windshield. They swept through a four-way stop, then toward another.

"Listening . . . listening between steps . . . cautious . . . nervous . . . taking the knife out of his overcoat pocket . . . smiling at the sharp edge of the blade . . . such a big knife . . ."

In the block she had specified they fishtailed to a stop at the curb in front of the third house on the right: a pair of matched magnolias, a winding walk, a two-story stucco with lights on downstairs.

"Goddamn," Goldman said, more reverently than not. "It fits her description perfectly."

2

BARNES GOT OUT of the car as the siren moaned into silence.

The revolving red emergency lights cast frenetic shadows on the wet pavement. Another black-and-white had pulled in behind the first, adding its beacons to the cascade of bloody color.

Several men had already climbed out of the second car. Two uniformed officers, Malone and Gonzales, hurried toward Barnes. Mayor Henderson, round and shiny in his black vinyl rain slicker, looked like a balloon bouncing along the street. Close behind him was whip-thin little Harry Oberlander, Henderson's most vocal critic on the city council.

The last man was Alan Tanner, Mary Tanner Bergen's brother. Ordinarily, he would have been in the first car with his sister; but he and Max had argued earlier and were keeping away from each other.

"Malone, Gonzales . . . split up," Barnes said. "Flank the house. Go around it and meet at the rear door. I'll take the front. Now move it!"

"What about me?" Goldman asked.

Barnes sighed. "You better stay here."

Goldman was relieved.

Taking the .357 Magnum from his holster, Barnes hurried up the tile walk. The name "Harrington" was printed on the mailbox. As he rang the doorbell, the rain suddenly lost most of its power. The downpour became a drizzle.

Alerted by the sirens, she had watched his approach from the window. She answered the door at once.

"Mrs. Harrington?"

"*Miss* Harrington. After the divorce, I took my maiden name."

She was a petite blonde in her early forties. She had a lush figure, but she wasn't carrying any excess weight.

Apparently, her primary occupation was taking good care of herself. Although she wore jeans and a T-shirt and didn't appear to be going out for the evening, her hair looked as if it had been styled minutes ago; her false eyelashes and makeup were perfectly applied; and her nails were freshly painted the color of orange sherbet.

"Are you alone?" Barnes asked.

Lasciviously, she said, "Why do you ask?"

"This is police business, Miss Harrington."

"What a shame." She had a drink in one hand. He knew it wasn't her first of the night.

"Are you alone?" he asked again.

"I live by myself."

"Is everything all right?"

"I don't like living by myself."

"That's not what I meant. Are you all right? Is there any trouble here?"

She looked at the revolver that he held at his side. "Should there be?"

Exasperated with her and with having to talk above the loud swing music that boomed behind her, he said, "Maybe. We think your life's in danger."

She laughed.

"I know it sounds melodramatic, but—"

"Who's after me?"

"The newspapers call him 'The Slasher.'"

She frowned, then instantly dropped the expression as if she had remembered that frowning caused wrinkles. "You're kidding."

"We have reason to believe you're his target tonight."

"What reason?"

"A clairvoyant."

"A what?"

Malone entered the living room behind her and switched off the stereo.

She turned, surprised.

Malone said, "We found something, Chief."

Barnes stepped into the house, uninvited. "Yeah?"

"The back door was open."

"Did you leave it open?" Barnes asked the woman.

"On a night like this?"

"Was it locked?"

"I don't know."

"There's blood on the door frame," Malone said. "More of it on the door between the laundry room and the kitchen."

"But he's gone?"

"Must have run when he heard the sirens."

Sweating, aware of his too-rapid heartbeat, wondering how to fit clairvoyance and the other psychic phenomena into his previously uncomplicated view of life, Barnes followed the younger officer through the kitchen and laundry room. The woman stayed close beside him, asking questions that he didn't bother answering.

Hector Gonzales was waiting at the back door.

"There's an alleyway behind that chain-link fence," Barnes told him. "Get back there and search for our man, two blocks in each direction."

The woman said, "I'm bewildered."

So am I, Barnes thought.

To Malone he said, "Beat the shrubs around both sides of the house. And check out that line of bushes near the fence."

"Right."

"And both of you, keep your guns drawn."

* * *

Waiting by the squad cars in front of the house, Harry Oberlander was baiting the mayor. He shook his head as if the very sight of Henderson amazed him. "What a mayor you are," he said with heavy sarcasm. "Hiring a witch to do police work."

Henderson responded like a weary giant spotting yet one more tiny challenger with delusions of grandeur. "She's not a witch."

"Don't you know there's no such thing as a witch?"

"Like I said, Councilman, she's not a witch."

"She's a fake."

"A clairvoyant."

"Clairvoyant, shmairvoyant."

"So clever with language."

"It's just a fancier name for a witch."

Dan Goldman watched Oberlander, as weary of the argument as the mayor was. There are no worse enemies, he thought, than two men who used to be best friends. He would have to separate them if Harry became dissatisfied with words and started to throw a few fast but largely ineffective punches at the mayor's well-padded belly. It had happened before.

"You know why I sold you my half of the furniture business?" Oberlander asked Henderson.

"You sold out because you didn't have any vision," Henderson said smugly.

"Vision, smision. I sold out because I knew a superstitious fool like you would run it into the ground sooner or later."

"The store's more profitable now than ever before," Henderson said.

"Luck! Blind luck!"

Fortunately, before the first punch could be thrown, Harley Barnes came to the front door of the house and shouted, "It's all right. Come on."

"Now we'll see who's the fool," Henderson said. "They must have caught him." He ran across the sidewalk and the slippery wet lawn with that unexpected grace peculiar to certain very fat men.

Oberlander scurried after him, an angry mouse snapping at the heels of a behemoth.

Suppressing a laugh, Goldman followed.

* * *

Alan Tanner sat behind the steering wheel in order to be in the front seat with his sister. When he saw Harley Barnes at the door of the house, he said, "Did they get the killer, Mary?"

"I don't know," she said. Her voice was hollow; she sounded drained.

"Wouldn't there have been a shot?"

"I don't know."

"There would have been *some* commotion."

"I guess so."

From the rear seat Max said urgently, "Mary, is it safe for Goldman?"

She sighed and shook her head and pressed her fingertips to her eyes. "I really can't say. I've lost the thread. I don't see anything else."

Max rolled down his window. The damp air carried his voice well. "Hey, Goldman!"

The officer was halfway across the lawn. He stopped and looked back.

"Maybe you'd better stay here," Max said.

"Harley wants me," Goldman said.

"Remember what my wife told you."

"It's all right," Goldman said. "Nothing's going to happen. They caught him."

"Are you sure of that?" Max asked.

But Goldman had already turned and was headed for the house again.

Alan said, "Mary?"

"Hmmmm?"

"Are you feeling well?"

"Well enough."

"You don't sound good."

"Just tired."

"He presses you much too hard," Alan told her solicitously. He didn't even glance back at Max. He spoke as if he and his sister were alone in the car. "He doesn't realize how fragile you are."

"I'm okay," she said.

Alan wouldn't quit. "He doesn't know how to prompt you, how to help you refine the visions. He doesn't have any finesse. He always presses too hard."

You creepy little bastard, Max thought, staring hard at his brother-in-law.

For Mary's sake, he said nothing. She was easily upset when the two men in her life argued. She preferred to pretend that they were charmed by each other. And while she never entirely took Alan's side, she always blamed Max when the argument became particularly bitter.

To get his mind off Alan, he studied the house. A shaft of light thrust through the open door, silhouetted some of the dense lumps of shrubbery. "Maybe we should lock the car doors," he said.

Mary turned sideways in her seat and stared at him. "Lock the doors?"

"For protection."

"I don't understand."

"For protection from what?" Alan asked.

"The cops are all up at the house, and none of us has a weapon."

"You think we'll need one?"

"It's a possibility."

"Are *you* getting psychic now?" Alan asked.

Max forced himself to smile. "Nothing psychic about it, I'm afraid. Just good sense." He locked his and Mary's doors, and when he saw that Alan wouldn't cooperate, he latched both doors on the driver's side.

"Feel safe now?" Alan asked.

Max watched the house.

* * *

Barnes, Henderson, and Oberlander crowded into the laundry room to examine the smears of blood that the killer had left behind.

Miss Harrington squeezed in beside the chief, determined not to miss any of the excitement. She appeared to be delighted to have been the madman's choice.

Dan Goldman preferred to remain in the kitchen. As Barnes explained how these few pieces of physical evidence matched the clairvoyant's visions, the mayor would begin to gloat. Harry Oberlander would be embarrassed, then outraged. The nasty bickering would quickly escalate into a loud and vicious exchange. Goldman had had enough of that.

Besides, the big kitchen deserved an appreciative inspection. It had been designed and furnished by someone who enjoyed cooking and who could afford the best.

Miss Harrington? Goldman wondered. She didn't seem to be a woman who would welcome the opportunity to pass several hours in front of a stove. No doubt, the cook had been her ex-husband.

Quite a lot of money had been spent to create a professional kitchen with a country home atmosphere. The floor was of Mexican tile with brown grouting. There were oak cabinets with porcelain hardware, white ceramic counter tops, two standard ovens and a microwave oven, two large refrigerator-freezers, two double sinks, an island cooking surface, a built-in appliance center, and a dozen other machines, tools, and gadgets.

Goldman liked to cook, but he had to make do with a battered gas range and the cheapest pots, pans, and utensils on the market.

His envious appraisal of the kitchen was interrupted when, from the corner of his eye, he saw a door opening beside and somewhat behind him, no more than a yard away. It had been ajar when he'd entered the room, but he hadn't thought anything of it. Now he turned and saw a man in a raincoat stepping out of a pantry that was lined with canned goods. The stranger's left hand was bloody, the thumb tucked into a tight fist.

She was right, Goldman thought. *Christ!*

In his raised right hand the killer held a butcher knife by its thick wooden handle.

Time ceased to have meaning for Goldman. Each second extended itself a hundredfold. Each moment expanded like a soap bubble, encapsulated him, separated him from the rest of the world where clocks maintained their proper pace.

In the distance Henderson and Oberlander were arguing again. It didn't seem possible that they were only one room away. They sounded extremely odd, as if they had been recorded at seventy-eight revolutions per minute and were being played back at forty-five.

The stranger stepped forward. Light slithered along the well-honed edge of the blade.

As if moving against incredible resistance, Goldman reached for the revolver at his hip.

The knife ripped into his chest. High and to the left. Too deep to contemplate.

Curiously he felt no pain, but the front of his shirt was suddenly soaked with blood.

Mary Bergen, he thought. How could you know? What are you?

He unsnapped his holster.

Too slow. Too damned slow!

Although he didn't realize that the blade had been wrenched loose from him, he watched with horror as the knife arched down again. The stranger jerked the weapon free, and Goldman collapsed against the wall, framed by a spray of his own blood.

There was still no pain, but his strength was draining out of him as if there was a tap in his ankle.

Can't fall down, he told himself. Don't dare fall down. Wouldn't have a chance.

But the killer was finished. He turned and ran toward the dining room.

Clutching his wounds with his weakening left hand, Goldman staggered after the man. By the time he reached the archway and leaned against it to catch his breath, the killer was nearly to the living room. Goldman had the gun out of his holster, but he found it too heavy to lift. To get Harley's attention, he fired into the floor. With that explosion time resumed its normal flow and pain finally smashed through his chest, and suddenly he found it difficult to breathe and his knees buckled and he went down.

* * *

Alan interrupted himself in the middle of a sentence. "What was that?"

"A shot," Max said.

Mary said, "Something's happened to Goldman. I know it as sure as I'm sitting here."

Someone rushed out of the house. His raincoat flapped and billowed like a cape.

"That's *him,*" Mary said.

When he saw the squad cars, the man stopped. Confused, he looked left and right, didn't seem to trust either route, and turned back toward the house.

Harley Barnes appeared at the open door. Even from where he sat, even through the dirty window and the shadows and the thin rain, Max could see the oversized revolver in the cop's hand. Obscenely, fire licked from the muzzle.

The madman spun as if in an inept ballet, then fell, rolled along the walk. Surprisingly, he scrambled to his feet and headed for the street again. He hadn't been hit. If he'd taken a bullet from the .357 Magnum, he would have stayed down.

Max was certain of that. He knew a great deal about firearms. He owned an extensive collection of guns.

Barnes fired again.

"Dammit!" Max said furiously. "Small town cops. Overarmed and undertrained. If that ass misses his man, he'll kill one of us!"

The third shot took the killer in the back as he reached the sidewalk.

Max could tell two things about the bullet. Because it didn't exit from the killer's chest and pierce the car window, it had been insufficiently packed with powder. It was designed for use on crowded streets; it had just enough punch to stop a guilty man without passing through him and harming others. Secondly, considering how it had lifted the man off his feet, the bullet was surely hollow-nosed.

After an instant of graceless flight, the killer slammed hard into the police cruiser. For a moment he clung to Mary's door. He slid down until he was peering at her. "Mary Bergen . . ." His voice was hoarse. He clawed at the window. "Mary Bergen." Blood spouted from his mouth and painted the glass.

Mary screamed.

The corpse dropped to the sidewalk.

3

THE AMBULANCE CARRYING Dan Goldman turned the corner as fast as it could without flipping on its side.

Max hoped the siren was fading more rapidly than the young patrolman's life.

On the sidewalk the dead man lay on his back. He stared at the sky and waited patiently for the coroner.

"She's upset about the killer knowing her name," Alan said.

"He saw her picture in her newspaper column," Max said. "Somehow he heard she was coming to town to find him."

"But only the mayor and the city council knew. And the cops."

"Somehow this guy heard. He knew she was in town and he recognized her. There's nothing supernatural about it. Is that what she thinks?"

"I know there's a simple explanation, and you know it. Deep down she knows it, too. But considering what she's seen in her life, she can't help wondering. Now, I've talked to Barnes. He can spare a man and a car for us. We should get Mary back to the hotel so she can lie down."

"We will," Max said, "when everything's settled with the mayor."

"That could be hours."

"Half an hour at most," Max said. "Now, if that's all you wanted to talk to me about—"

"She's dead tired."

"Aren't we all? She'll be okay."

"The loving husband."

"Go to hell."

They were standing behind the first squad car. Mary still sat inside with her eyes closed and her hands folded in her lap.

The rain had stopped. The air was moist and fragrant.

Glancing nervously at the people who had come out of their

homes to gather around the pathetic scene, Alan said, "There'll be reporters here any minute. I don't think she should have to put up with a lot of reporters tonight."

Max knew what his brother-in-law wanted. Tomorrow Alan began a two-week vacation. Before leaving he hoped to have a final conversation with his sister, just the two of them, one last uninterrupted hour in which to convince her that she had married a man who was terribly wrong for her.

His fists were the only tools Max had to prevent this domestic sedition. He was six inches taller and forty pounds heavier than Alan. He had shoulders and biceps designed for dock work, and the outsized hands of a basketball star. However, he knew that split lips and broken teeth and a cracked jaw would silence Alan Tanner only temporarily. Short of killing him, there was no way to put an end to his meddling.

Anyway, Max no longer tried to solve his problems with his fists. He had promised Mary and himself that his violent days were gone forever.

Other than strength and the will to use it, Alan had all the weapons in this intensely personal war. Not the least of them was his appearance. He had black hair and blue eyes, like Mary. He was handsome, while Max was so rough-hewn that he barely avoided ugliness. Alan's powerfully sensuous features, highlighted by a look of boyish innocence, could affect even a sister.

Especially a sister.

Alan's voice was as sweet and persuasive as an actor's. He was able to create moods and build drama with his voice. He employed it subtly to gain Mary's sympathy and to cause her to look upon her new husband with mild, unconscious, but insidious displeasure.

Max knew his mind was better than average, but he also knew that Alan was his intellectual superior. It wasn't the voice alone that won arguments. There was wit behind those mellifluous tones.

And charm?

Whenever Alan needed it, charm oozed from him.

I'd like to roll him up tight like an empty tube of toothpaste, Max thought. Squeeze all the charm out of him and see if there's any truth behind it.

Most important of all, Alan and Mary had shared thirty years; he was thirty-three and, as an older brother, was welded to her by blood, common experience, more than a little tragedy, and three decades of day-to-day life.

As the crowd grew around him, Max watched yet another police car approach. He said, "You're right. She shouldn't be here any longer than necessary."

"Of course not."

"I'll take her to the hotel right away."

"You?" Alan asked, surprised. "You have to stay here."

"Why?"

"You know why."

"Tell me anyway."

Grudgingly, Alan said, "You're better at this than I am."

"Better at what?" Max asked.

"You know why you need to hear it? Because it's all you've got going for you. It's the only thing you can use to hold her."

"Better at what?"

"So insecure."

"Better at what!"

"You're better at getting the money. Does that satisfy you?"

Mary made a good living as the author of a syndicated newspaper column about psychic phenomena. She had also earned a lot of money with three best-selling books about her career, and she could have survived quite well on her speaking fees alone if she'd wanted.

Although she traveled extensively, aiding authorities with investigations of violent homicides whenever they asked her to do so, she didn't profit from any of that. She didn't charge for her visions. Once she helped a famous actress locate a hundred-thousand-dollar diamond necklace that was lost, and she took no fee. She never required more than expenses—airline tickets, car rentals, meals, and lodging—from those whom she assisted; and she refused even that much if she thought she'd been of little or no service.

When Max first came into her life, the collection of expense money was her brother's duty. But Alan had no talent or taste for quibbling with mayors, councilmen, and bureaucrats. As often as not, when Mary had done her work and the guilty man had been found, the local politicians who had summoned her tried to get rid of her without paying what they owed. Alan seldom pressured them. As a result, tens of thousands of dollars in expenses were lost each year; and although Mary earned considerable sums, she was slowly going broke.

Within two months following the wedding Max straightened out Mary's financial affairs. He renegotiated her contract with the lecture bureau and doubled her speaking fee. When her contract with the newspaper syndicate came due for renewal, he made a far more advantageous deal than she had thought possible. And he never failed to get a check for expenses.

"Well?" Alan said.

"All right. You take her back to the hotel. But remember what you said. I'm better at getting the money. And I always will be."

"Of course. You have a nose for it," Alan said. His smile had no warmth. "You sniffed out Mary's money pretty damned fast, didn't you?"

"Go," Max said.

"Too much truth in that for you?"

"Get out of here before you find yourself looking up your own ass for the rest of your life."

Alan blinked.

Max didn't.

Alan walked over to Harley Barnes.

Gradually Max became aware of a number of people in the crowd who were staring at him. He stared back at them, one at a time. Each grew self-conscious and turned away—but each looked at him again as soon as he moved his gaze.

None of them was close enough to have heard the argument. He realized that they were staring because his face was contorted by rage, because his shoulders were drawn up like those of a stalking panther, because his huge hands were in tight fists at his sides. He tried to relax, to let his shoulders fall. And he put his hands in the pockets of his raincoat so that no one could see he was too infuriated to uncurl them.

4

THE HOTEL ROOM had four ugly lamps with garishly patterned shades, but only one of them was on.

In a black vinyl armchair that stood on a swivel base Alan folded his hands around a glass of Scotch that he wasn't drinking. The light fell over him from the left, carving his face with sharp shadows.

Mary was sitting up in bed, on top of the covers, well out of the light. She wished Max would get back so they could go out for a late supper and a couple of drinks. She was hungry and tired and emotionally exhausted.

"Still have a headache?" Alan asked.

"The aspirin helped."

"You're drawn . . . so pale."

"There's nothing wrong that eight hours of sleep won't cure."

"I worry about you," he said.

She smiled affectionately. "You've always worried about me, dear. Even when we were children."

"I care about you very much."

"I know that."

"You're my sister. I love you."

"I know, but—"

"He presses you too hard."

"Not this again, Alan."

"He does."

"I wish you and Max could get along."

"So do I. But we never will."

"But *why?*"

"Because I know what he is."

"And what's that?"

"For one thing, he's so different from you," Alan said. "He's not as sensitive as you are. He's not as kind." He seemed to be pleading with her. "You're gentle, and he's—"

"He can be gentle, too."

"Can he?"

"With me he can. He's sweet."

"You're entitled to your opinion."

"Oh, thank you very much," she said sarcastically. Anger flared briefly in her but was quickly extinguished. She couldn't stay angry with Alan for more than a minute. Even a minute was stretching it.

"Mary, I don't want to argue with you."

"Then don't."

"We never had cross words, not in thirty years . . . until he came into the picture."

"I'm not up to this tonight."

"You're not up to anything because he presses you too hard and too fast when he's guiding you through your visions."

"He does it well."

"Not as well as I did it."

"At first he was too insistent," she admitted. "Too anxious. But not anymore."

Alan put down his Scotch, got up, turned his back on her. He went to the window. Moody silence enveloped him.

She closed her eyes and wished Max would get back.

After a minute Alan walked away from the window. He stood at the foot of the bed, staring down at her. "I'm afraid to go away on vacation."

Without opening her eyes, she said, "Afraid of what?"

"I don't want to leave you alone."

"I won't be alone. I'll be with Max."

"That's what I mean—alone with Max."

"Alan, for Christ's sake!"

"I mean it."

She opened her eyes, sat up straighter. "You're being silly. Ridiculous. I won't listen to any more of this."

"If I didn't care what happens to you, I could walk out right now. Whether you want to hear it or not, I'm going to say what I think is true about him."

She sighed.

"He's an opportunist," Alan said.

"So what?"

"He likes money."

"So do I. So do you."

"He likes it too much."

She smiled indulgently. "I'm not sure you can ever like it too much, dear."

"Don't you understand?"

"Enlighten me."

Alan hesitated. There was sadness in his beautiful eyes. "Max likes *other people's* money too much."

She stared at him, surprised. "Look . . . if you're saying he married me for my money—"

"That's precisely what I'm saying."

"Then it's *you* who's pressing me too hard." There was steel in her voice now.

He changed his tone with her, spoke softly. "All I'm trying to do is make you face facts. I don't—"

She raised herself up, away from the headboard. "Am I so ugly that no one would want me if I were poor?"

"You're beautiful. You know that."

She wasn't satisfied. "Then am I some mindless little twit who bores men to death?"

"Don't shout," Alan said. "Calm down. Please." He seemed genuinely grieved that he had hurt her. But he didn't change the subject. "Plenty of men would give everything they own to marry you. And for all the right reasons. Why you ever picked Max—"

"He was the first decent prospect, the first full-fledged man who asked."

"That's not true. I know of four others who asked."

"The first two were spineless wonders," she said. "The third one was about as gentle and considerate in bed as a bull is in the ring. The other one was virtually impotent. Max wasn't any of that. He was different, interesting, exciting."

"You didn't marry him because he was exciting, or because he was intelligent or mysterious or romantic. You married him because he was big, strong, and gruff. A perfect father image."

"Since when have you practiced psychiatry?"

She knew Alan didn't want to pick at her like this. He continued only because he felt she needed to hear it. He was being a conscientious big brother. Even though he was misguided, his intentions were admirable. If she hadn't been certain of that, she would have asked him to leave.

"I don't have to be a psychiatrist to know that you need to lean on someone. You always have. From the day you realized what your clairvoyance was, what it meant, you've been frightened of it, unable to deal with it yourself. You leaned on me for a while. But I wasn't tall enough or broad-shouldered enough to fill the role for long."

"Alan, for the first time in my life I have the urge to slap your face."

He came around and sat down on the edge of the bed. He took her left hand in both of his. "Mary, he was a newspaper hack, a washed up reporter who hadn't covered a major story in ten years. You knew him just six weeks before you were married."

"That's all the longer I *needed* to know him." She relaxed, squeezed Alan's hand. "It's working out fine, dear. You should be happy for me."

"You've only been married four months."

"Long enough to like him even better than I did when he proposed."

"He's a dangerous man. You know his past."

"A few fights in barrooms . . . and he doesn't go to barrooms anymore."

"It's not as innocent as that. He nearly killed some people in those brawls."

"When they've had too much to drink and are feeling mean, some men will go after the biggest man in the room. Max was a natural target. He didn't start any of those fights."

"So he says."

"No one ever pressed charges."

"Maybe they were afraid to."

"He's changed. What he needed was someone who loved him, someone he could feel responsible for. He needed me."

Alan nodded forlornly. "Want a drink?"

"I'll wait for Max."

He drank his Scotch in three swallows. "You're absolutely sure about him?"

"About Max? Positive."

He went to the window again, studied the night sky for a moment. "I don't think I'll be returning to work with you after my vacation."

She got up, went to him, took hold of his shoulder and turned him around. "Say again?"

"I'm a fifth wheel now."

"Nonsense. You take care of so much of my business—"

"That's nothing a secretary couldn't handle," Alan said. "Before Max, I was vital. I was your guide through the visions. But there's nothing important for me to do anymore. And I don't need this constant friction with Max."

"But what will you do?"

"I'm not sure. I think I'll start by taking two months vacation instead of two weeks. I can afford it. You've been very generous to me and—"

"Not generous. You earned your share. Alan—"

"I've got enough money put away to keep me for years. Maybe I'll go back to the university . . . finish that degree in political science."

"Will you move out of the house in Bel Air?"

"That would be best. I can find an apartment."

"Will you live with Jennifer?"

"She dropped me," he said.

"What?"

"For another guy."

"I didn't know."

"I didn't want to talk about it."

"I'm sorry."

"Don't be. She wasn't my type."

"You two seemed happy."

"We were . . . briefly."

"What went wrong?"

"Everything."

"You won't move far away, will you?"

"Probably just to Westwood."

"Oh, then we'll practically be neighbors."

"That's right."

"We'll have lunch once a week."

"All right," he said.

"And dinner occasionally."

"Without Max?" he asked.

"Just you and me."

"Sounds lovely."

A childlike tear rolled out of the corner of her eye.

"No need for that," he said, wiping it away.

"I'll miss you."

"A brother and sister can't live in the same house forever. It's unnatural."

The sound of a key in the lock made them turn to the door.
Max came in and stripped off his raincoat.

Mary went to him, kissed him on the cheek.

Putting an arm around her, refusing to acknowledge Alan, Max asked, "Feeling better?"

"Just tired," she said.

"Everything went smoothly in spite of Oberlander," Max said. "I got the check for expenses."

"You always do," she said proudly.

During that exchange Alan went to the door and opened it. "I'll be going."

Only minutes ago she had hoped he would leave before Max returned in order to avoid one of those tiresome quarrels. Now she felt that Alan was drifting out of her life, and she was unwilling to let go of him so soon or so easily. "Can't you stay for another drink?"

He looked at Max and shook his head. "I don't think that would be wise."

Max said nothing. He didn't move, smile, or even blink. His arm at Mary's waist was like a stone bannister against which she rested.

She said, "We haven't talked about what happened tonight. There's so much to be discussed."

"Later," Alan said.

"You're still just going to spend your vacation driving up the coast?"

"Yeah. I'll spend some time in San Francisco. I know a girl there who's invited me for Christmas. Maybe after that I'll head for Seattle."

"You'll call me?"

"Sure."

"When?"

"A week or so."

"Christmas Day?"

"All right."

"I'll miss you, Alan."

"Watch out for yourself."

"I'll watch out for her," Max said.

Alan ignored him. To Mary he said, "Be careful, will you? And remember what I said."

He went out, closing the door behind him, leaving her alone with Max.

* * *

The small, downtown tavern was dimly lit, quite busy as late evening approached, but cozy in spite of the crowd. Max and Mary sat in a corner booth, and the bartender made two perfect vodka martinis. Later they ate roast beef sandwiches and split a bottle of red wine.

When she had finished half of her large sandwich, she pushed the rest of it aside, poured a third glass of wine for herself, and said, "I wonder if Dan Goldman's hospital bills will be covered."

"The town carries a comprehensive insurance policy on its cops," Max said. "Goldman got hurt in the line of duty, so he won't be stuck for a penny of it."

"How can you be so sure?"

"I knew you'd want me to be."

"I don't understand."

"I knew you'd wonder about Goldman's hospital bills, so I asked the mayor."

"Even if the bills are covered," she said, "I guess he'll lose some pay while he's off work."

"No," Max said. "I asked about that, too."

She was surprised. "What are you—a mind reader?"

"I just know you too well. You're the softest touch there ever was."

"I am not. I just think we should do something nice for him."

Max put down his sandwich. "We can buy him either a new electric range or maybe a microwave oven."

She blinked. "What?"

"I asked some of Goldman's buddies what he needs. Seems he's a serious amateur chef, but his kitchen leaves a lot to be desired."

She smiled. "We'll get him the range *and* the oven, and the best set of pots and pans—"

"Hold on a minute," Max said. "He's got an apartment kitchen, not a restaurant. Besides, why do you think you owe him *anything?*"

Staring into her wine, she said, "If I hadn't come to town, he wouldn't have been hurt."

"Mary Bergen, the female Atlas, carrying the world on her shoulders." He reached across the table and took her hand.

"Do you remember the first conversation we ever had?"

"How could I forget? I thought you were weird."

The night they'd met he had been uncharacteristically shy. They'd been guests at the same party. He'd seemed at ease and self-confident with everyone but her. His approach had been so self-conscious and awkward that she felt sorry for him. He had begun with one of those analyze-yourself party games.

She smiled, remembering. "You asked me what machine I would choose to be if I could be any machine in the world. Weird."

"The last woman who answered that question said she'd be a Rolls Royce and go to all the best places. But you said you'd be some piece of medical equipment that saves lives."

"Was that a good answer?"

"At the time," Max said, "it sounded phony. But now I know what you are, and I realize you were serious."

"And what am I?"

"The kind of person who always asks for whom the bell tolls—and always cries buckets at even slightly sad movies."

She sipped her wine. "I played the game right back at you that night, asked you what machine you'd be. Remember?"

Max nodded. He pushed his unfinished sandwich aside, picked up his wine. "I said I'd be a computer dating service so I could hook you up with me."

She laughed girlishly. "I liked it then, and I like it now. It was a surprise finding a romantic under that big tough exterior."

Max leaned across the table, spoke softly. "Know what machine I'd be tonight?" He pointed to the colorfully lighted juke box at the far end of the bar. "I'd be that music machine. And no matter what buttons people pushed, I'd play love songs for you."

"Oh, Max, that's positively saccharine."

"But you like it."

"I love it. After all, I'm the lady who cries buckets at even slightly sad movies."

5

THE NIGHTMARE WOKE HER, but the dream continued. For a minute after she rose up in fear from her pillows, colorful snatches of the nightmare swam in the air before her. Ethereal snapshots. Blood. Shattered bodies. Broken skulls. They were more vivid than any visions she'd ever known.

The shadows of the hotel room settled over her once more. When she grew accustomed enough to the darkness to see the outlines of the furniture, she got up.

The room was a carousel. She reached out for a brass pole that wasn't there, for something to steady her.

When she regained her balance, she went into the bathroom. She didn't close the door because she worried she might wake Max. For the same reason, she didn't use the main light. Instead, she turned on the much dimmer, orange-filtered heat lamp.

In that eerie light her mirror image disturbed her: dark rings around the eyes, skin slack and damp. She was used to a reflection that was the envy of most women: silky black hair, blue eyes, fine features, a flawless complexion. Now the person looking back at her seemed a stranger, an alien.

She felt personally threatened by what she had seen. The dead bodies in the nightmare were the first parts of a chain in which she might be the final link.

She drew a glass of cold water, drank it, then another. The tumbler rattled against her teeth. She had to use both hands to hold it.

Each time she shut her eyes, she saw the same remnant of the nightmare. A dark-haired girl with one blue eye gazing sightlessly at the ceiling. The other eye swollen in a macabre wink. Face torn, bruised, misshapen.

Worst of all, Mary felt that if the blood were swabbed from

that face, and if its smashed features were restored, she would
know it at once.

She put the glass down, leaned against the sink.

Who? she thought. Who was that girl?

The distorted face would not resolve itself.

As if she craved more fear than the dream had given her,
she remembered the psychopath who had died that same night:
his twisted features; his marble-chip teeth; his hands pressed
to the squad car windows; his whispery voice, cool as cellar
air when he spoke her name.

He had been an omen, a warning to her.

But an omen of what?

There might be nothing mysterious about his knowing her
name. He could have heard she was in town, even though that
information was limited to a select few. He might have recognized her from the photograph that accompanied her column,
although the picture was not a good one and was six years old.
That was Alan's explanation.

Although she had no good reason to disagree with Alan,
she knew that his explanation was inadequate.

Maybe the madman had known her because he'd had his
first (and necessarily last) telepathic experience in the instant
that death seized him.

Or perhaps there was a meaning to the incident that couldn't
be defined in rational terms. When she recalled the madman's
demonic face, one thought circled through her mind: *He's a
messenger from Hell, a messenger from Hell*.... She didn't
know what that meant. But she didn't dismiss the thought
simply because it had a supernatural ring to it.

Through her extensive travels, through her many conversations with clairvoyants like Peter Hurkos and Gerard Croiset,
through her conversations and correspondence with other
psychically gifted people, she had come to think anything was
possible. She'd been in homes where poltergeists were active,
where dishes and paintings and bric-a-brac and heavy furniture
sailed through the air and exploded against walls when no one
had touched them or been near them. She hadn't decided whether
she'd seen ghosts at work or, instead, the unconscious telekinetic powers of someone in the house; but she did know
that *something* was there. She had seen Ted Serios create his
famous psychic photographs, which *Time* and *Popular Pho-
tography* and many other national publications had tried un-

successfully to debunk. He projected his thoughts onto unexposed film, and he did so under the intense scrutiny of skeptical scientists. She had seen an Indian mystic—a fakir but not a faker—do the impossible. He planted a seed in a pot of earth, covered it with a light muslin sheet, then went into a deep trance. Within five hours, while Mary watched, the seed germinated, the plant grew, and fruit appeared—several tiny mangoes. As a result of two decades of contact with the extraordinary in life, she scoffed at nothing. Until someone proved beyond doubt that all psychic and supernatural phenomena were pieces of a hoax (which no one ever would), she would put as much faith in the unnatural, supernatural, and suprarational as she did in what more dogmatic people believed to be the one, true, natural, and only world.

. . . *messenger from Hell.*

Although she was half convinced that life existed after death, she didn't believe that it was accurately described by the Judeo-Christian myths. She didn't accept the reality of Heaven and Hell. That was too simplistic. Yet, if she didn't believe, why this unshakable certainty that the madman was a satanic omen? Why phrase the premonition in religious terms?

She shuddered. She was cold to her bones.

She returned to the bedroom but left on the bathroom light. She was uneasy in the dark. She put on her robe.

Max snored peacefully. She stroked his cheek with her fingertips.

He was instantly awake. "What's the matter?"

"I'm scared. I need to talk. I can't stand to be alone."

He closed his hand around her wrist. "I'm here."

"I saw something awful . . . horrible." She shuddered again.

He sat up, switched on the lamp, looked around the room.

"Visions," she said.

Still holding her wrist, he pulled her down to the bed.

"They started when I was asleep," she said, "and went on after I woke up."

"Started when you were sleeping? That's never happened before, has it?"

"Never."

"So maybe it was a dream."

"I know the difference."

He let go of her wrist, pushed his hair back from his forehead. "A vision of what?"

"Dead people."

"An accident?"

"Murder. Beaten and stabbed."

"Where?"

"Quite a distance from here."

"Name of the town?"

"It's south of us."

"That's all you've got?"

"I think it's in Orange County. Maybe Santa Ana. Or Newport Beach. Laguna Beach. Anaheim. Someplace like that."

"How many dead?"

"A lot. Four or five women. All in one place. And..."

"And what?"

"They're the first of many."

"You sense that?"

"Yes."

"Sense it psychically?"

"Yes."

"The first of how many?"

"I don't know."

"You saw the killer?"

"No."

"Pick up anything about him?"

"No."

"Not even the color of his hair?"

"Nothing, Max."

"Have these killings taken place yet?"

"I don't think so. But I can't be sure. I was so surprised by the visions that I didn't make any attempt to hold on to them. I didn't pursue them like I should have."

He got out of bed and slipped into his own robe. She stood up, moved against him. "You're shivering," he said.

She wanted to be loved and sheltered. "It was horrible."

"They always are."

"This was worse than usual."

"Well, it's over."

"No. Maybe it is over or shortly will be for those women. But not for us. We're going to get tangled up in this one. Oh, God, so many bodies, so much blood. And I think I knew one of the dead girls."

"Who was she?" he asked, holding her still closer.

"The face I saw was so badly disfigured. I couldn't tell who she was, but she seemed familiar."

"It had to be a dream," he said reassuringly. "The visions don't come to you out of the blue. You've always had to concentrate, focus your attention in order to pick them up. Like when you start tracking a killer, you have to handle something that belonged to his victim before you can receive images of him."

He was telling her what she already knew, soothing her in the manner of a father explaining to his still frightened young daughter that the ghosts she had seen in the dark bedroom were only the draft-stirred curtains she could now see with all the lights on.

Actually it didn't matter to her what he said. Just hearing him speak and feeling him close, Mary grew calm.

"Even when you're searching for a lost ring or necklace or brooch," Max said, "you have to see the box or drawer where it was kept. So what you saw tonight *had* to be a dream because you didn't seek it."

"I feel better."

"Good."

"But not because I believe it was a dream. I know it was a vision. Those women were real. They're either dead by now or they soon will be." She thought of the brutally beaten faces and she said, "God help them."

"Mary—"

"It was *real*," she insisted, letting go of his hand and sitting on the mattress. "And it's going to involve us."

"You mean the police will ask for your help?"

"More than that. It's going to affect us . . . intimately. It's the start of something that'll change our lives."

"How can you know that?"

"The same way I know everything else about it. I sense it psychically."

"Whether or not it's going to change our life," he said, "is there any way we can help those women?"

"We know so little. If we called the police, we couldn't tell them anything worthwhile."

"And since you don't know what town it will happen in, which police department would we call? Can you pick up the vision again?"

"No use trying. It's gone."

"Maybe it'll return spontaneously, just the way it came the first time."

"Maybe." The possibility chilled her. "I hope not. As it is, I've got too many nasty visions in my life. I don't want them to start flashing on me when I'm not prepared, when I'm not *asking* for them. If that became a regular thing, I'd end up in a madhouse."

"If there isn't anything we can do about what you saw," Max said, "then we have to forget about it for tonight. You need a drink."

"I had some water."

"Would *I* ever suggest water? I meant something with more bite."

She smiled. "At this hour of the morning?"

"It's not morning. We went to bed early, remember. And we've been asleep only half an hour or so."

She looked at the travel clock. Eleven-ten. "I thought I'd been conked out for hours."

"Minutes," he said. "Vodka and tonic?"

"Scotch, if you're having it."

He went to the small breakfast table by the window. The liquor bottles, glasses, and ice were there. In spite of his size, he was not awkward. He moved like a wild animal—fluidly, silently. Even the preparation of drinks was a study in grace when Max did it.

If everyone were like him, Mary thought, the word "clumsy" wouldn't exist.

He sat beside her on the edge of the bed. "Will you be able to get back to sleep?"

"I doubt it."

"Drink up."

She sipped the Scotch. It burned her throat.

"What are you worrying about?" he asked.

"Nothing."

"You're worrying about the vision."

"Not at all."

"Look, worry accomplishes nothing," he said. "And whatever you do, don't think about a blue giraffe standing in the center of a giant custard pie."

She stared at him, incredulous.

Grinning, he said, "What are you worrying about now?"

"What else? A blue giraffe in a custard pie."

"See? I stopped you from worrying about the vision."

She laughed. He had such a stern, forbidding face that his humor always came as a surprise.

"Speaking of blue," he said, "you look perfect in that robe."

"I've worn it before."

"And every time you wear it you're breathtaking. Perfect."

She kissed him. She explored his lips with her tongue, then teasingly drew back.

"You look perfect in it, but you'd look even better out of it." He put his drink beside her on the nightstand and untied the sash that was knotted at her waist, opened the long blue robe.

A pleasant tremor passed through her. The cool air caressed her bare skin. She felt soft, vulnerable; she needed him.

With his heavy hands, now light as wings, he traced lazy circles on her breasts, cupped them, pressed them together, gently massaged them. He got on his knees before her, nuzzled her cleavage and kissed her nipples.

She took his head in her hands, pushed her fingers through his lush, shining hair.

Alan was wrong about him.

"My lovely Max," she said.

He moved his lips down her taut belly as she lay back, kissed her thighs, delicately licked the warm center of her. He slipped his hands under her buttocks, lifted slightly.

After many minutes during which her murmurs rose and fell, rose and fell again like the enigmatic susurration of the sea, he raised his head and said, "I love you."

"Then love me."

He took off his robe and joined her on the bed.

* * *

Agreeably exhausted, they separated at midnight, but the spell was not broken. Still enchanted, eyes closed, she drifted. In some ways she was more intensely aware of her body than she had been during intercourse.

Within minutes, however, memories of the vision returned to her: bloodied and crumpled faces. With her eyes closed, the backs of her lids were like twin projection screens on which she saw nothing but carnage.

She opened her eyes and the dark room appeared to crawl with strange shapes. Although she didn't want to disturb Max, she couldn't keep herself from tossing and turning.

Eventually he switched on the light. "You need a sedative." He swung his legs out of bed.

"I'll get it," she said.

"Stay put."

A minute later he came back from the bathroom with a glass of water and one of the capsules that she too frequently required.

"Maybe I shouldn't take it on top of liquor," she said.

"You drank only half of your Scotch."

"I had vodka before that."

"The vodka's through your system by now."

She took the sedative. It stuck in her throat. She choked it down with another swallow of water.

In bed again, he held her hand. He was still holding it when the chemically induced sleep finally began to creep over her.

As consciousness spun away from her like a child's ball rolling down a hillside, she thought about how wrong Alan was about Max, how terribly and completely wrong.

Tuesday,
December 22

6

"ANAHEIM POLICE."

"Are you a police officer, Miss?"

"I'm the receptionist."

"Could I speak to an officer?"

"What's the nature of your complaint?"

"Oh, no complaint. I think you people do a wonderful job."

"I meant, are you reporting a crime?"

"I'm not sure. A very strange thing happened here."

"What is your name?"

"Alice. Alice Barnable."

"Your address?"

"Peregrine Apartments on Euclid Avenue. I'm in apartment B."

"I'll connect you with someone."

"Sergeant Erdman speaking."

"Are you really a sergeant?"

"Who's this?"

"Mrs. Alice Barnable."

"What can I do for you?"

"Are you really a sergeant? You sound too young."

"I've been a policeman for twenty years. If you—"

"I'm seventy-eight, but I'm not senile."

"I didn't say you were."

"So many people treat us senior citizens as if we're children."

"I don't, Mrs. Barnable. My mother's seventy-five, and she's sharper than I am."

"So you better believe what I've got to tell you."

"And what's that?"

"Four nurses share an apartment above mine, and I know they're in some sort of bad trouble. I called up there, but no one answers the phone."

"How do you know they're in trouble?"

"There's a puddle of blood in my spare bathroom."

"Whose blood? I'm afraid I don't follow you."

"You see, the water pipes that serve the apartment above mine are exposed, and they run up one corner of my spare bath. Now, I don't want you to think I live in a cheap place. The pipes are painted white, hardly noticeable. The building's old but elegant in its way. It's not cheap. It's quaint. My Charlie left me enough to let me live very comfortably."

"I'm sure he did, Mrs. Barnable. What about the blood?"

"Those pipes run through a hole in the ceiling. The hole's a tiny bit bigger than it needs to be. Just a quarter of an inch of space all the way around the pipe. During the night, blood dripped out of that hole. The pipes are streaked with it, and there's a large sticky spot on my floor."

"You're sure it's blood? It might be rusty water or—"

"Now you're treating me as if I'm a child, Sergeant Erdman."

"Sorry."

"I know blood when I see it. And what I wondered—I wondered if maybe your people should take a look upstairs."

* * *

Patrolmen Stambaugh and Pollini found the door to the apartment ajar. It was spotted with fingerprints that were cast in dried blood.

"Think he's still in there?" Stambaugh asked.

"Never can tell. Back me up."

Pollini went inside with his gun drawn and Stambaugh followed.

The living room was inexpensively but pleasantly furnished with wicker and rattan. On the white walls were colorful framed prints of palm trees and native villages and bare-breasted, nut-brown girls in striped sarongs.

The first body was in the kitchen. A young woman in black and green pajamas. On the floor. On her back. Long yellow hair streaked with clotted red bands spread around her like a fan. She had been stabbed—and kicked in the face more than once.

"Christ," Stambaugh said.

"Something, huh?"

"Don't you feel sick?"

"Seen it before."

Pollini pointed to several items on the counter by the sink—a paper plate, two slices of bread, a jar of mustard, a tomato, a package of cheese.

"Important?" Stambaugh asked.

"She woke up during the night. Maybe she was an insomniac. She was making a snack when he came in. Doesn't look like she put up a fight. He either surprised her, or she knew and trusted him."

"Should we be talking like this?"

"Why not?"

Stambaugh gestured toward the rooms that they hadn't yet investigated.

"The killer? He's long gone."

Stambaugh greatly admired his partner. He was eight years younger than Pollini. He'd been a cop only six months, while the older man had been on the force for seven years. In his view, Pollini had everything that a great lawman required—intelligence, courage, and street wisdom.

Most important of all, Pollini was able to do his job without letting it touch him. He didn't flinch at the sight of shattered bodies, not even when he encountered the most pathetic victim of all—the battered child. Pollini was nothing less than a rock.

Although he tried to imitate his mentor, Stambaugh usually got sick to his stomach in the midst of too much spilled blood.

"Come on," Pollini said.

He led Stambaugh back through the hall to the spare bath, where the harsh light glared on blood-splashed porcelain and on the hideously stained white vanity top.

"There was a struggle this time," Stambaugh said.

"But not much of one. It was over in seconds."

Another young woman, wearing only panties, was curled fetally in a corner of the bathroom. She had been stabbed repeatedly in the breasts and stomach, back and buttocks. There were between fifty and a hundred wounds.

Her blood had pooled around the pipes that came up from Alice Barnable's first-floor apartment.

"Funny," Pollini said.

"Funny?" Stambaugh had never seen such slaughter. He could not comprehend the violent mind behind it.

"Funny that he didn't rape either of them."

"Is that what he should have done?"

"His kind does, ninety percent of the time."

Across the hall the spare bedroom contained two unmade beds but no bodies.

In the master suite they found a nude redhead on the bed nearest the door. Her throat had been cut.

"No struggle at all," Pollini said. "He caught her while she was sleeping. Doesn't look like he raped this one either."

Stambaugh nodded. He was unable to speak.

Both women in the master bedroom appeared to be Catholics who were, if not devout, at least attentive to their faith. A number of religious objects were scattered on the floor.

A damaged crucifix lay beside the redhead's nightstand. The wooden cross had been broken into four pieces. The aluminum image of Christ was bent at the waist, so that its crown of thorns touched its bare feet; and its head was twisted around so that Christ was looking over his shoulder.

"This wasn't just broken in a scuffle," Pollini said, stooping over the remains of the icon. "The killer pulled this off the wall and spent a good bit of time demolishing it."

Two small religious statues had been on the redhead's dresser. These were also broken. Some of the pieces had been ground into chalky dust; there were a few white heel prints on the carpet.

"He sure has something against Catholics," Pollini said. "Or against religion in general."

Stambaugh reluctantly followed him to the last bed.

The fourth dead woman had been stabbed repeatedly and strangled with a rosary.

In life she had been beautiful. Even now, naked and cold, her hair matted with blood, nose broken, one eye swollen shut, face dark with bruises, there were still traces of beauty. Alive, her blue eyes would have been as clear as mountain lakes. Washed and combed, her hair would have been thick, lustrous. She had long shapely legs, a narrow waist, a flat belly and lovely breasts.

I've seen women like her, Stambaugh thought sadly. She would have walked with her shoulders back, with evident pride in herself, with joy apparent in every step.

"She was a nurse," Pollini said.

Stambaugh looked at the uniform and cap that were on a chair near the bed. His legs felt weak.

"What's the matter?" Pollini asked.

Stambaugh hesitated, cleared his throat. "Well, my sister's a nurse."

"This isn't your sister, is it?"

"No. But she's about my sister's age."

"You know her? She work with your sister?"

"Never saw her before," Stambaugh said.

"Then what's wrong?"

"This girl might have been my sister."

"You cracking up on me?"

"I'm okay. I'm fine."

"You'll get used to this stuff."

Stambaugh said nothing.

"This one was raped," Pollini said.

Stambaugh swallowed hard. He was dizzy.

"See that?" Pollini asked.

"What?"

"On the pubic hair. It's semen."

"Oh."

"I wonder if he had her before or after."

"Before or after what?"

"Before or after he killed her."

Stambaugh hurried into the master bath, dropped to his knees before the toilet, and threw up.

When his stomach spasms passed, he knew that in the past ten minutes he had learned something important about himself. In spite of what he'd thought this morning, he *never* wanted to be like Ted Pollini.

7

MAX CAME BACK to the room at eleven-thirty, just as she finished dressing. He kissed her lightly on the mouth. He smelled of soap, shaving lotion, and the cherry-scented pipe tobacco that he favored.

"Out for a walk?" Mary asked.

"When did you wake up?"

"Only an hour ago."

"I was up at eight-thirty."

"I slept *ten* hours. When I finally managed to throw myself out of bed, I felt dopey. I shouldn't have taken the sedative on top of liquor."

"You needed it."

"I didn't need to feel the way I felt this morning."

"You look wonderful now."

"Where have you been?"

"At the coffee shop downstairs. Had some toast and orange juice. Read the papers."

"Anything that's connected with what I saw last night?"

"The local paper has a nice story. You and Barnes catching The Slasher. They say Goldman is already off the critical list."

"That's not what I meant. The dead women in the vision. What about them?"

"Nothing in the papers."

"There will be this afternoon."

A worried look crossed his face. He put a hand on her shoulder. "You've got to relax once in a while. You've got to let your head clear out now and then. Don't run after this one, Mary. Forget about it. Please. For me?"

"I can't forget," she said unhappily. She wished desperately that she could.

* * *

Before leaving town, they stopped at an appliance store, chose and paid for an electric range and microwave oven for Dan Goldman.

Later they got off the freeway at Ventura to have lunch at a restaurant they knew. They ordered salads, manicotti, and a bottle of Cabernet Sauvignon by Robert Mondavi.

From their table they had a view of the ocean. The slate-gray water looked like a mirror reflecting the turbulent sky. The surf was high and fast. A few gulls swooped along the shoreline.

"It'll be good to get home," Max said. "We should be in Bel Air before two o'clock."

"The way you drive, we'll be there long before."

"We can go over to Beverly Hills for a few hours of Christmas shopping."

"Since we're going to get home in time, I'd rather see my analyst. I've got a four-thirty appointment. I've been missing too many of them lately. I'll do my shopping tomorrow. Besides, I haven't given any thought to Christmas gifts. I don't have any idea what to get you."

"I can see your problem," he said. "I *am* the man who has everything."

"Oh, are you?"

"Naturally. I have you."

"That's corny."

"But I mean it."

"You make me blush."

"That's never been difficult."

She put her right hand to her cheek. "I can feel it. I wish I could control it."

"I'm glad you can't," he said. "It's charming. It's a sign of your innocence."

"Me? Innocent?"

"As a baby," he said.

"Remember me in bed last night?"

"How could I forget?"

"Was that innocence?"

"That was heaven."

"So there."

"But you're still blushing."

"Oh, drink your wine and shut up."

"Still blushing," he said.

"I'm flushed from the wine."

"Still blushing."

"Damn you," she said affectionately.

"*Still* blushing."

She laughed.

Beyond the window thick curdled clouds continued to roll in from the ocean.

Over the spumoni and coffee Mary asked, "What do you think of adoption?"

He shook his head in mock despair. "We're too old to find parents now. Who would want kids as big as us?"

"Be serious," she said.

He stared at her for a long moment, then put down his spoon without eating the spumoni on it. "You really mean you and me . . . adopting a child?"

She was encouraged by the wonder in his voice. "We've talked about having a family," she said. "And since I'll never be able to have a baby of my own . . ."

"But maybe you will."

"No, no," she said. "The doctor made that very clear to me."

"Doctors have been known to be mistaken."

"Not this time," she said, almost too softly to be heard.

"There's too much wrong . . . inside of me. I'll never have a baby, Max. Never."

"Adoption . . ." Max thought about it while he sipped his coffee. Gradually he began to grin. "Yeah. It would be nice. A cute little baby girl."

"I was thinking about a little boy."

"Well, sure as hell this is one thing we can't compromise on."

"We can," she said quickly. "We'll adopt a girl *and* a boy."

"You've thought of everything, haven't you?"

"Oh, Max, you really do like the idea. I can tell. We could talk to an adoption agency this week. And if—"

"Hold on," he said, his smile fading. "We've been married only four months. We should take our time, get to know each other and ourselves better than we do. Then we'll be *ready* for children."

She didn't hide her disappointment. "How long will that take?"

"It'll take as long as it takes. Six months . . . a year."

"Look, I know you. You know me. We love each other and we like each other. We've got intelligence, common sense, and loads of money. What else do we need to be good parents?"

"We need to be at peace with ourselves, in ourselves," he said.

"You don't fight anymore. You're at peace with yourself."

"I'm only halfway there," he said. "And you've got things to face, too."

Defiantly, although she knew the answer, she said, "Like what?"

"You've got to face up to what happened twenty-four years ago, remember what you've refused to remember . . . every detail of the beating you took . . . everything about what that man did to you when you were six years old. Until you come to terms with that, you'll continue to have the nightmares. You'll never know real peace of mind until those memories are confronted and exorcised."

She tossed her head, throwing her long hair over her shoulders. "I don't have to face what happened then to be a good parent now."

"I think you do," he said.

"But Max, there are so many kids without homes, without hope or a future. Right now we could give two of them—"

He squeezed her hand. "You're playing Atlas again. Mary, I understand you. There's more love in you than in anyone I've ever known. You want to share it; that's the meaning of you. And I promised you'll have the opportunity. But adoption is a big step. We'll take it only when we're ready."

She couldn't get angry. She smiled and said, "I'll wear you down. I promise."

He sighed. "You probably will."

* * *

Mary didn't like to drive fast. When she was nine years old her father died in an accident. She'd been in the car when it happened. To her, the automobile was a treacherous machine.

As a passenger, she endured high speeds only when Max was at the wheel. With him in command, she was able to relax and even to feel exhilarated as the scenery whipped past her

window. Max was her guardian. He watched over her and
protected her. It was inconceivable that anything bad could
happen to her when she was with him.

He took great pleasure in handling the Mercedes at speeds
that tested his skills and his ability to avoid police detection.
He enjoyed the car as much as he did his gun collection; and
when he drove, he was as single-minded as when he made
love. On a long, uncrowded straight stretch of freeway, with
all his attention riveted on the car beneath him and on the
blurred pavement that succumbed to him, he rarely had patience
for conversation. He looked like a bird of prey, flint-eyed,
silent, hunched over the steering wheel.

When he drove like that, Mary could see the recklessness,
the taste for excitement and violence that had gotten him into
dozens of fights. Oddly, she wasn't frightened by that aspect
of him; instead, she found him more attractive than ever.

They rocketed toward Los Angeles at ninety miles an hour.

* * *

The eighteen-room English Tudor house in Bel Air looked cool
and elegant in the shade of thirty-foot trees. The two-acre estate
had cost her virtually every dollar that she had earned from
her first two best-sellers, but she had never regretted the cost.

When they parked in the circular drive, Emmet Churchill
came out to greet them. He had gray hair and a neat mustache.
He was sixty years old, but his face was unlined. A life in
service had been remarkably agreeable to both Emmet and his
wife. "Good trip, Mr. Bergen?"

"Fine," Max said. "Had it up to one-twenty for a few miles,
and Mary didn't scream once."

"I would have," Emmet said.

Mary had expected to find another Mercedes in the driveway. "Isn't Alan home?"

"He stopped by for fresh clothes," Emmet said. "But he
was anxious to be off on vacation."

She was disappointed. She'd hoped for another chance to
convince him that he and Max *could* get along if they tried.
"How's Anna?" she asked Emmet.

"Couldn't be better. When you called this morning to say
that you'd be home, she started planning dinner right away.
She's in the kitchen now."

"As soon as Max freshens up, he'll be going to Beverly Hills to do some shopping," Mary told Emmet. "You'll want to get our luggage out of the Mercedes before he leaves."

"Right away."

She started toward the front door. "And would you get my car out of the garage? I've got a four-thirty appointment with Dr. Cauvel. I want—"

The man coming at her, relentless, power in the blow, a knife deep in her stomach, blade twisting, flesh tearing, blood erupting, pain erupting, blackness flowing, flowing...

* * *

She regained consciousness as Max put her down on the bed in the second-floor master suite. She clung to him. She couldn't stop shaking.

"Are you all right?"

"Hold me," she said.

He did. "Easy. Easy now."

She could feel the strong, unhurried beat of his heart. After a while she said, "I'm thirsty."

"Is that all? Aren't you hurt? Should I call a doctor?"

"Just get me some water."

"You passed out."

"I'm fine now."

When he came back from the bathroom with the water, he helped her sit up. He held the glass, tilted it as she drank, nursed her as if she were a sick child. When she was finished, he said, "What happened?"

Leaning against the headboard, she said, "Another vision that I didn't ask for. Only . . . it's different from anything that's come before."

She must have gone pale, for he said, "Calm down. It's over."

He looked good. Marvelous. So big and reliable.

She did calm down somewhat, merely because he told her she should.

"I didn't just *see* the damned thing, Max. I *felt* it. A knife. I felt a knife going into me, ripping me apart . . ."

She put one hand on her belly. There was no wound. No bruise. The flesh wasn't even tender.

"Let me get this straight," he said. "You saw yourself being stabbed to death?"

"No."

"What *did* you see?"

She got up, waved him away as he moved to support her. She went to the window and looked out at the forty-foot pool behind the main house, at the lush grounds and at the Churchills' little house at the far end of the property. Ordinarily she would have been calmed further by this evidence of prosperity; but now it had no effect on her. "I saw another woman. Not me. But I felt her pain as if it were mine."

"That's never happened before."

"It did this time."

"Have you ever heard of another clairvoyant having the same experience? Hurkos? Croiset? Dykshoorn?"

"No." She turned from the window. "What's it mean? What's going to happen to me?"

"Nothing will happen to you." Convinced that she wasn't ill, he began the gentle interrogation that could guide her through a vision in progress or through the memory of a vision that had passed. "Has this thing you just saw happened yet?"

"No."

"This woman who will be stabbed . . . was she one of those you saw in the nightmare last evening?"

"No. A new one."

"Did you see her face clearly?"

"I did. But only briefly."

Mary sat in a wing-back chair by the window. Her hands, against the brown crushed-velvet upholstery, were pale, almost translucent. She felt lighter than air, as if her existence were tenuous, as if she were fading away.

"What did this woman look like?" Max asked.

"Pretty."

He paced before her. "Color of hair?"

"Brunette."

"Eyes?"

"Green or blue."

"Young?"

"Yes. About my age."

"Did you sense her name?"

"No. But I think I've seen her before."

"You thought the same of one of them last night."

She nodded.

"What gives you the idea you know her?"

"I can't say. It's just an impression."

"Was the scene of this crime the same as in last night's vision?"

"No. This woman will be murdered . . . in a beauty parlor."

"At a hairdresser's?"

"Yes. The beautician is a man."

"What will happen to him?"

"He'll be killed, too."

"Any other victims?"

"A third. Another woman."

She had sensed a great deal in the few seconds that the psychic images had coruscated through her mind. However, with each datum came the brutal recollection of that knife she had shared mystically with the dying woman.

"What's the name of the beauty shop?" Max asked.

"I don't know."

"Where's it located?"

"Not far from here."

"In Orange County again?"

"Yes."

"Which town?"

"I don't know."

He sighed, sat down in the armchair opposite hers. "Is the killer the same as the one you saw last night?"

"No doubt about it."

"So he's a repeater, a psychopath, a mass murderer. He's going to kill four or five people in one place and three in another."

"That may only be the start," she said softly.

"What does he look like?"

"I still don't know."

"Is he a big man or small?"

"I don't know."

"What's his name?"

"I wish I knew."

"Is he young or old?"

"I don't even know that."

The room was stuffy. The air was stale, almost rank. She got up and opened the window.

"If you can't get an image of him," Max said, "how can you tell it's the same killer in both visions?"

"I just *can,* that's all."

She sat down, face to the window.

She felt hollow, light. She could imagine being carried off by the breeze, slight as it was. The unbidden visions had sucked a lot of energy from her. She wouldn't be able to endure many more of them. Certainly not a life full of them.

Pretty soon, she thought, I won't need a tornado like Dorothy did. Just a puff of air will carry *me* off to Oz.

"What can we do to keep him from killing?" Max asked.

"Nothing."

"Then let's put him out of our minds for now."

She scowled. "Know when I feel worst? You know when I feel so awful I hardly want to live?"

He waited.

Her hands were in her lap, her fingers at war with one another. "It's when I know something horrible will happen— but I don't know enough to stop it from happening. If I must have this power, why wasn't I given it without strings attached? Why can't I turn it on and off like a television set? Why does it sometimes get all cloudy for me when I need it the most? Am I supposed to be tormented? Is it a nasty joke? A lot of people are going to die because I can't see clearly. Dammit, dammit, dammit!" She jumped up, strode to the television. She turned the set on, off, on, off, on, off, with nearly enough force to break the switch.

"You can't feel responsible for what you see in your visions," he said.

"But I do."

"You've got to change."

"I won't. I can't."

He stood up, went to her, took her hand from the television controls. "Why don't you freshen up? We'll do some shopping."

"Not me," she said. "I have an appointment with Dr. Cauvel."

"That's two and a half hours from now."

"I'm not up to shopping," she said. "You go. I'll make the rounds tomorrow."

"I can't leave you here alone."

"I won't be alone. Anna and Emmet are here."

"You shouldn't drive."

"Why not?"

"What if you have another attack while you're behind the wheel?"

"Oh. Then Emmet can drive me."

"What'll you do until you see the analyst?"

"Write a column," she said.

"We sent a packet to the syndicate last week. We're already twenty columns ahead of schedule."

Although she didn't feel well, she managed a light tone. "We're twenty ahead because you wrote fifteen of them. It's time I did my share. Being twenty-one ahead won't hurt."

"There's some material on my desk about that woman in North Carolina who can predict the sex of unborn babies just by touching the mother. They're studying her at Duke University."

"Then that's what I'll write about."

"Well, if you're positive . . ."

"I am. Now scoot over to Gucci, Giorgio's, The French Corner, Juel Park, Courrèges, Van Cleef and Arpels—and buy me beautiful things for Christmas."

Trying to keep from smiling, he said, "But I already have something picked out at Woolworth's."

"Oh," she said, playing along with him, "then you won't mind that I'm only getting you a gift certificate for some McDonald's hamburgers."

He pretended to be disappointed. "Well, I might stop at Gucci and Edwards Lowell for a few things that'll go with the Woolworth's piece."

She grinned. "You do that. Then maybe I'll let you sleep in here tonight instead of on the couch."

He laughed and kissed her.

"Mmmm," she said. "Again."

She knew that she was loved, and that knowledge compensated somewhat for the horror of the past few days.

8

THE FOCAL POINT of Dr. Cauvel's office was a collection of hundreds of glass dogs that were displayed on glass and chrome shelves to one side of his desk. No member of the menagerie was larger than Mary's hand, and most were a great deal smaller than that. There were blue dogs, brown dogs, red dogs, clear dogs, milky white dogs, black dogs, orange and yellow and purple and green dogs, transparent and opaque, striped and polka-dotted, hand-blown and solid glass dogs. Some of them were lying down, some sitting, standing, pointing, running. There were basset hounds, greyhounds, airedales, German shepherds, Pekingese, terriers, Saint Bernards, and a dozen other breeds. A bitch with a litter of fragile glass puppies stood near a comic scene of dogs playing tiny glass instruments, flutes and drums and bugles for beagles. Several curious figures shone darkly in the silent zoo: snarling hellhounds, demons with dog faces and forked tongues.

Glass was also the focal point of the doctor himself. He wore thick spectacles that made his eyes appear abnormally large. He was short, athletic looking, and compulsively neat about himself. The spectacles were never smudged; he polished them continually.

Mary and the doctor sat across from each other at a folding table in the middle of the room.

The psychiatrist shuffled a deck of playing cards. He dealt ten of them face-down in a single row.

She picked up a six-inch loop of wire that he had provided and held it over the cards. She moved it back and forth. Twice it dipped toward the table as if invisible fingers were tugging it out of her hands. After less than a minute of dowsing, she put down the loop and indicated two of the ten cards. "These are the highest values in the batch."

"What are they?" Cauvel asked..

"One might be an ace."

"Of which suit?"

"I don't know."

He turned them over. An ace of clubs. A queen of hearts. She relaxed.

He revealed the other cards. The highest value was a jack.

"Incredible," he said. "This is one of the most difficult tests we've tried. But out of ten attempts, you've been ninety percent accurate. Ever think of going to Las Vegas?"

"To break the bank at the twenty-one tables?"

"Why not?" he asked.

"The only way I'd have a chance is if they spread out the cards and let me use a wire loop on them before they dealt."

Like all his movements and expressions, his smile was economical. "Not likely."

For the past two years her Tuesday and Friday appointments had begun at four-thirty and ended at six o'clock. On these days she was Cauvel's final patient. During the first three quarters of an hour she participated in some experiments in extrasensory perception for a series of articles he intended to publish in a professional journal. He devoted the second forty-five minutes to treating her in his capacity as a psychiatrist. In return for her cooperation he waived his fee.

She could afford to pay for treatment. She permitted the current arrangement because the experiments interested her.

"Brandy?" he asked.

"Please."

He poured Remy Martin for both of them.

They moved from the card table to a pair of armchairs that faced each other across a small round cocktail table.

Cauvel used no standard technique with his patients. His style was very much his own. She liked his quiet, friendly approach.

"Where would you like to begin?" he asked.

"I don't know."

"Take your time."

"I don't want to begin at all."

"You always say that, and you always begin."

"Not today. I'd just like to sit here."

He nodded, sipped his brandy.

"Why am I always so difficult for you?" she asked.

"I can't answer that. *You* can."

"Why don't I want to talk to you?"

"Oh, you do want to talk. Otherwise you wouldn't be here."

Frowning, she said, "Help me start."

"What were you thinking about on your way here?"

"That's no place to start."

"Try it."

"Well . . . I was thinking about what I am."

"And what's that?"

"A clairvoyant."

"What about it?"

"Why me? Why not someone else?"

"The top researchers in this field believe we all have the same paranormal talents."

"Maybe," she said. "But most people don't have it to the extent that I do."

"We just don't recognize our potential," he said. "Only a handful of people have found a way to use their ESP."

"So why did *I* find a way?"

"Haven't all of the best clairvoyants suffered head injuries at some time prior to the discovery of their psychic powers?"

"Peter Hurkos did," she said. "And a number of others. But not all of us."

"Did you?"

"Suffer a head injury? No."

"Yes, you did."

She sipped her brandy. "What a wonderful taste."

"You were injured when you were six years old. You've mentioned it a few times, but you've never wanted to pursue it."

"And I don't want to pursue it now."

"You should," Cauvel said. "Your reluctance to discuss it is proof that—"

"You're talking too much today." Her voice was hard, too loud. "I pay you to listen."

"You don't pay me at all." As always, he spoke gently.

"I could walk out of here right now."

He took off his glasses and polished them with his handkerchief.

"Without me," she said sharply, disliking his studied calm, "you wouldn't have the data to write those articles that make you a big man among the other shrinks."

"The articles aren't that important. If you want so much to

walk out, do it. Shall we terminate our arrangement?"

She sagged back into her chair. "Sorry." She seldom raised her voice. It wasn't like her to shout at him. She was blushing.

"No need to apologize," he said. "But don't you see that this experience twenty-four years ago might be the root of your problem? It could be the underlying cause of your insomnia, of your periodic deep depressions, of your anxiety attacks."

She felt weak. She closed her eyes. "You want me to pursue it."

"That would be a good idea."

"Help me start."

"You were six years old."

"Six..."

"Your father had money then."

"Quite a lot of it."

"You lived on a small estate."

"Twenty acres," she said. "Most of it landscaped. There was a full-time... a full-time..."

"Gardener."

"Gardener," she said. She wasn't blushing anymore. Her cheeks were cold. Her hands were icy.

"What was his name?"

"I don't remember."

"Of course you do."

"Berton Mitchell."

"Did you like him?"

"At first I did."

"You said once that he teased you."

"In a fun way. And he had a special name for me."

"What did he call you?"

"Contrary. As if that were my real name."

"*Were* you contrary?"

"Not the least bit. He was teasing. He got it from the nursery rhyme. 'Mary, Mary, quite contrary'..."

"When did you stop liking Berton Mitchell?"

She wanted to be home with Max. She could almost feel his arms around her.

"When did you stop liking him, Mary?"

"That day in August."

"What happened?"

"You know."

"Yes, I do know."

"Well then."

"But we never seem to get further into this thing unless we start from the top each time."

"I don't *want* to get further into it."

But he was relentless. "What happened that day in August when you were six years old?"

"Have you gotten any new glass dogs recently?"

"What did Berton Mitchell do that day in August?"

"He tried to rape me."

* * *

Six P.M. Early winter night. The air was cool and fresh.

He left the car at the coffee shop and walked north along the highway, his back to the traffic.

He had a knife in one pocket, a revolver in the other. He kept his hands on both weapons.

His shoes crunched in the gravel.

The wind from the passing cars buffeted him, mussed his hair, pasted his overcoat to his legs.

The beauty shop, Hair Today, occupied a small detached building on Main Street, just north of the Santa Ana city limits. With its imitation thatched roof, leaded windows, plaster and exposed-beam exterior, the place resembled a cottage in the English countryside—except for the floodlights shining on the front of it, and except for the pink and green paint job.

The block was strictly commercial. Service stations, fast-food restaurants, real estate offices, dozens of small businesses, all of them nestled in neon and palm trees and jade-plant hedges, flourished like ugly flowers in the money-scented Orange County air. South of Hair Today was the sales lot of an imported automobile dealership. Row after row of sleek machines huddled in the night. Only the windshields and chrome gleamed malevolently under mercury-vapor lights. North, beyond the beauty shop, lay a three-screen motion picture theater, and beyond that a shopping center.

A dirty white Cadillac and a shiny Triumph stood on the macadam parking area in front of Hair Today.

He crossed the lot, walked between the cars, opened the cottage door, and went inside.

The narrow front room was a lounge where women marked time until their appointments. The carpet was purple and plush, the chairs bright yellow, the drapes white. There were end tables, ashtrays, and stacks of magazines, but at this late hour there were no customers waiting.

At the rear of the room was a purple and white counter. A cash register rested on it, and a woman with bleached blonde hair sat on a stool behind it.

In back of the woman a curtained archway led to the working part of the shop. The sound of a hand-held hair dryer penetrated the curtain like the buzz of angry bees.

"We're closed," the bleached blonde said.

He went to the counter.

"Are you looking for someone?" she said.

He took the revolver out of his pocket. It felt good in his hand. It felt like justice.

She stared at the gun, then into his eyes. She licked her lips. "What do you want?"

He didn't speak.

She said, "Now wait."

He pulled the trigger. The sound was masked somewhat by the noisy dryer.

She fell off the stool and didn't get up.

The hair dryer shut off. From the back room someone said, "Tina?"

He walked around the dead woman, parted the curtains and stepped through them.

Of the four salon chairs, three were empty. The last customer of the day sat in the fourth chair. She was young and pretty, with an impossibly creamy complexion. Her hair was straight and wet.

The hairdresser was a burly man, bald, with a bristling black mustache. He wore a purple uniform shirt with his first name, Kyle, embroidered in yellow on the breast pocket.

The woman drew a deep breath, but she couldn't find the courage to scream.

"Who are you?" Kyle asked.

He shot Kyle twice.

* * *

"My father wasn't at home that day," Mary said.

"And your mother?"

"She was up at the main house. Drunk as usual."

"And your brother?"

"Alan was in his room, working on his model airplanes."

"The gardener, Berton Mitchell?"

"His wife and son were away for the week. Mitchell . . . got me into his place, enticed me into it."

"Where was this?"

"Down at the far end of the estate, a little cottage with a green shingle roof. He often told me that elves lived with his family."

An awesome force pressed against her from all sides. She felt as if she was enfolded by leather wings, muscular wings that were draining the heat from her, squeezing the life out of her.

"Go on," Cauvel said.

Relentlessly the warmth dropped out of her like mercury falling in a thermometer. She was a cold, hollow reed of glass, brittle, breakable. "More brandy?"

"When you've finished telling me," Cauvel said.

"I need help with this."

"I'm here to help you, Mary."

"If I tell, he'll hurt me."

"Who? Mitchell? You don't believe that. You know he's dead. He was found guilty of child molestation, of assault with intent to kill. He hung himself in his cell. I'm the only one here, and I won't let anyone hurt you."

"I was alone with him."

"You're speaking so softly I can't hear you."

"I was alone with him," she said again. "He . . . touched . . . me . . . exposed himself."

"Were you frightened?"

"Yes."

The pressure was intense, unbearable, and getting worse.

Cauvel didn't speak, and she said, "I was frightened because he wanted me . . . to do things."

"What things?"

The air was foul. Although only she and the doctor were in the room, she felt that some creature had its lips to hers and was forcing its rank breath into her lungs.

"I need brandy," she said.

"What you need is to tell me all of this, to remember every last detail, to get it out in the open once and for all. What things did he want you to do?"

"Help me. You've got to guide me."

"He wanted to have intercourse, didn't he?"

"I'm not sure."

Her hands were numb. She could feel cords biting into them. But there were no cords.

"Oral intercourse?" Cauvel asked.

"But not only that."

Her ankles were sore. She could feel cords that were not there. She moved her feet. They were leaden.

"What else did he want to do?" Cauvel asked.

"I don't recall."

"You can remember if you want to."

"No. Honestly, I can't. I can't."

"What else did he want you to do?"

The embrace of the imaginary wings was so tight that she had difficulty breathing. She could hear them beating the air—*wicka-wicka-wicka* . . .

She stood up, walked away from the chair.

The wings held her.

"What else did he want you to do?" Cauvel asked.

"Something awful, unspeakable."

"A sex act of some sort?"

Wicka-wicka-wicka . . .

"Not just sex. More than that," she said.

"What was it?"

"Dirty. Filthy."

"In what way?"

"Eyes watching me."

"Mitchell's eyes?"

"Not his."

"Who then?"

"I can't remember."

"You can."

Wicka-wicka . . .

"Wings," she said.

"Rings? You're speaking too softly again?"

"Wings," she said. "Wings."

"What do you mean?"

She was shaking, vibrating. She was afraid her legs would fail her. She returned to the armchair. "Wings. I can hear them flapping. I can *feel* them."

"You mean Mitchell kept a bird in the house?"

"I don't know."

"A parrot perhaps?"

"I couldn't say."

"Work at remembering it, Mary. Don't let go of this thought. You've never mentioned wings before. It's important."

"They were everywhere."

"The wings?"

"All over me. Little wings."

"Think. What did he do to you?"

She was silent a long while. The pressure began to ease a bit. The sound of wings faded.

"Mary?"

Finally she said, "That's all. I can't recall anything else."

"There is a way to unlock those memories," he said.

"Hypnosis," she replied.

"It works."

"I'm afraid to remember."

"You should be afraid *not* to remember."

"If I remember, I'll die."

"That's ridiculous, and you know it."

She pushed her hair back from her face. For his benefit, she forced a smile. "I don't hear the wings now. I can't feel them. We don't need to talk about wings anymore."

"Of course we do."

"I *won't* talk about wings, dammit!" She shook her head violently. She was surprised and frightened by her own vehemence. "Not today anyway."

"All right," Cauvel said. "I'll accept that. That's not the same thing as saying you don't *need* to talk." He began to polish his glasses once more. "Let's go back to what you remember. Berton Mitchell beat you."

"I suppose he did."

"You were found in his place?"

"In his living room."

"And you were badly beaten?"

"Yes."

"And later you told them he did it."

"But I can't remember it happening. I recall the pain, terrible pain. But only for an instant."

"You could have lost consciousness with the first blow."

"That's what everyone said. He must have kept hitting me

after I passed out. I couldn't have stood up to him for long. I was just a little girl."

"He used a knife, too?"

"I was cut all over."

"How long were you in the hospital?"

"More than two weeks."

"How many stitches for the wounds?"

"More than a hundred altogether."

* * *

The beauty shop smelled of shampoo, cream rinse, and cologne. He could also smell the woman's sweat.

The floor was littered with hair. It swirled around them as he moved onto her and into her.

She refused to respond to him. She neither welcomed him nor struggled against him. She lay still. Her eyes were like the eyes of the dead.

He didn't hate her for that. In the long run he'd never cared for passion in his women. For the first few months a new lover's aggression and delight in sex was tolerable. He could be tender for a short time. But always, after a few months, he needed to see fear in them. That was what brought him to climax. The more they feared him, the better he liked them.

As he lay on her, he could feel this woman's heart thumping wildly, accelerated by terror. That excited him, and he began to move faster within her.

* * *

"You took a number of Mitchell's blows on your head," Cauvel said.

"My face was black and blue. My father called me his little patchwork doll."

"Did you suffer a concussion?"

"I see where all of this is leading," she said. "But no. No concussion. Absolutely not."

"When did your visions begin?"

"Later the same year."

"A few minutes ago you asked me why you'd been singled out to be a clairvoyant. Well, there's nothing mysterious about it really. As in the case of Peter Hurkos, your psychic talent came after a serious head injury."

"Not serious enough."

He stopped polishing his spectacles, put them on, and studied her with huge, magnified eyes. "Is it possible that a severe psychological shock could trigger psychic abilities in the same way that certain head injuries seem to do?"

She shrugged.

"If you didn't acquire your power as a result of a physical trauma, then maybe you acquired it because of a *psychological* trauma. Do you suppose that's possible?"

"It could be," she said.

"Either way," he said, thrusting a bony finger at her, as if repeatedly tapping a window between them, "either way, your clairvoyance probably goes back to Berton Mitchell, to what he did to you that you can't remember."

"Maybe."

"And your insomnia goes back to Berton Mitchell. Your periodic depressions go back to him. What he did to you is the underlying cause of your anxiety attacks. I tell you, Mary, the sooner you face up to this, the better. If you ever let me use hypnosis to regress you and guide you through the memories, then you'll never need my help again."

"I'll always need your help."

He scowled. His deeply tanned face was scored by lines like saber slashes. An ambitious portrait painter would have wanted to catch him with that expression, for it made him look fierce, yet fair and reliable. It was that expression that drew her to him at a party three years ago; and his distant but paternal manner caused her to seek his advice when her dependency on sleeping pills became absolute.

"If you'll always need my help," he said, "then I'm not helping you at all. As a psychiatrist, I must make you find all the strength you need inside yourself."

She went to the bar and picked up the decanter of brandy. "You said I could have another if I kept talking a while."

"I never break a promise." He joined her at the bar. "The day's nearly over. I'll have another, too."

As she poured for them, she said, "You're wrong about Mitchell."

"In what sense?"

"I don't think all of my problems date back to him. Some of them started the day my father died."

"I've heard you expound on that theory before."

"I was in the car with him when he was killed. I was in the back seat and he was driving. I saw him die. His blood sprayed all over me. I was only nine. And the years after he died weren't easy. In three years my mother lost all the money my father left us. We went from rich to poor between my ninth and twelfth birthdays. I think an experience like that would leave some scars, don't you?"

"It has," he said. He picked up his brandy glass. "But it's not responsible for the *worst* scars."

"How do you know?"

"You're able to talk about it."

"So?"

"But you aren't able to talk about what happened with Berton Mitchell."

* * *

When he finished with the woman, he stood, pulled up his pants, zipped his fly. He hadn't even taken off his coat.

He stepped back from her, looked at her.

Given the opportunity, she made no effort to cover herself. Her skirt was bunched around her hips. Her blouse was unbuttoned; one plump breast was visible. Her hands were fisted. He fingernails had gouged her palms, and ribbons of blood were on her hands. Terrorized, reduced to little more than a cowering animal, she represented his ideal woman.

He took the knife out of his coat pocket.

He expected her to scream and scramble away from him, but as he moved in for the kill, she lay as if she were dead already. She was past fear now, past feeling anything.

Kneeling beside her, he placed the point of the blade at her throat. The flesh dimpled around it, but she didn't blink.

He raised the blade high, held it in her line of sight, over her breasts.

No response.

He was disappointed. When time and circumstance allowed, he preferred to kill slowly. To get any thrill from that game, he required a lively woman for prey.

Angry with her for spoiling the moment, he rammed the knife down.

* * *

Mary Bergen gasped.

The razor edge ripping her skin, opening muscle, opening the reservoir of blood, opening the dark place where pain was stored . . .

She leaned into the corner formed by the wall and the side of the antique oak bar. She was only half aware that she knocked over an unopened bottle of Scotch.

"What's the matter?" Cauvel asked.

"It hurts."

He touched her shoulder. "Are you sick? Can I help?"

"Not sick. The vision. I feel it."

The knife again, thrust deep . . .

She put both hands to her stomach, trying to contain the eruption of pain. "I won't faint this time. I won't!"

"A vision of what?" Cauvel asked worriedly.

"The beauty shop. The same one I saw a few hours ago. Only it's happening now. The slaughter . . . God almighty . . . happening somewhere, happening right this minute." She put her hands to her face, but the images would not be shut out. "Oh, God. Sweet God. Help me."

"What do you see?"

"A dead man on the floor."

"The floor of the beauty shop?"

"He's bald . . . mustache . . . purple shirt."

"What is it you're feeling?"

The knife . . .

She was sweating. Crying.

"Mary? *Mary?*"

"I feel . . . the woman . . . being stabbed."

"What woman? There's a woman?"

"Mustn't black out."

She started to sag, and he held her by both shoulders.

She saw the knife gouging flesh again, but she felt no pain this time. The woman in the vision was dead; therefore, there was no more pain to share.

"Have to see his face, have to get his name," she said.

The killer standing up from the body, standing in a cape, no, a long coat, an overcoat...

"Can't lose the thread. Mustn't lose the vision. Have to hold it, have to find where he is, who he is, *what* he is, stop him from doing these awful things."

The killer standing, standing with the butcher knife in one hand, standing in shadow, his face in shadow but turning now, turning very slowly and deliberately, turning so that she'll be able to see his face, turning as if he is looking for her—

"He knows I'm with him," she said.

"Who knows?"

"He knows I'm watching."

She didn't understand how that could be true. Yet the killer knew about her. She was certain of that, and she was scared.

Suddenly half a dozen glass dogs leaped from the display shelves, flew through the air, and smashed with a great deal of force into the wall beside Mary.

She screamed.

Cauvel turned to see who had thrown them. "What the hell?"

As if they had come to life and had acquired wings, a dozen glass dogs swept off the top shelf. They spun, glittering like fragments of an exploded prism, to the high center of the room. They bounced off the ceiling, struck one another with the musical rattle of Chinese wind chimes.

Then they streaked toward Mary.

She raised her arms, covered her face.

The miniatures battered her harder than she had expected. They stung like bees.

"Stop them!" she said, not certain to whom she was speaking.

A hellhound with pointy horns struck the doctor in the forehead between the eyes and drew blood.

Cauvel turned away from the shelves, moved against her, tried to shield her with his body.

Another ten or fifteen dogs bulleted around the room. Two of them smashed through a stained glass panel in the bar. Others burst to pieces on the wall around Mary, icing her hair with chunks and slivers of colored glass.

"It's trying to kill me!" She was struggling unsuccessfully to avoid hysteria.

Cauvel pressed her into the corner.

More glass dogs whistled across the room, swooped over the psychiatrist's desk, scattered a sheaf of onionskin papers. The figurines clattered against the venetian blinds without shattering, rose up again, zigzagged crazily from one end of the chamber to the other, then pelted Cauvel's shoulders and back, rained fragments over Mary's bowed head.

Yet another squadron of dogs took flight. They danced in the air, swarmed ominously, fluttered against Mary, flew away, came back with greater determination, struck her with incredible force, stung, bruised, hung over her like locusts.

As suddenly as the macabre assault began, it ended. Almost a hundred glass miniatures remained on the display shelves, but they did not move.

Mary and Cauvel huddled together, not trusting the calm, waiting for another attack.

Silence prevailed.

Eventually he let go of her and stepped back.

She was unable to control the tremors that broke like waves within her.

"Are you all right?" he asked, oblivious to the blood on his own face.

"I wasn't meant to see him," she said.

Cauvel was dazed. He stared, uncomprehendingly.

"His face," she said. "I wasn't meant to see it."

"What are you talking about?"

"When I tried to see the killer in the vision," she said, "I was stopped. What stopped me?"

Cauvel gazed at the shards of glass on all sides of them. He began to pick splinters of glass from the shoulders and sleeves of his suit jacket. "Did you do this? Did you make the dogs fly?"

"Me?"

"Who else?"

"Oh, no. How could I?"

"Someone did."

"Some*thing.*"

He stared at her.

"It was a . . . spirit," she said.

"I don't believe in life after death."

"I wasn't sure about that myself. Until now."

"So we're haunted?"

"What else?"

"Many possibilities." He looked concerned about her.

"I'm not crazy," she said.

"Did I say you were?"

"We've seen a poltergeist in action."

"I don't believe in them either," he said.

"I do. I've seen them work before. I was never sure if they were spirits or not. But now I am."

"Mary—"

"A poltergeist. It came to stop me from seeing the killer's face."

Behind them the display shelves toppled and struck the floor with a thunderous crash.

9

MAX WAS NOT at home.

Without him Mary felt that the house was a mausoleum. Her footsteps on the hardwood floor seemed louder than usual, the echoes full of sinister voices.

"He called earlier," Anna Churchill said, as she wiped her hands on her apron. "He asked me to delay dinner half an hour."

"Why?"

"He said to tell you he wouldn't be back until eight o'clock because Woolworth's is open late for Christmas shopping."

She knew that Max had meant to make her laugh with that message, but she couldn't even smile. The only thing that would lift her spirits was the sight of him. She didn't want to be alone.

As she went through the parlor on her way to the mahogany staircase, she felt dwarfed by the heavy European furniture. With the memory of the poltergeist fresh in her mind, she expected each piece of furniture to come to life, and she didn't know how she would survive if the chairs and sofas and corner cabinets began to rush at her with murderous intent.

The furniture did not move.

Upstairs, in her bathroom, she took a bottle of valium from the medicine cabinet. She had been able to conceal her nervousness when she was with Emmet and Anna; but now her hands shook so badly that she needed almost a minute to get the safety cap off the container. She poured a glass of cold water, swallowed one of the capsules. One didn't seem like much. She felt she could use two. Maybe three. "God, no," she said, and she quickly replaced the cap before temptation got the better of good judgment.

As she was leaving the bathroom, the empty water glass fell to the floor, shattered. Startled, she whirled around. She was sure she hadn't set the tumbler on the edge of the sink. It had not fallen: something had knocked it off.

"Max, please come home," she said softly.

* * *

She waited for him in the second-floor den, his favorite room, a room crammed full of guns and books. Antique rifles expertly restored and mounted in wall display boxes. Matched sets of Hemingway, Stevenson, Poe, Shaw, Fitzgerald, Dickens. A pair of 1872 No. 3 Colt Derringers in a silk-lined, brass-bound carrying case. Novels by John D. MacDonald, Clavell, Bellow, Woolrich, Levin, Vidal; volumes of nonfiction by Gay Talese, Colin Wilson, Hellman, Toland, Shirer. Shotguns, rifles, revolvers, automatic pistols. Raymond Chandler, Dashiell Hammett, Ross MacDonald, Mary McCarthy, James M. Cain, Jessamyn West.

Guns and books were an odd combination, Mary thought. However, next to her, they were the two things that Max liked most.

She tried to read a current bestseller that she had been meaning to begin for weeks, but her mind wandered. She put the book aside, went to Max's desk, sat down. She took a pen and a writing tablet from the center drawer.

For a while she stared at the blank page. Finally she wrote:

Page 1
Questions:
Why am I having these visions when I don't seek them out?
Why, suddenly, for the first time, am I able to feel the pain that the victims in the visions feel?
Why hasn't any other clairvoyant ever felt his visions?
How could the killer in the beauty shop possibly know I was watching?
Why would a poltergeist attempt to keep me from seeing this killer's face?
What does all of this mean?

Ever since she was a child, through major and minor crises, she had felt that it helped to write down her problems. When they were before her, summarized in a few words, somehow more concrete in ink than in reality, they usually ceased to appear insoluble.

After she finished composing the list, she read each question carefully, first silently and then aloud.

On the next page of the tablet she wrote: *Answers*.

She thought for a few minutes. Then: *I don't have any answers*.

"Dammit!" she said.

She threw the pen across the room.

* * *

"Harley Barnes speaking."

"Chief Barnes, this is Mary Bergen."

"Why, hello. Are you still in town?"

"No. I'm calling from Bel Air."

"What can I do for you?"

"I'm writing a column about what happened last night, and I had some questions. The man we caught last night . . . what was his name?"

"Can't you get it with your clairvoyance?"

"I'm afraid not. I can't see everything I want."

"Name's Richard Lingard."

"A resident of your town, or an outsider?"

"Born and raised here. I knew his dad and mom. He owned a pharmacy."

"His age?"

"Early thirties, thereabouts."

"Is he . . . was he married?"

"Divorced years ago. No children, thank God."

"Are you sure . . ."

"Sure there aren't children? Oh, yes. Positive."

"No. I meant . . . is he . . . really dead?"

"Dead? Of course he's dead. Didn't you see him?"

"I just thought . . . Have you found anything unusual about him?"

"Unusual? In what way?"

"Did his neighbors think he was odd in any way?"

"They liked him. Everyone liked him."

"Was anything strange found in his home?"

"Nothing. He lived like anyone else. It's frightening how ordinary he was. If Dick Lingard could turn out to be a psychopathic killer, then who can you trust?"

"No one."

"Mrs. Bergen . . ." Barnes hesitated. "Did you take the knife?"

"What knife?"

"Lingard's knife."

"You can't find it?"

"It vanished from the scene."

"Vanished? Does that happen often?"

"Never before to me."

"I don't have it."

"Perhaps your brother picked it up."

"Alan wouldn't do that."

"Or your husband?"

"We've worked with the police many times, Chief. We know enough not to make souvenirs out of the evidence."

"We've searched Mrs. Harrington's place from top to bottom. The knife isn't there."

"Maybe Lingard dropped it on the front lawn."

"We've gone over every inch of that, too."

"He might have dropped it in the gutter when he collapsed against your squad car."

"Or on the sidewalk. We didn't search for the knife immediately, like we should have done, and there was a large crowd of spectators. Maybe one of them picked it up. We'll ask around. I imagine we'll come across the thing. At least we don't need it for any trial. Death solved that problem. There's no way a smart attorney can get Richard Lingard out on the streets again."

* * *

At seven-thirty the all-news radio station in Los Angeles carried a story about four young nurses who had been found beaten and stabbed to death in their Anaheim apartment.

Beverly Pulchaski.

Susan Haven.

Linda Proctor.

Marie Sanzini.

Mary didn't recognize even one of them.

Perplexed, she sat back from the edge of her chair. She recalled the battered face in last night's vision: the black-haired, blue-eyed woman. She was *certain* she knew that face.

* * *

8:00 P.M.

She met Max at the front door. When he came inside and closed the door, he put his arms around her. His clothes were cold, crisp with the night air, but the warmth of his body pressed through the fabric.

"Six hours of shopping," she said, "and no packages?"

"I left them to be gift-wrapped. I'll pick them up tomorrow."

Grinning, she said, "I didn't know Woolworth's did gift-wrapping."

He kissed her cheek. "Missed you."

She leaned back in his arms. "Hey, where's your overcoat? You'll catch the flu."

"It got splashed with mud," he said. "I dropped it off at the dry cleaner's."

"How'd it get muddy?"

"I had a flat tire."

"A Mercedes *wouldn't*."

"Ours did. The spot where I had to change it was muddy. I got splashed by a passing car."

"Did you get his license number? If you did, I'll—"

"Unfortunately I didn't," Max said. "At the time it happened I thought, 'If I could get the bastard's number, Mary would find out who he is and thrash him within an inch of his life.'"

"Nobody hurts my Max and gets away with it."

"I also cut my finger changing the tire," he said, holding up his right hand. The cuff of the shirt sleeve was soaked with blood, and one finger was bound in a bloody handkerchief. "There's a sharp metal edge on the jack," he said.

She took hold of his wrist. "So much blood! Let's see the cut."

"It's nothing." He pulled his hand away before she could remove the handkerchief. "It's stopped bleeding."

"Maybe it needs stitches."

"It needs pressure, that's all. It's a deep cut, but the area's too small to take stitches. And the sight will ruin your dinner."

"Let me look. I'm a big girl now. Besides, it has to be

properly cleaned and bandaged."

"I'll take care of that," he said. "You go ahead to the table. I'll join you in a few minutes."

"You can't handle it yourself."

"Of course I can. I wasn't always married, you know. I lived alone for years." He kissed her forehead. "Let's not upset Mrs. Churchill. If we don't get to the table soon, she'll be in tears."

With his good hand he pushed Mary toward the dining room.

"If you bleed to death," she said, "I'll never forgive you."

Laughing, he hurried to the staircase and climbed the steps two at a time to the second floor.

* * *

Dinner was to Mary's taste, hearty yet not heavy. They had onion soup, salad, châteaubriand with bearnaise sauce, and strips of zucchini marinated in oil and garlic, then broiled briefly.

Over coffee in the library, drifting on a pool of serenity formed by a second valium taken just before Max arrived for dinner, she told him about her day: Cauvel, the pain-filled vision, the poltergeist that had kept her from probing the vision for the name and face of the killer. They discussed the radio report of the dead nurses in Anaheim, which he had also heard, and last of all she told him about her conversation with Harley Barnes.

"You're emphasizing the missing knife," Max said. "Isn't Barnes' explanation credible enough? A spectator *could* have taken it."

"Could have—but didn't."

"Then who did?"

She was beside him on the sofa. She kicked off her shoes, drew one leg under her, delaying until she could summon the right words. This was a delicate situation. If Max was unable to believe what she had to tell him, he would think her at least *slightly* mad.

"These visions are totally different from any I've ever known," she said at last. "Which means the killer, the source of the psychic emanations, is different from any killer I've ever tracked before. He isn't an ordinary man. I've been trying to find a theory that will make sense of what's happened to me since last night, and when I talked with Barnes I found the key. The missing knife is the key. Don't you see? Richard Lingard has the knife."

"Lingard? He's dead. Barnes shot him. Lingard couldn't have taken his knife anywhere but to a drawer in the morgue."

"He could have taken it wherever he wanted. Barnes killed Lingard's body. Lingard's spirit took the knife."

Max was amazed. "I don't believe in ghosts. And even if spirits *do* exist, they don't have substance, at least not as we think of it. So how could Lingard's spirit, a thing of no substance, carry off a very substantial knife?"

"A spirit has no substance, but it does have *power*," she said emphatically. "Two months ago, when you helped me cover that story in Connecticut, you saw a poltergeist in action."

"What of it?"

"Well, a poltergeist has no apparent substance, yet it tosses around solid objects, doesn't it?"

Reluctantly he said, "Yes. But I don't believe a poltergeist is the spirit of a dead person."

"What else could it be?" Before he responded she said, "Lingard's spirit carried away the butcher knife. I *know* it."

He drank his coffee in three long swallows. "Suppose that's true. Where's his spirit now?"

"In possession of someone living."

"What?"

"As soon as Lingard's body died, his spirit slipped out of it and into someone else."

Max got up, walked to the bookshelves. He looked at Mary with eyes that studied, weighed, and judged. "In every session with Cauvel, you've come closer to remembering what Berton Mitchell did to you."

"So you think that because I'm on the verge of knowing, I might be seeking escape from the truth, escape in madness."

"Can you face up to what he did?"

"I've lived with it for years, even if I have suppressed it."

"Living with it and accepting it are two different things."

"If you think I'm a candidate for a padded room, you don't know me," she said, irritated in spite of the valium.

"I don't think that. But demonic possession?"

"Not demonic. I'm talking about something less grand than that. This is the possession of a living person by the spirit of someone dead."

His square, almost ugly face was creased with worry. He spread his arms, his hands, palms up, a supplicant bear. "And who is this living person?"

"The man who killed those nurses in Anaheim. He's possessed by Lingard, and that's why the psychic emanations he puts out are so different."

Max returned to the sofa. "I can't accept it."

"That doesn't mean I'm wrong."

"The poltergeist phenomena in Cauvel's office . . . You think—"

"That was Lingard," she said.

"There's a problem with that theory," he said.

She raised her eyebrows.

"How could Lingard's spirit be in two places at once?" he asked. "How could Lingard be in possession of a man who he's forcing to commit murder—and at the same time be throwing glass dogs around Cauvel's office?"

"I don't know. Who's to say what a ghost can do?"

* * *

At ten o'clock, Max came to the master bedroom. He had gone downstairs to the library for a novel and had returned carrying a thick volume—not the book he'd been after. "I talked to Dr. Cauvel just now," he said.

Mary was sitting up in bed. She used a flap of the dust jacket to mark her place in the book she was reading. "What did the good doctor have to say?"

"He thinks *you* are the poltergeist."

"Me?"

"He says you were under stress—"

"Aren't we all?"

"Especially you."

"Was I?"

"Because you remembered about Berton Mitchell."

"I've remembered about him before."

"This time you recalled more than ever. Cauvel says you were under great psychological stress in his office, and that *you* caused the glass dogs to fly about."

She smiled. "A man your size looks just too cute in pajamas."

"Mary—"

"Especially yellow pajamas. You should wear just a robe."

"You're avoiding this." He came to the foot of the bed. "What about the glass dogs?"

"Cauvel just wants me to pay for them," she said airily.

"He didn't mention money."

"That's what he was angling for."

"He's not the type," Max said.

"I'll pay half the value of the dogs."

Exasperated, Max said, "Mary, that's not necessary."

"I know," she said lightly. "I didn't break them."

"I mean, Cauvel isn't asking to be paid. You're trying to avoid the main issue."

"Okay, okay. So *how* did I cause glass dogs to fly about?"

"Unconsciously. Cauvel says—"

"Psychiatrists always blame the unconscious."

"Who's to say they're wrong?"

"They're stupid."

"Mary—"

"And you're stupid for believing Cauvel."

She didn't want to argue, but she couldn't control herself. She was frightened by the direction the conversation was taking, although she didn't know why she should be. She was terrified of some knowledge that lay within her, but she couldn't understand what that might be.

Standing like a preacher, holding his book as if it were a Bible, Max said, "Will you listen?"

She shook her head to indicate she found him too irritating to bear. "If I'm responsible for his figurines getting busted up, am I also to blame for the bad weather in the East, for the war in Africa, for inflation, for poverty, for the recent crop failures?"

"Sarcasm."

"You encourage it."

The tranquilizer was doing her no good whatsoever. She was tense. Trembling. Like a shallow-water, feathery sea anemone quivering in the subtle currents that preceded a storm, she was nervously aware of unseen forces that could destroy her.

Suddenly she felt threatened by Max.

That doesn't make sense, she thought. Max isn't any danger to me. He's trying to help me find the truth, that's all.

Dizzy, confused, on the verge of anomie, she leaned back against her pillows.

Max opened his book and read in a quiet but urgent voice: "'Telekinesis is the ability to move objects or to cause changes within objects solely by the force of the mind. The phenomenon has most often and most reliably been reported in times of crises or in severe stress situations. For example, automobiles have been levitated from injured people, debris from the dying in fire-swept or collapsed buildings.'"

"I *know* what telekinesis is," she said.

Max ignored her, kept reading: "'Telekinesis is often mistaken for the work of poltergeists, which are playful and occasionally malevolent spirits. The existence of poltergeists as astral beings is debatable and certainly unproven. It should be noted that in most houses where poltergeists have appeared, there resides an adolescent with serious identity problems, *or some other person under severe nervous strain*. A good argument could be made that the phenomena often attributed to poltergeists are usually the product of unconscious telekinesis.'"

"This is ridiculous," she said. "Why would I pitch those dogs around just when I was about to see the killer's face in the vision?"

"You really didn't want to see his face, so your subconscious threw those figurines to distract you from the vision."

"That's absurd! I *wanted* to see it. I want to stop this man before he kills again."

Max's hard gray eyes were like knives, dissecting her. "Are you sure you want to stop him?"

"What kind of question is that?"

He sighed. "Do you know what I think? I think you've sensed, through your clairvoyance, that this psychopath will kill you if you pursue him. You've seen a possible future, and you're trying like hell to avoid it."

Surprised, she said, "Nothing of the sort."

"The pain you felt—"

"Was the pain of the victims. It wasn't a foreshadowing of my own death."

"Maybe you haven't foreseen the danger consciously," Max said. "But subconsciously, perhaps, you've seen yourself as a victim if you pursue this case. That would explain why you're trying to mislead yourself with poltergeists and with talk about possession."

"I'm not going to die," she said sharply. "I'm not hiding from anything like that."

"Why are you afraid to even consider it?"

"I'm not afraid."

"I think you are."

"I'm not a coward. And I'm not a liar."

"Mary, I'm trying to help you."

"Then believe me!"

He looked at her quizzically. "You don't have to shout."

"You never hear me unless I shout!"

"Mary, why do you want to argue?"

I don't, she thought. Stop me. Hold me.

"*You* started this," she said.

"I only asked you to consider an alternative to this business about possession. You're overreacting."

I know, she thought. I know I am. And I don't know why. I don't want to hurt you. I need you.

But all she said was, "Listening to you, I'd think I was never right about anything. I'm always overreacting or mistaken or misled or confused. You treat me as if I'm a child."

"You're treating *yourself* with condescension."

"Just a silly little child."

Hug me, kiss me, love me, she thought. Please make me stop this. I don't want to argue. I'm scared.

He started toward the bedroom door. "This isn't the time to talk. You're not in the mood for constructive criticism."

"Because I'm behaving like a child?"

"Yes."

"Sometimes you fucking piss me off."

He stopped, turned back to her. "That's like a child," he said calmly. "Like a child who's trying to shock a grownup with a lot of dirty words."

She opened her book to the page she had marked and, refusing to acknowledge him, she pretended to read.

* * *

She would rather have suffered disabling pain than even temporary estrangement from Max. When they argued, which was

rarely, she felt miserable. The two or three hours of silence
that invariably followed a disagreement, and which were usually her fault, were unbearable.

She spent the remainder of the evening in bed with a copy
of *The Occult* by Colin Wilson. As she began each page, she
could not remember what had been on the page before it.

Max stayed on his side of the bed, reading a novel and
smoking his pipe. He might as well have been a thousand miles
away.

The eleven o'clock television news, which she switched on
by remote control, headlined a grisly story about slaughter
in a Santa Ana beauty salon. There was film of the blood-
smeared shop and interviews with police officials who had
nothing to say.

"You see?" Mary said. "I was right about the nurses. I was
right about the beauty salon. And, by God, I'm right about
Richard Lingard, too."

Even as she spoke, she regretted the words, and especially
her tone of voice.

He looked at her but said nothing.

She looked away, down at her book. She hadn't meant to
revive the argument. Quite the opposite. She wanted to get him
talking once more. She wanted to hear his voice.

Although she often started arguments, she had never been
able to initiate the conclusion of one. Psychologically, she
wasn't capable of making the first gesture for peace. She left
that move to the men. Always. She knew that wasn't fair, but
she could not change.

She supposed that this inadequacy dated back to her father's
violent death. He had left her so suddenly that she still sometimes felt abandoned. All of her adult life she had worried
about men walking out on her before *she* was prepared to end
the relationship.

And of course she wasn't ever going to be ready to end her
marriage; that was for keeps. Therefore, whenever she and
Max argued, whenever she had reason to worry about his leaving, she forced him to pick up the olive branch. It was a test
which he could pass only if he would sacrifice more pride than
she; and when he had done that, he would have proved that
he loved her and that he would never leave her as her father
had done.

The death of her father *was* more important than whatever Berton Mitchell had done to her.

Why couldn't Dr. Cauvel see that?

* * *

In the dark bedroom, when it became evident that neither of them could sleep, Max touched her. His hands affected her in the same way that the rapidly vibrating tines of a tuning fork would affect fine crystal. She trembled uncontrollably and shattered. She broke against him, weeping.

He didn't speak. Words no longer mattered.

He held her for a few minutes, and then he began to stroke her. He slid one hand over her silk pajamas, along her flank, across her buttocks. Slow, warm movement. And then he popped open two buttons on her blouse, slipped his hand inside, felt her warm breast, his fingers lingering on her nipple only for an instant. She put her open mouth to his neck, against the hard muscle. His strong pulse was transmitted to her through her tender lips. He undressed her and then himself. The bandage on his hand brushed her bare thigh.

"Your finger," she said.

"It'll be fine."

"The cut might come open," she said. "It might start to bleed again."

"*Sshhh*," he said.

He was not in the mood to be patient, and although she hadn't said a word, he sensed she was equally anxious. He rose above her in the lightless air, as if taking flight, then settled over her. Although she had expected nothing more than the special joy of closeness, she climaxed within a minute. Not intensely. A gentle rush of pleasure. However, when she came a second time, moments before he finished far down inside of her, she cried out with delight.

For a while she lay at his side, holding his hand. Finally she said, "Don't ever leave me. Stay with me as long as I live."

"As long as you live," Max promised.

* * *

At five-thirty on Wednesday morning, in the middle of a nightmare vision of the killer's next crime, Mary was catapulted from sleep by the sound of gunfire. A single shot, ear-splitting, too close. Even as the *boom* was bouncing off the bedroom walls, she sat up, threw off the blanket and sheet, swung her legs out of bed. "Max! What's wrong? Max!"

Beside her, he switched on the lamp, jumped up from the bed. He stood, swaying, blinking.

The sudden light hurt her eyes. Although she was squinting, she could see there was no intruder in the room.

Max reached for the loaded handgun that he kept on the nightstand. It was not there.

"Where's the pistol?" he asked.

"I didn't touch it," she said.

Then, as her eyes adjusted to the light, she saw the gun. It was floating in the air near the foot of the bed, floating five feet above the floor, as if it were suspended from wires, except that there were no wires. The barrel was pointed at her.

The poltergeist.

"Jesus!" Max said.

Although no visible finger pulled the trigger, a second shot exploded. The bullet tore into the headboard inches from Mary's face.

She panicked. Gasping, whimpering, she ran across the room, hunched as if she were crippled. The gun traversed to the left, covering her. She came to a corner, stopped. Trapped. She realized she should have gone in the opposite direction, where she could have at least locked herself in the bathroom.

The third shot smashed into the floor beside her feet. Bits of a throw rug and splinters of wood sprayed up.

"Max!"

He grabbed at the gun, but it slid away from him, rose and fell and swung from side to side, bobbled and weaved, forced him into a clumsy ballet.

She looked for something to hide behind.

There was nothing.

The fourth shot passed over her head, piercing a framed, glass-covered watercolor of Newport Beach harbor.

Max connected with the pistol, clutched it. The barrel twisted in his hands until it was pointed at his chest. Sweating, cursing, he struggled to pull the weapon from a pair of hands that he couldn't see. Surprisingly, after a few seconds, the unseen contestant surrendered, and Max staggered backward with the prize.

She stood with her back to the wall, hands to her face. She couldn't take her eyes from the barrel of the gun.

"It's safe now," Max said. "It's over." He started toward her.

"For God's sake, unload it!" she said, pointing at the gun in his hand.

He stopped, stared at the pistol, and then took the magazine out of the handgrip.

"All of the bullets should be taken from the clip," she said.

"I doubt that's necessary if I—"

"Do it!"

His big hands were shaking as he took the bullets from the magazine. He placed all of the pieces on the bed: pistol, empty magazine, unspent ammunition. For a minute he studied the items, as she did, waiting for one of them to rise off the blanket.

Nothing moved.

"What was it?" he asked.

"Poltergeist."

"Whatever it was—is it still here?"

She closed her eyes, tried to relax, tried to *feel*. After a while she said, "No. It's gone."

Wednesday,
December 23

10

Percy Osterman, the Orange County sheriff, opened the door for Max and Mary, motioned for them to go ahead of him.

The room was gray. The paint was gray, the floor tile gray, the windowsills gray with dust. A set of gray metal storage shelves was bolted to one wall, and the wall opposite the shelves contained a lot of built-in file drawers with burnished steel fronts. The few pieces of furniture were fashioned of tubular steel and gray vinyl. The screens over the ceiling lights were gray, and the fuzzy fluorescent illumination transformed the scene into a chiaroscuro print.

The only spots of brightness in the room were the well scrubbed porcelain sinks and the slanted autopsy table, which was fiercely white with polished, gleaming stainless steel fixtures.

The sheriff was all hard lines and sharp angles. He was nearly as tall as Max, but forty pounds lighter and far less muscular. Yet he did not appear wasted or weak. His hands were large, boney, almost fleshless, the fingers like talons. His shoulders sloped forward. His neck was thin with a prominent adam's apple. In his pinched, sun-browned face, his eyes were quick, nervous, a curious pale shade of amber.

Osterman's frown was ominous, his smile easy and kind. He was not smiling when he opened one of the six large drawers and pulled the shroud from the face of the corpse.

Mary stepped away from Max, moved closer to the dead man.

"Kyle Nolan," Osterman said. "Owned the beauty shop. Worked there as a hair stylist."

Nolan was short, broad-shouldered, barrel-chested. Bald. A bushy mustache. Shave off the mustache, Mary thought, and he'd look like that actor, Edward Asner.

She put one hand on the drawer and waited for a rush of

psychic impressions. Although she didn't understand how or why, she knew that, for a time after passing away, the dead maintained a bubble of energy around them, an invisible capsule that contained memories, vivid scenes of their lives and especially of their last minutes. Ordinarily, contact with the victim of a murder, or with the victim's belongings, would generate a torrent of clairvoyant images, sometimes clear as reality and sometimes hopelessly blurry and meaningless, most of them dealing with the moment of death and with the identity of the killer.

In this case, for the first time in her experience, she sensed absolutely nothing. Not even a shapeless flurry of movement or color.

She touched the dead man's cold face.

Still nothing.

Osterman closed the drawer, opened the one next to it. As he folded back the shroud, he said, "Tina Nolan. Kyle's wife."

Tina was an attractive but hard-faced woman with brittle, bleached hair that her husband should have found professionally embarrassing. Although they had been closed hours ago by the coroner, her eyes had come open again. She stared at Mary as if she were trying to impart some dreadfully important news; but in the end she provided nothing more than poor Kyle had done.

The woman in the third drawer was in her late twenties. She had once been beautiful.

"Rochelle Drake," Percy Osterman said. "Nolan's last customer for the day."

"Rochelle Drake?" Max said. He came closer, peered into the drawer. "Don't I know that name?"

"Recognize her?" Sheriff Osterman asked.

Max shook his head. "No. But . . . Mary? Does that name mean anything to you?"

"No," she said.

"When you foresaw these killings, you said you thought you knew one of the victims."

"I was wrong," she said. "These people are strangers."

"That's odd," Max said. "I'd swear . . . well, I don't know *what* I'd swear . . . except this one's name . . . Rochelle Drake . . . it's familiar."

Mary was not paying much attention to him, for she perceived a familiar electricity in the air, a stirring of psychic forces. The Drake woman was going to provide what the other bodies should have offered but didn't. Mary opened her mind to the psychic emanations, made herself as receptive as she could, and put her hand on the dead woman's forehead.

Wicka-wicka-wicka!

Wings.

Startled, Mary pulled her hand away from the corpse as if she had been bitten.

She felt wings, leathery wings, shuddering like the membranes of drums.

This isn't possible, she thought frantically. The wings have something to do with Berton Mitchell. Not with this dead woman. Not with the man who killed her. The wings have to do with the past, not the present. Berton Mitchell couldn't be involved in this. He hung himself in a jail cell nearly twenty-four years ago.

But now she could smell the wings as well as feel them, smell the wings and the creatures behind them—a dank, musty, musky odor that nauseated her.

What if the man who murdered Rochelle Drake and the others was not possessed by the spirit of Richard Lingard? What if, instead, he was possessed by the soul of another psychopath, by the spirit of Berton Mitchell? Wasn't it conceivable that Lingard himself had been possessed by Berton Mitchell? And when Barnes shot Lingard, perhaps Mitchell's spirit moved on to another host. Perhaps she had unknowingly crossed the path of an old nemesis. Perhaps she would spend the remainder of her life in pursuit of Berton Mitchell. Perhaps she would be compelled to follow him from one host to another until he finally found the opportunity to kill her.

No. That was madness. She was thinking like a lunatic.

Max asked, "Is something wrong?"

Wings brushed her face, her neck, shoulders and breasts and belly, fluttered against her ankles and up her calves and then against her inner thighs.

She was determined not to succumb to fear. But she was also half convinced that if she didn't stop thinking about the wings, they would carry her off into everlasting darkness. A ridiculous notion. Nevertheless, she turned away from the morgue drawer.

"Are you receiving something?" Max asked.

"Not now," she lied.

"But you were?"

"For an instant."

"What did you see?" he asked.

"Nothing important. Just meaningless movement."

"Can you pick it up again?" Max asked.

"No."

She mustn't pursue it. If she did, she would see what lay behind those wings. She must never see what lay behind those wings.

Osterman closed the drawer.

Mary sighed with relief.

* * *

Sheriff Osterman went with them to the far corner of the municipal parking lot, where they'd left their car.

The December sky was like the morgue—shades of gray. The fast-moving clouds were reflected in the polished hood of the Mercedes.

Shivering, Mary put her hands in her coat pockets and hunched her shoulders against the wind.

"Heard good things about you," Osterman told Mary in his peculiarly economical way of speaking. "Often thought about working with you. Pleased when you called this morning. Hoped you'd come up with a lead."

"I hoped so, too," she said.

"Foresaw these murders, did you?"

"Yes," she said.

"Those nurses in Anaheim, too?"

"That's right."

"Same killer, you think?"

"Yes," she said.

Osterman nodded. "We think so, too. Have some evidence of it."

"What sort of evidence?" Max asked.

"When he killed the nurses," Osterman said, each word sharp and quick, "he busted up some stuff. Religious things. Two crucifixes. Statuette of the Virgin Mary. Even strangled one girl with a rosary. Found something similar in this beauty shop case."

"What?" Mary asked.

"Pretty ugly bit of business. Maybe you don't want to hear it."

"I'm used to hearing and seeing ugly things," she said.

He regarded her for a moment, amber eyes hooded. "Guess that's true." He leaned against the Mercedes. "This woman in the beauty shop. Rochelle Drake. She wore a necklace. A gold cross. He raped her, killed her. Tore the cross off her neck. Pushed it up . . . inside of her."

Mary felt ill. She hugged herself.

"Then he's a psychopath with some sort of religious hang-up," Max said.

"Appears so," Osterman said. He looked at Mary and asked, "So where do you go from here?"

"Down to the shore," she said.

"King's Point," Max said.

"Why there?"

She hesitated, glanced at Max. "That's where the next murders will take place."

Osterman did not seem surprised. "Had another vision, did you?"

"Early this morning," she said.

"When will it happen?"

"Tomorrow night," she said.

"Christmas Eve?"

"Yes."

"Where in King's Point?"

"On the harbor," she said.

"Pretty good-sized harbor."

"It'll be near the shops and restaurants."

"How many will he kill?" Osterman asked.

"I'm not sure."

She was so *cold*, colder than could be accounted for by the California winter day and the wind, cold in the pit of her stomach, cold in her heart. She was wearing a stylish but thinly lined calfskin coat from North Beach Leather. She wished she'd chosen her heaviest fur.

"Maybe I'll be able to stop him before he kills anyone else," she said.

"You feel a responsibility to stop him?" Osterman asked.

"I won't have peace of mind until I do."

"Wouldn't want this talent you've got."

"I never asked for it," she said.

A truck rumbled by in the street. Osterman waited for the noise to die down.

"King's Point used to be in my jurisdiction," he said. "Two years ago they voted in their own police force. Now I can't poke my nose in unless they ask. Or unless a case that starts in the county ends up on their doorstep."

"I wish I could be working with you," Mary said.

"You'll be working with a jackass," Osterman said.

"Excuse me?"

"Chief of police at King's Point. Name's Patmore. John Patmore. A jackass. He gives you trouble, tell him to call me. He kind of respects me, but he's still a jackass."

"We'll use your name if we have to," Mary said. "But we aren't entirely without influence down there. We know the owner of the *King's Point Press*."

Osterman smiled. "Lou Pasternak?"

"You know him?"

"Damned good newspaperman."

"Yes, he is."

"Quite a character, too."

"A little bit of one," she agreed.

The sheriff offered his hand to Mary, then to Max. "Hope you two do my job for me this time."

"Thanks for your help," Max said.

"Don't hesitate to ask for more if you need it. It's been my pleasure."

As Mary got into the Mercedes, a gust of wind sang in the power lines overhead.

* * *

They reached King's Point at two-thirty in the afternoon. Their first glimpse of it, as they topped a rise in the road, was from high above the harbor.

The sky was low. Thick gray clouds scudded inland. A mile offshore the ocean was shrouded in mist; and closer to the beach formidable waves churned beneath half a dozen scuba-suited surfers, fell frothily onto the sand, and exploded into spray against the stone breakwaters on both sides of the harbor entrance.

The town was on the Pacific Coast Highway, a few miles south of Laguna Beach, in a perpetually smogless pocket of sunshine and money. The sun was in hiding today, but the money was everywhere evident. Houses on the verdant hillsides were priced from $75,000 to $500,000, nearly all of them with well manicured decorative gardens and ocean views. Waterfront homes with docks were not as expensive as those in Newport Beach, but real estate brokers had no time for would-be customers who flinched at a base price of a quarter million dollars. In the flat land between harbor and hills the houses were cheaper—there were some apartment buildings, too—but even they were expensive by most standards.

The travel guides said that King's Point was "charming" and "quaint" and "picturesque," and for once they were telling the truth. The lawns were lush and green; the many small parks were filled with palms of all varieties, oleander, jade plants, magnolia trees, schefflera, dracaena, olive trees, and seasonal flowers. The houses were well cared for, freshly painted every year or two as protection against the corrosive sea air. Businessmen were required to forgo the most offensive neon signs, and were forbidden by law to paint their stores in anything but soft natural tones.

The residents of King's Point appeared to think that with the proper local ordinances they could keep out everything that made the rest of the world a less desirable place to live. And they *did* keep out much that was tasteless, cheap, and gaudy.

But they can't keep out everything they don't want, Mary thought. A killer has come in from outside. He's walking among them now. They can't use local ordinances to keep out death.

From spring through early autumn the population of King's Point was sixty percent higher than in the winter. During these vacation months the motels were booked weeks in advance, the restaurants raised their prices except for locals who were recognized, the shops hired extra help, and the white beaches were crowded. Now, two days before Christmas, the town was quiet. When Max turned off the main highway onto a city street, they encountered very little traffic.

King's Point Police Headquarters was a single-story brick building of absolutely no architectural period, style, charm, integrity, or responsibility. It looked like an oversized, flat-roofed storage shed with windows. Even three blocks from the harbor, in the flats below the hills, in a limbo between the highest-value real estate parcels—waterfront and view—it was no credit to its neighborhood.

Inside, the public reception room was depressingly institutional: brown tile floor, muddy green walls, washed-out green ceiling, strictly utilitarian furniture. Tax money had purchased three desks, six-drawer filing cabinets, IBM typewriters, a copier, a small refrigerator, a United States flag, a glass-fronted case full of riot guns and pistols, a dispatcher's corner with radio—and a civilian secretary (Mrs. Vidette Yancy, according to the name plate on her desk) who was in her fifties, a woman with tightly curled white hair, pale skin, bright red lipstick, and an enormous bosom.

"I'd like to see Chief Patmore," Mary said.

Mrs. Yancy took a minute to correct a word she had just typed. "Him?" she said at last. "He's out."

"When will he be back?"

"The chief? Tomorrow morning."

"Could you give us his home address?" Max asked, leaning against the formica counter that separated the foyer from the work area.

"His home address?" Mrs. Yancy said. "Surely. I can give you that. But he isn't at home."

"Where is he?" Mary asked impatiently.

"Where is he? Why, he's up in Santa Barbara. He won't be back until ten tomorrow morning."

Mary turned to Max. "Maybe we should talk to a deputy."

"Deputy?" Mrs. Yancy said. "There are five officers under the chief. Of course, only two of them are on duty right now."

"If this guy's like we've heard," Max said, "it won't do any good to talk to subordinates. He'll expect to be dealt with directly."

"Time's running out," Mary said.

"Don't we have until seven o'clock tomorrow evening?" Max asked.

"If my vision's accurate, we do."

"Then if we see Patmore early tomorrow, that'll be soon enough."

"The officers on duty are out on patrol right now," Mrs. Yancy said. "Did you want to report a crime?"

"Not exactly," Mary said.

"Not exactly? Well, I have the forms right here, you know."

She opened a desk drawer, began to rummage through it. "I can take down the information and have an officer get back to you."

"Never mind," Max said. "We'll be in tomorrow at ten o'clock."

*   *   *

At the bay end of the harbor, valuable shoreline was occupied by commercial enterprises—yacht clubs, yacht sales offices, dry docks, restaurants, and shops. Each of these businesses was as clean and attractive and well maintained as the many expensive homes that lined both sides of the harbor channel.

The Laughing Dolphin was a restaurant and cocktail lounge that fronted on the harbor. On the second level a narrow open-air deck was suspended over the water. In good weather patrons could get pleasantly drunk while the sun warmed their faces. This afternoon the deck was deserted. Max and Mary had it to themselves.

Holding a mug of coffee laced with brandy, Mary leaned against the wooden railing.

If you stepped out of the brisk sea breezes, the day was only chilly; but the wind from the ocean was downright cold. It nipped at her face and brought a healthy color to her cheeks.

When she looked up and to her right, she could see the Spanish Court, the hotel where she and Max had reserved a room. It stood on the north hill, high above the harbor. It was majestic, all white plaster and natural woods and red tile.

Closer to hand, eight dinghies were sailing in formation, snaking back and forth across the smooth slate-colored water. Against a backdrop of sixty-, eighty-, and hundred-foot sailing ships and motor yachts, the small vessels were lovely and amusing. Even today, without the sun upon them, their sails were dazzlingly white. Their graceful progress was a definition of serenity.

"Study the boats, the houses, the entire harbor," Max said. "Maybe something you see will trigger the vision."

"I don't think so," she said. "It was knocked out of my mind forever when I woke up and found I was being shot at."

"You've got to try."

"Do I?"

"Isn't that why you wanted to come?"

"If I don't go after this killer," she said, "he'll eventually come after me."

The wind gusted suddenly, flapped Mary's leather coat against her legs, rattled the large plate-glass windows of the cocktail lounge behind them.

She sipped her coffee. Tentacles of steam writhed across her face and dissolved in the wintry air.

Max said, "Maybe it'll help if you tell me again how it's going to happen." When she didn't answer, he coaxed her. "Tomorrow night at seven o'clock. Not too far from where we're standing right now."

"Within a couple of blocks," she said.

"You said he'll come with a butcher knife."

"Lingard's knife."

"Some knife, anyway."

"Lingard's," she insisted.

"You said he'll stab two people."

"Yes, two."

"Kill them?"

"Maybe one of them."

"But not the other."

"At least one will live. Maybe both."

"Who are these people he'll stab?"

"I don't know their names," she said.

"What do they look like?"

"I couldn't see their faces."

"Young women, like in Anaheim?"

"I really don't know."

"What about the high-powered rifle?"

"I saw it in the vision."

"He's got a butcher knife and a gun?"

"After he's stabbed those two people," she said, "he'll take the rifle up into a tower. He intends to shoot everyone."

"Everyone?"

"A lot of people, as many as he can."

At the far end of the harbor, a dozen sea gulls kited in from the ocean, riding very high on the wind, white feathers silhouetted dramatically against the stormy sky.

"How many will he kill?" Max asked.

"The vision ended before I could see."

"Which tower will he use?"

"I don't know."

"Look around," Max said. "Look at each one of them. Try to sense which it will be."

To her right, three hundred yards farther around the bend of the harbor's bay end and five hundred yards from the Laughing Dolphin, the Roman Catholic Church of the Holy Trinity lay one block from the waterfront. She had been inside it once. It was a brooding Gothic structure, an impressive fortress of weathered granite and darkly beautiful stained glass windows. The hundred-foot bell tower, which had a low-walled open deck directly beneath its peaked roof, was the highest point within two blocks of the harbor.

The sound of sea gulls distracted her for a moment. Above the formation of sailboats that were playing follow the leader, still soaring inland, the gulls began to squeal with excitement. Their sharp voices were like fingernails scraped across a blackboard.

She tried not to hear the birds, concentrated on Trinity. She received nothing. No images. No psychic vibrations. Not the vaguest premonition that the killer would strike out at King's Point from Trinity's bell tower.

St. Luke's Lutheran Church was between Mary and the Church of the Holy Trinity. It was two hundred yards north and half a block from the harbor. It was a Spanish-style building with massive carved oak doors, and a bell tower slightly more than half as high as the one at the Catholic church.

Nothing from St. Luke's either.

Just the ghostly wind and the cries of agitated sea gulls.

The third tower was to her left, two hundred yards away, at the edge of the water. It was only four stories high, part of Kimball's Games and Snacks, a clapboard and cedar-shingled pavilion that housed an amusement arcade. In the summer camera-laden tourists climbed to the top and took photographs of the harbor. Now the place was closed for the season, quiet, empty.

"Will it be Kimball's tower?" Max asked.

"I don't know," she said. "It could be any of them."

"You've got to try harder," he said.

She closed her eyes and concentrated.

Screeching angrily, a gull swooped down, flashed past their faces with only eight or ten inches to spare.

Mary jumped back in surprise, dropped her coffee mug.

"You okay?" Max asked.

"Startled. That's all."

"Did it touch you?"

"No."

"They don't dive that close unless you trespass on their nesting grounds. But there's nowhere around here they'd lay eggs. Besides, it's not the time of year for that."

The dozen gulls that had entered the harbor a few minutes ago were circling overhead. They weren't taking advantage of the wind currents as gulls usually do; there was nothing lazy or graceful about their flight. Instead, they twisted and fluttered and soared and dived and darted frantically among one another within a tightly defined sphere of air. They seemed tortured. It was surprising that they didn't collide. Screeching at one another, they performed an unnatural, frenzied dance in midair.

"What's upset them?" Max wondered.

"Me," she said.

"You? What did you do?"

She was trembling. "I tried to use my clairvoyance to see which tower the killer will use."

"So?"

"The gulls are here to stop me from doing that."

Astounded, he said, "Mary, that makes no sense. Trained gulls?"

"Not trained. Controlled."

"Controlled by whom? Who sent them?"

She stared at the birds.

"Who?" he asked again. "Lingard's ghost?"

"Maybe," she said.

He touched her shoulder. "Mary—"

"You saw the poltergeist that was after me, dammit!"

In a let's-calm-down-and-be-reasonable tone of voice that drove her mad, he said, "Whatever causes poltergeist phenomena can lift and hurl inanimate objects—but not living animals."

"Listen," she said, "you don't know everything. You don't know—" She looked away from him, looked up.

"What's wrong?" he asked.

"The birds."

The gulls still capered maniacally overhead, but they were silent. Perfectly silent.

"Strange," Max said.

"I'm going inside," she said.

She almost reached the mullioned door that connected the deck to the second-floor cocktail lounge when a sea gull struck her from behind, between the shoulders, like a hammer blow. She stumbled and instinctively put one arm across her face. The wings beat at her neck. Battered the back of her head. Thundered in her ears. These weren't like the wings that she associated with Berton Mitchell. Those wings had been leathery, membranous. These were feathered. But that didn't make the sea gulls any less frightening. She thought of the bird's wickedly sharp, hooked beak, thought of it pecking out her eyes, and she screamed.

Max shouted something that she couldn't hear.

She started to reach for the bird, realized it might tear her fingers, jerked her hand back.

Max knocked the gull away from her. It flopped on the deck, temporarily stunned.

Max opened the door, pushed her inside, went in after her, and pulled the door shut.

The bartender had seen the attack, and he was hurrying around the end of the counter, wiping his hands on a towel.

A heavyset, red-haired man at the bar swiveled around on his stool to see what was happening.

In one of the black vinyl booths by the windows a young couple—a pretty blonde in a green dress and a dark, intense man—looked up from their drinks.

Before the bartender had taken three steps, a sea gull struck the mullioned door behind Max. Two small panes broke inward. Glass tinkled musically on the floor.

The cocktail waitress dropped her tray and ran toward the stairs that led down to the restaurant foyer.

With a sound like a shotgun blast, another gull slammed into one of the five-foot by six-foot windows that overlooked the harbor. The glass cracked but held. The injured bird toppled backwards to the deck outside, leaving a smear of blackish blood to mark the collision.

"They'll kill me."

"No," Max said.

"That's what they want!"

He held her protectively, but for the first time since she had known him, his arms didn't seem big enough, his chest broad enough, his body strong enough to guarantee her safety.

A sea gull caromed off the window beside the young couple's table. The glass cracked in a jagged, lightning-bolt pattern. The pretty blonde shrieked and scrambled out of the booth.

An instant after her companion prudently followed her, another gull rammed the same window and shattered it. Large shards of glass collapsed onto the dark pine table, bounced up in many smaller pieces, and showered over the vinyl where the couple had been sitting.

The decapitated gull landed in the center of the table; and its bloody head plopped into the woman's martini.

Two more gulls flew in through the broken window.

"Don't let them!" Mary shouted hysterically. "Don't let them, don't, don't, oh don't, *please* don't!"

The young couple went to their knees, taking shelter behind and half beneath a table.

Max pushed Mary into the nearest corner. He shielded her as best he could with his body. One of the birds sailed straight at him. He threw up one arm to ward it off. The creature squealed in anger, shied away, circled through the room.

The other gull attempted to land on one of the round tables in the middle of the lounge. Its wings knocked over a centerpiece—a copper and stained-glass lantern with a candle inside—and the candle set fire to the tablecloth.

The bartender used his damp towel to extinguish the flame.

The gull swooped from the table to the shelves of liquor behind the bar. Two, three, four, half a dozen, eight bottles crashed to the floor. On his stool, a few feet from the crazed gull, the red-haired man was too bewildered to be frightened. He watched the bird with fascination as it flapped and kicked and sent more bottles to the floor. The fragrance of whiskey blossomed through the room.

The first gull flew at Max again. It came in above him, fluttered wildly in the corner, then with malign intelligence dropped behind his back, onto Mary's head.

Its feet tangled in her hair.

"God, no! No!"

She grabbed at the bird, not caring about its beak, not caring if it pecked her fingers. It was unclean. She had to get if off her. Max reached for it, too. Then it rose from her, up and away once more, circling into the room. In a second, however, it darted back and thumped into the wall beside her head. It dropped to the floor at her feet and twitched spasmodically.

Gasping for breath, her hands to her face and fingers spread, she backed away from it.

"It's terror-stricken," Max said.

"Kill it!" She hardly recognized her own voice; it was altered by fear and hatred.

He hesitated. "I don't think it's dangerous anymore."

"Kill it before it flies up!"

He kicked the bird into the corner, raised his foot, and with evident reluctance stepped on its head.

Gagging, Mary turned away.

The other gull flew away from the bar and left the room through the broken window.

Everything was quiet, still.

At last the intense, dark-skinned young man stood up, helped the blonde to her feet.

The heavyset, red-haired man at the bar tossed down his drink in one gulp.

"Christ, what a mess!" the bartender said. "What happened? Did anyone ever see gulls act like that before?"

Max touched her cheek. "Are you okay?"

She leaned on him and wept.

11

6:30.

Lights speckled the nighttime King's Point hills like orange flame gleaming from within a jack-o'-lantern with a thousand eyes. To the west the ocean and sky melted into a single black shroud.

Max parked at the curb, switched off the headlights. He leaned over and kissed Mary. "You look lovely tonight."

She smiled. Surprisingly, in spite of what had happened to her today, she felt lovely, feminine, buoyant. "That makes six times you've told me."

"Seven's a lucky number. You look lovely tonight." He kissed her again. "Do you feel better? Are you relaxed?"

"The man who invented valium should be made a saint."

"*You* should be made a saint," he said. "Now don't move. I'm feeling terribly chivalrous. I'll come around and open your door."

The wind from the sea was no stronger than it had been during the day, although with nightfall it grew colder and seemed also to grow noisier. It shook badly fitted shutters until they clattered. It worried loosely hinged garage doors, made them groan and creak. It scraped tree branches against the side of the house, tipped over empty trash barrels, stirred brittle feathered-end palm fronds together in a chorus of snakelike hissing, and rolled a few discarded soda cans along the streets.

Sheltered from the worst of the wind by dense shrubs, pine trees and date palms, the small single-story house at 440 Ocean Hill Lane looked warm and cozy. Soft light radiated from the leaded windows. A carriage lamp glowed beside the front door.

Lou Pasternak—owner, publisher, and editor of the twice-a-week *King's Point Press*—answered the bell and hustled them inside. While they told each other how well they looked and how happy they were to see each other again, Pasternak kissed Mary on the cheek, shook hands with Max, and hung their coats in the closet.

Being in Lou's presence was, she thought, as relaxing as taking a tranquilizer. Except for Max and her own brother, Mary liked Lou more than any other man she'd ever met. He was intelligent, kind, too generous. He was also the worst cynic she had ever met, but the cynicism was tempered by humility and a marvelous sense of humor.

She worried about him because he drank too much. But he knew he did, and he was able to talk about his drinking dispassionately. He argued that if you understood how screwed up the world was, if you saw how like a paradise it *could* be, if you understood that what could be never *would* be because most people were hopeless jackasses—well, then you needed a crutch to get through life with your sanity intact. For some people, he said, it was money or drugs or any of a hundred other things. His crutch was Scotch. And damned good bourbon.

"My mother," Mary sometimes said to him, "led a miserable life as an alcoholic."

"Your mother," Lou always responded, "sounds like an alcoholic who didn't know how to hold her liquor. There's nothing worse than a sloppy drunk—unless it's a self-pitying drunk."

His drinking didn't appear to interfere with the full life he led. He had built and still operated an extremely successful business. His editorials and reportage had won several national awards. At forty-five, although he had never been married, he had more women friends than any man Mary knew. At the moment he lived alone, but that would not last.

Although she had seen him consume Herculean quantities of liquor, she had never seen him drunk. He did not stagger, slur his speech, become maudlin or loud or obnoxious. He not only could hold his liquor, he thrived on it.

"I don't drink to escape my responsibilities," he had once told her. "I drink to escape the consequences of other people's inability to meet *their* responsibilities."

"Alcohol killed my mother," she warned him. "I don't want to see you die."

"We all die, my dear. It's just as good to drop of a rotted liver as it is to be felled by cancer or a stroke. Actually, I think it's better."

She loved him as much as she loved Max, though in different ways.

He was a stocky man, a full foot shorter than Max's six-four, even slightly shorter than Mary. He was solidly constructed. His neck, shoulders, arms, and chest were thick with muscle, powerful. He was wearing a white shirt; the sleeves were rolled up; and his forearms were matted with hair.

His face was in stark contrast to his body. He had the fine features of an inbred aristocrat. He combed his brown hair straight back from his face. His brow was high; his lively brown eyes were deeply set and sensitive; his nose was narrow, the nostrils delicate; and his mouth was almost prim. He wore wire-rimmed spectacles that made him look as if he was a college professor.

"Bourbon and ice," he said, picking up a tall glass from the slate-topped foyer table. "My third since I got home from work. In case the wind blows down the power lines later on, I intend to be so lit up that I can do my bedtime reading by my own light."

Although there were armchairs and a comfortable sofa, the living room was primarily furnished with books, magazines, record albums, and paintings. Stacks of books stood beside and behind the couch; books filled the space under the coffee table; recent issues of magazines overflowed a rack meant to hold a hundred of them. The one wall that was free of records and books was covered with original oils, pastels, and watercolors by local painters. Dozens of pieces in every imaginable style had been squeezed so close that their beauty overlapped; they intruded upon one another; but Lou's taste was so good that even under these circumstances the eye was caught and held by each work at some point during a long evening. One of the armchairs was more tattered and lumpy than the other. That was where Lou sat, reading half a dozen books each week, drinking too much, and listening to opera, Benny Goodman, or Bach.

It was the friendliest room Mary had ever seen.

Lou brought their drinks. He put Bach, interpreted by Eugene Ormandy, on the stereo at low volume. "Now let's hear the whole story. Since you called this morning, I've been half crazy wondering what this is about. You were so mysterious."

Interrupted frequently by Lou's questions, digressing into discussions of poltergeists, Mary told him everything. She began with the tracking down of Richard Lingard and ended with the sea gull attack at the Laughing Dolphin.

When she finished, the house was abnormally quiet. A grandfather clock ticked solemnly in the dining room.

Thinking about what she had said, Lou poured himself more bourbon. When he returned to his armchair, he said, "So tomorrow night at seven o'clock this killer will stab two people, perhaps killing one of them. Then he'll climb a tower and start to shoot."

"You believe me?" she asked.

"Of course. I've followed your work for years, haven't I?"

"You believe about Lingard's spirit?"

"If you say I should, why wouldn't I?"

She glanced at Max.

"Will this man have anyone to shoot at tomorrow night?" Max asked. "Won't just about everyone be at home with their families on Christmas Eve?"

"Oh," Lou said, "he'll have plenty of targets around the harbor. There'll be Christmas Eve parties on dozens of boats. People on the decks. People on the docks. People everywhere."

"I don't think we can stop the stabbings from taking place," Mary said. "But maybe we can keep him from shooting anyone. Policemen can be stationed in all three towers."

"One problem," Lou said.

"What's that?"

"John Patmore."

"Your chief of police."

"Unfortunately, he is. It's not going to be easy to convince him that he should heed your visions."

"If he thinks there's even the slightest chance I might be right," Mary said, "why shouldn't he cooperate? After all, his job is to protect the people of King's Point."

Lou smiled crookedly. "My dear, you should know by now that many cops don't see their jobs quite the same way as taxpayers do. Some cops think that all they're required to do is wear fancy fascist uniforms, ride around in flashy patrol cars, collect envelopes of graft money, and retire at the public expense after twenty or thirty years of 'service.'"

"You're too cynical," she said.

"Percy Osterman told us Patmore's difficult," Max added.

"Difficult? He's stupid," Lou said. "Ignorant beyond description. The only reason you can't accuse him of being scatterbrained is because he doesn't have any brains to scatter. I'm sure he's never heard the word 'clairvoyant.' And when we are finally able to make him understand what it means, he won't believe it. If something's not within his personal experience, he doesn't accept its existence. I'm positive he'd argue against the reality of Europe simply because he's never been there."

"He can call some police chiefs I've worked with," Mary said. "They'll convince him I'm genuine."

"If he's never met them, he won't believe a word they say. I tell you, Mary, if ignorance is really bliss, then he's the happiest man in the world."

"Sheriff Osterman said we could tell Patmore to call him for an endorsement," Max said.

Lou nodded. "That might help. Patmore's impressed with Osterman. And I'll go with you to see him if you'd like. But I've got to warn you that I won't help your cause very much. Patmore hates me."

"I can't imagine why," Max said. "Except, you probably talk like this about him to his face."

Grinning, Lou said, "I've never been able to hide my true feelings, and that's a fact. You've met Mrs. Yancy, his flunky?"

"She was the only one in the office this afternoon," Max said.

"Isn't she a gem?"

"Is she?"

"A miracle worker," Lou said. "It's a miracle when she works."

"She *didn't* seem too efficient," Mary said.

Lou said, "She's a steady worker—and if she gets any steadier, she'll be motionless."

Mary laughed, sipped her dry sherry.

"Now, getting back to those sea gulls," Lou said. "Do—"

"No more about the gulls," Mary said. "No more about any of that. Tomorrow's soon enough. Tonight I want to forget about clairvoyance and talk about something else. Anything else."

* * *

Dinner was filet mignon, salad, baked potatoes, and cold asparagus spears.

As Max was opening the bottle of red wine they'd brought as a gift, Lou noticed the bandage. "Max, what happened to your finger?"

"Oh . . . I cut it changing a flat tire."

"Stitches?"

"It wasn't that serious."

"He should have seen a doctor," Mary said. "He wouldn't even let me look at it. There was so much blood—blood all over his shirt."

"I thought you might have been in a fight again," Lou said.

"I don't go to bars anymore," Max said. "I don't fight these days."

Lou looked at Mary, raised an eyebrow.

"It's true," she said.

"You worked two years for me," Lou said. "In all that time you never went more than a month or six weeks without getting in a bad fight. You went to the worst bars along the coast— biker bars and worse, to all the places where you were most likely to wind up in trouble. Sometimes I wondered if you went drinking more for the fighting than for the liquor."

"Maybe I did," Max said, frowning. "I had problems. What I needed was someone who needed me. Now I've got Mary, and I don't fight."

Although he had promised not to talk about clairvoyance anymore that night, Lou found himself unable to drop the subject during dinner. "Do you think the killer knows you're in town?"

"I don't know," Mary said.

"If he's possessed by a spirit, and if the same spirit possessed those gulls, then surely he knows."

"I guess he does."

"Won't he play it safe until after you leave town?"

"Maybe he will," she said. "But I doubt it."

"He wants to get caught?"

"Or he wants to catch me."

"What do you mean by that?"

"I don't know."

"If—"

"Can we change the subject?"

* * *

After she had finished eating, Mary excused herself from the table and went to the bathroom at the far end of the house.

When he was alone with Max, Lou asked, "What about this notion of hers?"

"That Lingard's come back from the dead?"

"Do you put any stock in that?"

"You're the student of the occult," Max said. "You're the one with hundreds of books on the subject. Besides, you've known her longer than I have. You're the one who introduced us. What do you think?"

"I've got an open mind," Lou said. "I gather you don't."

"Her analyst says *she* threw those glass dogs."

"Unconscious telekinesis?" Lou asked.

"That's right."

"Has she ever shown telekinetic ability before?"

"No," Max said.

"What about the revolver?"

"I think she was controlling that, too."

"Shooting at herself?"

"Yes," Max said.

"And she was guiding the sea gulls?"

"Yes."

"Controlling living animals . . . that's not telekinesis."

"It's telepathy of a sort," Max said.

Lou refilled his wine glass. "That's rare."

"It has to be telepathy. I can't believe those sea gulls were guided by a dead man's spirit."

"Why would she want to kill herself?"

"She doesn't," Max said.

"Well, if *she* is the poltergeist behind these phenomena, if *she* levitated that revolver, then it seems to me that she was trying to kill herself."

"If she was suicidal," Max said, "she wouldn't have missed. But she *did* miss with the glass dogs, with the revolver, and with the gulls.

"Then what's she doing?" Lou asked. "Why is she playing the part of a poltergeist?"

Max frowned. "I have a theory. I think there's something special about this case, something unusual. She's foreseen something about it that she refuses to face up to. Something devastating. Something that would completely unhinge her if she thought about it for long. So she pushed it out of her mind.

Of course, she could only push it out of her *conscious* mind. The subconscious never forgets. Now, every time she attempts to pursue a vision that's connected to this case, her subconscious uses the poltergeist phenomena to distract her."

"Because her subconscious knows it will be harmful for her to pursue this man."

"That's right."

An icy tremor passed through Lou Pasternak. "What could she have foreseen?"

"Maybe this psychopath will kill her," Max said.

The thought of Mary dead hit Lou with surprising force. He had known her for more than a decade, had liked her from the moment he met her, and had grown to like her more each year. Liked her? Only that? No. He loved her, too. In a fatherly way. She was so gentle, good-natured. So vulnerable. But until this moment he had not realized how deeply he had come to love her. Mary dead and gone? He felt sick, feverish.

Max watched him with steady gray eyes that revealed nothing of his own emotions. He appeared unaffected, unmoved by the prospect of his wife's death.

He's had more time to consider it than I have, Lou thought. He's had time to become accustomed to the idea of Mary dead. He cares as much as I do, but his feelings have settled from the surface into darker, more affecting regions.

"Or maybe the psychopath will kill me," Max said.

"The two of you should give up on this one," Lou said. "Go home right now. Stay out of it."

"But if she *did* foresee something of that sort," Max said, "won't it happen regardless of what we do to avoid it?"

"I don't believe in predestination."

"Neither do I. Yet... what she foresees always seems to happen. So if we don't go after this killer, will he come after us?"

"Damn you," Lou said. "You've made me stone cold sober." He drank his wine, poured more.

"There's something else," Max said. "When she was six years old, a man apparently sexually molested her."

"Berton Mitchell," Lou said.

"How much has she told you about that?"

"Not much. The general outlines of it. I gather she can't remember most of it."

"Did she tell you what happened to Mitchell?"

"He was found guilty," Lou said. "He hung himself in his prison cell, didn't he?"

"Do you know that for a fact?"

"She told me."

"But do you know it for a fact?"

Lou was puzzled. "Why would she lie?"

"I'm not saying she lied. But what if no one ever told her the truth?"

"I don't follow you."

"Suppose," Max said, "that Berton Mitchell was never sentenced to a prison term. Suppose he had a good attorney who got him off scot-free even though he was guilty. It happens. If you were the father of a six-year-old girl who'd been molested and horribly traumatized, would you want to tell her that her assailant had walked away unpunished? Wouldn't you worry that she might suffer even more serious psychological damage if she knew that the monster who had abused her was on the streets, free to try for her again? If Berton Mitchell was acquitted, Mary's father might have decided the best thing was for her to believe that Mitchell was dead."

"Surely she would have discovered the truth when she got older," Lou said.

"Not necessarily. Not if she didn't want to discover it."

"Alan would have told her."

"Maybe Alan never knew the truth either," Max said. "He was only nine at the time. Their father would have lied to both of them. And if—"

Lou held up one hand for silence. "Let's say you're right. Let's say Berton Mitchell was acquitted. What's that have to do with this case?"

Max picked up his fork and poked at the rumpled pile of potato skin on his plate. "I told you I think Mary's foreseen something that terrifies her."

"That she'll be killed. Or you will."

"Perhaps that's it. But maybe she's also seen that the killer we're after is . . . Berton Mitchell."

"He'd be sixty years old if he was alive!"

"Is there some law that says all psychopathic killers have to be young?" Max asked.

* * *

In the bathroom Mary washed her hands, picked up the towel, looked in the mirror above the washbasin—and did not see her own face. Instead, she saw the face of a total stranger—a young woman with pale yellow hair and even paler skin and wide-set blue eyes, her features distorted by terror.

The mirror had become a window on another dimension, for it did not reflect anything in the bathroom. The blonde woman's face was disembodied, floating in misty shadows. Above and to the right of her, the only other object in the void beyond the mirror was a golden crucifix.

Mary dropped the towel, backed away from the sink until she bumped into the wall.

In the mirror a man's hand, also disembodied, appeared in the foreground of the surrealistic collage of psychic images. It was gripping a butcher knife.

Mary had never received a clairvoyant vision in this fashion. For a moment she didn't know what to expect. She didn't know what she should do; she was afraid both to move and to stay still.

The disembodied hand raised the knife. The blonde's face receded like a ball flying away, whirling and spinning and tumbling through endless space. The hand and the butcher knife receded, too, in pursuit of her.

Concentrate, Mary told herself. For God's sake, don't let the vision get away from you. Hold on to it at all costs. Hold it and expand upon it. Develop it until it provides the name of the man whose hand holds the knife.

The crucifix swelled until it filled the mirror. Then, in perfect, eerie silence, the icon exploded into a dozen jagged pieces and was gone.

Concentrate...

The woman's face reappeared. And the knife loomed large in the mirror. The blade gave off a fierce light of its own, as if it were made of neon tubing.

"Who are you?" Mary asked aloud. "You with the knife. Who in the hell are you?"

Suddenly the hand was no longer disembodied. The woman's face vanished, and the shoulder and the back of a man's head entered the scene, cloaked in shadow. The killer started to turn slowly, turned through laces of wan light and shifting shadows, turned so he would be facing out from the mirror, turned as if he knew Mary was now behind him, turned slowly and silently, turned as if in response to her request for his name . . .

Worried that she might lose the vision an instant before she had her answer, as had happened to her in Dr. Cauvel's office the day before, Mary said, "Who? Who are you? I demand to know!"

To her right, six feet away, the latch on the bathroom window opened with a sharp *click!*

Startled, Mary looked away from the image in the mirror. The window slid up.

The wind threw aside the flimsy brown and black curtains and rushed into the room, making banshee noises as it came.

The night beyond the window was dark, far darker than she had ever seen.

Over the howling of the wind came another sound: *wicka-wicka-wicka!*

Wings. Leathery wings. Just beyond the window.

Wicka-wicka-wicka!

Perhaps it was a coincidental sound. The curtain rod vibrating in its fixtures? A branch or shrub rustling rhythmically against the side of the house?

Whatever the cause of it, she was certain she was not merely imagining the sound this time; nor was she receiving it as part of her psychic impressions. Some creature was actually close at hand, beyond that open window, some unimaginably bizarre creature with wings.

No. Insanity.

Well, go look, she told herself. Go see what it is that has these wings. See if it's anything at all. End this forever.

She couldn't move.

Wicka-wicka-wicka!

Max, help me, she said. But the words formed without sound.

To her left, beside the sink, the door of the medicine cabinet was wrenched open by invisible hands. Thrown shut. Wrenched open. Thrown shut. The next time it came open, it stayed that way. All of the contents of the cabinet—bottles of Anacin, aspirin, cold tablets, iodine, cough syrup, laxatives; tubes of toothpaste, skin cream, shampoo; boxes of throat lozenges, Band-Aids, gauze pads—leaped from the shelves to the floor.

The shower curtain was flung back by an invisible hand, and the shower rod sagged and bent as if someone quite heavy was hanging from it. The rod tore out of the wall and fell into the tub.

The commode seat began to bash itself up and down, faster and faster, making an incredible din.

She took one step toward the bathroom door.

It swung open as if urging her to leave—then a second later went shut with a crash like a thunderclap. It opened and closed itself repeatedly, almost in time with the clatter of the commode seat.

She put her back to the wall once more, afraid to move.

"Mary!"

Max and Lou were on the other side of the door, briefly visible as it swung open. They were staring, amazed.

The door closed with even greater power than it had before, flew open, shut, open, shut.

Max tried to come in as the door opened again, but it slammed in his face. The next time it opened he grabbed the doorknob and forced his way inside.

The door stopped moving.

The wind at the window decreased to a slight draft.

There were no wings beating now.

Stillness.

Silence.

Mary looked at the mirror above the washbasin and saw that, while the images in it had changed, it was still not an ordinary mirror and did not reflect the room in front of it. The pale blonde, the crucifix, and the man with the butcher knife were gone. The mirror was black—except for the very bottom of it, where blood appeared to seep through the glass and over the frame, where it dripped into the room, as if the world on the other side was nothing but a lake of gore with a surface that reached slightly above the lower edge of the mirror. The blood splashed on the faucets that were directly below the mirror, spattered the white porcelain sink.

Confused, Max said, "What the devil is this? What's happening here?" He looked from the mirror to Mary. "Are you hurt? Have you cut yourself?"

"No," she said. And only then did she realize that *he* saw the blood, too.

Max touched the rim of the mirror. Impossibly, incredibly, the blood came off on his fingers.

Lou squeezed into the small bathroom to have a better look.

Gradually the blood—on the mirror, faucets, porcelain, and on Max's finger—became less vivid, less brilliantly red, less substantial, faded until it was gone, as if it had never been.

* * *

Mary sat on the living room sofa and accepted a glass of brandy from Lou. When she brushed her hair back from her forehead, it felt greasy and cold. There was no color in her face. Her hands were clammy. The brandy burned her throat and brought a welcome warmth.

Standing in front of her, Max said, "What you saw in that mirror before we came after you—does that mean someone will die tonight?"

"Yes," Mary said. "The girl I saw. She'll die. She'll be stabbed before morning."

"What's her name?"

"I didn't see it."

"Where does she live?"

"Here in King's Point. But I didn't sense any address for her."

"Does she live on the hills, in the flats, or around the harbor?"

"It could be any place," Mary said.

"What does she look like?"

"She's got very light yellow hair, almost white. Kinky hair, worn long. Pale skin. Big blue eyes. She's young, in her twenties, very cute. Delicate. No, a better word . . . ethereal."

Max turned to Lou as the newspaperman finished a double shot of Wild Turkey. The way he tossed it back, he might as well have been drinking milk or cyanide. "This is your town, Lou. Do you know anyone who fits that description?"

"We've got ten thousand permanent residents," Lou said. "I don't know all of them. I don't *want* to know all of them. Nine tenths of them are hopeless jackasses, dullards, and bores. Besides, a lot of pretty young blondes are drawn to the Southern California beach life. Sun, sand, sea, sensitivity sessions, sex, and syphilis. In this town there must be at least two hundred tender, achingly ethereal blondes who could be the one Mary saw."

Unconsciously Max had picked up a copy of *The Nation* and had rolled it into a tight tube. He slapped it into the palm of his left hand. "If we don't locate the girl, she'll be killed tonight."

Mary's fear had metamorphosed into a depression like an endless plain of ashes; but beneath the ashes were scattered glowing coals of anger. She was not angry with Max or Lou or with herself, but with fate. Even as the anger built, she knew it was a luxury, that it had no effect or meaning; for the only weapon anyone had against fate was resignation.

"You forget what it means when I foresee something," she told Max. "It doesn't matter if we find this girl and warn her. Nothing matters. She'll die anyway. *I've seen it!* I can't see the names of the winning horses in tomorrow's races. I can't see what stocks will rise in price and which will fall next week. All I can see is people dying." She stood up. "Jesus, but I'm sick of the way I have to live. I'm sick of seeing violence and being unable to prevent it. I'm sick of seeing innocent people in trouble and being unable to help them. I'm tired of a life filled with corpses and violated women and battered children and blood and knives and guns."

"I know," Max said gently. "I know."

She went to the bar and jerked the stopper from the bottle of brandy. "I don't want to be a funnel for other people's misery! I want to be a mechanism for the destruction of that misery, for the amelioration of that misery, for the prevention of it." She poured herself a brandy. "If I'm going to have the all-seeing eye of a god, then dammit, I should have the power of a god, too. I should be able to reach out with that power right this minute and find the man we're after. I should be able to squeeze his heart in a vise of power until it bursts. But I'm not a god. I'm not even a complete mechanism. I'm like half a radio set. I can receive, but I can't transmit. I can be affected, but I can't cause an effect." She drank the brandy as quickly and smoothly as Lou might have done. "I hate it. Hate it. Why do *I* have to have this power? Why *me?*"

* * *

Later, at the front door, Lou said, "I wish you'd stay here tonight."

"We've seen your guest room," Max said. "Magazines and books, but no furniture. We appreciate your intellect and the size of your library, but we don't relish sleeping on stacks of old paperbacks."

"I could use the living room sofa tonight," Lou said. "You two could sleep in my room."

Mary kissed him on the cheek. "You're a darling man. But we'll be fine. Really we will. At least until tomorrow night."

Thursday,
December 24

12

AT ONE O'CLOCK in the morning, rain slashed inland from the sea. It made the bare earth slick, flattened the dry grass, bounced off the macadam roadway.

He parked the Mercedes at the end of the paved lane, switched off the engine. Darkness wrapped the car. There was so little light that he could not even see his own hands on the steering wheel. The only sound was the incessant drumming of the rain on the hood and roof.

He decided to wait until the storm passed. The rainy season had come to Southern California; however, sudden cloudbursts like this one seldom lasted long.

The butcher knife was on the seat beside him. He felt for it, picked it up. He could barely see it in the poor light; but he was thrilled by the feel of it as much as by the sight of the well-honed blade. He pressed one finger to the cutting edge, not firmly enough to draw his own blood but hard enough to feel the energy of death lying inert but ready within the tempered steel.

At one-ten the rain slowed to a drizzle. Five minutes after that, it stopped altogether. He opened the car door and got out.

The air was clean and cool. The wind had died down.

Three quarters of a mile to his left and below him, the night around the harbor was strung with lights like Christmas decorations.

The only nearby light came from one of three cottages that stood two hundred yards to the west. These houses were lined up along the cliff, facing seaward, presenting their back doors to the dead-end macadam road. The northernmost cottage, which belonged to Erika Larsson, was seventy yards from its neighbor and stood in a cluster of trees; lights shone from many of its windows.

As he had expected, Erika was awake. Probably working.

One of her somber watercolors. Or a disquieting oil painting full of brooding faces rendered in blues and deep greens. She did most of her painting in the calm, early morning hours and went to bed at dawn.

He walked around the back of the Mercedes and opened the trunk. It was littered with guns—an Italian shotgun, two rifles, and seven handguns—and boxes of ammunition. He chose a .45 Auto Colt, a custom-made collector's piece, all the metalwork heavily engraved with wild animals fleeing from the muzzle back toward the handgrip. It was already loaded. All of the guns were loaded. He put the Colt in his jacket pocket and closed the trunk.

Holding the knife at his side, he walked down the dirt lane toward the lighted house. The night was so unrelievedly dark that he occasionally stumbled over the driveway ruts. His shoes squished in the mud.

* * *

Mary murmured in her sleep.

In her dream she was with her father. He looked as he had when she was nine years old; and she was a child again. They were sitting on a velvety green lawn. The sun was high; it came straight down on top of them; and they cast no shadows.

"If I help people with my ESP, maybe they'll love me. I want people to love me, Daddy."

"Well, Sweetcakes, I love you."

"But you'll leave me."

"Leave my little girl? Nonsense."

"You'll die in the car. Die and leave me."

"You mustn't say things like that."

"But—"

"If I did die, you'd still have your mother."

"She's left me already. Left me for her whiskey."

"No, no. Your mother still loves you."

"She loves whiskey. She forgets my name."

"Your brother loves you."

"No, he doesn't."

"Mary, what a terrible thing to say!"

"I don't blame Alan for not loving me. All his pets die because of me."

"That's not your fault."

"You know it is. But even if Alan loves me, he'll leave me someday. Then I'll be alone."

"Someday you'll meet a man who'll marry you and love you."

"Maybe he'll love me for a little while. But then he'll leave, won't he? Like everyone leaves. I need protection against being left alone. I'm scared of being alone. I need lots of people who love me. If lots and lots of people love me, they won't all be able to go away at the same time."

"Look at the time! I've got to be going."

"Daddy, you can't leave me."

"I don't have any choice."

"I found Elmo this morning."

"Alan's cat?"

"I found him all bloody."

"Found him where?"

"At the playhouse."

"Not another dead animal?"

"Someone cut him to pieces."

"Does Alan know?"

"Not yet. Daddy, he'll cry."

"Jesus, the poor kid."

"He'll be awful mad at me."

"Mary . . . you didn't . . ."

"No! Daddy, I wouldn't do something like that."

"After what happened last week . . ."

"It wasn't me! It wasn't!"

"Okay, then it was the Mitchell boy again."

"I wish Mrs. Mitchell would move out of town."

"Berton Mitchell's boy cut up Elmo. Alan won't be mad at you."

"But it's because I had his daddy sent away that he's coming here and killing all of Alan's pets."

"Alan understands. He doesn't hold you responsible."

"Alan's still mad because I threw his turtles in the creek last week."

"You haven't explained why you did that."

"Something told me to."

"You deserved your punishment, you know. They were Alan's turtles, not yours."

"Something told me to."

"Who told you to?"

"Something. Something."
"Mary, you're a strange child at times."
"Stay here, and I'll be good."
"Got to go."
"I'll be alone if you go."
"Got to go."
"I'll be alone with the wings."
"Good-bye."
"Daddy, the wings!"

Whimpering, weighted down in sleep by the sedative she'd taken, Mary turned over, unaware that she was alone in bed.

* * *

He pushed up the unlocked bedroom window and slipped inside without making a sound.

Toward the front of the cottage a stereo was playing one of Joan Baez' most soulful albums.

He crossed the bedroom and went down the narrow hall to the living room. Erika Larsson was sitting on a high wooden stool with her back to him. She was at a large easel, working on an oil painting.

The girl's black cat, Samantha, was curled up on an easy chair. It raised its head and stared at him with yellow eyes as he came out of the hallway.

There was a pleasant odor in the air. She had made herself some popcorn not long ago.

He was only ten feet from her when she sensed him and turned. "You," she said.

She was as beautiful as he remembered her. Thick, kinky blond hair. Pale, almost translucent skin. Huge blue eyes. She was wearing jeans and a T-shirt, and her dark nipples were prominent against the thin white material.

She got up from the stool. "What are you doing here?"

He didn't answer.

The black cat knew something was terribly wrong. It jumped down from the chair and ran into the kitchen.

He took another step toward Erika.

She edged around the easel. "Get out of here."

He knocked over the easel.

"What do you want?" she asked.

He held up the knife.

"No. Oh, no."

She backed up against the windows that looked out on the Pacific Ocean.

She held her hands in front of her, as if she would push him away when he tried to close the last few feet between them.

"Mary will know," Erika said.

He said nothing.

"Mary will see who did it," she said.

He reached for her.

"She'll turn you over to the cops. Mary will know!"

* * *

Near dawn.

The black cat named Samantha came out of the kitchen cabinet in which she had hidden and fallen asleep. She yawned and stretched. Then she stood for a minute with her head held high, listening.

The cottage was quiet. The wind soughed softly across the roof.

At last, Samantha padded into the living room. The Christmas tree had been knocked on its side. Ornaments were strewn across the floor; and many of them had been stamped to slivers and dust. Samantha sniffed at a broken glass angel, pushed at its head with one paw. She tasted a crushed candy cane and investigated a broken crucifix that had once hung on the living room wall above the hall door. She nosed around a discarded pair of jeans and a rumpled white T-shirt.

Finally, warily, Samantha circled the body of Erika Larsson and tasted the blood as she had tasted the candy cane.

13

LIKE SCARECROWS FLAPPING on an empty snow-covered field, nightmares had studded her sleep. Most of them were based upon the worst moments of her childhood. This morning filthy rags of those dreams hung around her and made her uneasy, nervous.

Ordinarily, after she showered and before she dressed, she half dried her hair with a towel, then applied one hundred vigorous brush strokes. Now, curiously disturbed by her nakedness, she counted the twenty-eighth stroke and knew that she couldn't wait through seventy-two more before putting on her clothes.

She usually enjoyed performing this and other morning rituals in the nude. She admitted to being an exhibitionist. (See me, see my lovely breasts and ass and legs, see how unmarked, see how very pretty, like me, love me, love me.) But she was motivated by more than exhibitionism. She felt that by beginning the day unclothed, she acquired a sense of lightness and freedom that stayed with her through the afternoon. Dr. Cauvel said that perhaps by starting each day naked, she was trying to prove to herself that her nightly dreams had left no sign on her, that Berton Mitchell had left no sign on her; but she couldn't see the logic in that bit of analysis.

Sometimes Max would sit in perfect silence and watch as she brushed her hair and exercised in the nude. He could make her blush by referring to his voyeurism as "reading beautiful poetry."

But now Max was in the shower. There was no one in the motel room to read her poetry. Yet she felt that someone was staring at her.

Shivering, she put on a brassiere and panties.

When she opened the closet to get slacks and a blouse, she

saw Max's muddy shoes and mud-streaked, blood-stained jacket. As she was examining the dark reddish blots on the jacket, Max came out of the bathroom. He was drying his hair with a towel, and another towel was wrapped around his waist.

"Did you hurt yourself?" she asked.

"All I did was take a shower."

She didn't smile. She held up the soiled jacket.

"Oh," he said. "The cut on my finger came open."

"How did that happen?"

"The bandage tore loose when I tripped and fell."

"Fell? When was this?"

"Last night," he said. "After you took your sedative you went right to sleep, but I couldn't keep my eyes closed. I went for a walk. I was three blocks from the hotel when it started to rain. It was a regular cloudburst. Surprised the hell out of me. I started to run back. Took a short cut through the vacant lot next door, tripped on a stone and fell. Pretty stupid of me. The bandage came off my finger and the cut popped open."

She winced. Looking down at the jacket in her hands, she said, "You bled a lot."

"Like a stuck pig." He held up his hand. The injured finger was swathed in clean gauze and adhesive tape. "It still aches."

He tossed aside the towel with which he'd been drying his hair, took the jacket from her, turned it over in his hands. "I don't think any dry cleaner is going to make this look like new." He took the jacket to the wastebasket and threw it away.

"You should have awakened me when you came in last night," Mary said.

"You were a mile under."

"You should have tried."

"What for? It wasn't anything serious. I applied pressure for fifteen minutes, until the bleeding completely stopped. Then I put on a new bandage. Nothing to worry about."

"You should see a doctor."

He shook his head. "No need."

"Well, it's apparently not healing."

"Give it time. It had just begun to heal when I fell and pulled it open," he said. "I'll be more careful."

"The next time you change bandages," she said, "I want to see the cut. If it isn't healing, you'll go to a doctor even if I have to drag you there."

He came to her and put his hands on her slender shoulders. "Yes, Mother." He had a charming smile which he reserved almost exclusively for her.

She sighed and leaned against his chest, where she could hear the slow, steady beat of his heart. "I worry about you."

"I know," he said.

"Because I love you."

"I know."

"Because I'd die if I lost you."

He unhooked her brassiere.

"But we don't have time," she said.

"We'll skip breakfast."

She moved her hands over him. He was solid, powerful. His size and strength had tremendous impact on her. She felt drugged and excited at the same time. Her eyes grew heavy, her legs weak; yet, in her breasts and belly and thighs, she felt an extraordinary heat and tension. The texture of his skin, the steeliness of his muscle and sinew and bone mesmerized her.

He stripped her, then took off the towel he had been wearing around his waist. He kissed her throat. She felt weightless. His hands slid down her back and cupped her buttocks.

"You could hold me so tight," she said, "squeeze me so tight that you'd cut off my breath. You're strong enough to break my neck."

"I don't want to break your neck," he murmured.

"But you could. So easily."

He took her earlobe between his lips.

"If you . . . broke my neck . . . I don't think . . . I'd care."

He moved one hand between them and touched the moist center of her.

"You'd be so gentle," she said dreamily. "Even as you broke me, you'd be gentle. There wouldn't be pain. You wouldn't allow pain."

He took her to the bed.

As he entered her, as the piston of lovemaking grew slick with her clear oils, she thought about being crushed to death in his arms, and she thought how odd it was for her to consider such a thing, and how much stranger still to consider it without fear and with something very like desire, a melancholy longing, a curiously pleasant anticipation, not a death wish but a sweet resignation, and she knew that Dr. Cauvel would say this was a sign of her sickness, that now she was prepared to surrender even her ultimate responsibility (the fundamental responsibility for her own life, for deciding whether or not she was worthy of life), and he would say that she needed to rely more on herself and less on Max, but she didn't care, didn't care at all; she just felt the power, Max's power, and began to call his name, dug her fingers into his unyielding muscle and surrendered willingly.

* * *

"Roger Fullet speaking."

"Your name fits. Fullet, you're full of it."

"Lou? Is that you? Lou Pasternak?"

"I called and asked for Roger Fullet, the reporter, and was promptly told it's now Roger Fullet, the editor."

"It happened a month ago."

"The *Los Angeles Times* is degenerating swiftly."

"They finally recognized brilliance."

"Oh? You mean after just promoting you they're giving your job to someone else?"

"Very funny."

"Thank you."

"You're a funny man."

"Thank you."

"Plastic surgery might help."

"Watch it, Fullet. You're no match for me."

"Sorry. Lost my head."

"It wouldn't be the first time."

"Hey, Lou, I've got an office with this job that's almost as large as your whole shop."

"They gave you an office so they could lock you in it and keep you out from under foot."

"I dine with the brass."

"Because they don't trust you with the silver."

"Christ, it's good to hear your voice."

"How are Peggy and the kids?"

"Fine. Wonderful. Everyone's healthy."

"Give them my love and wish them a merry Christmas for me."

"I will. You'll have to come visit for a weekend soon. You

know we haven't seen each other in six months? We live so close, only an hour or so apart. Lou, why don't we get together more often?"

"Maybe subconsciously we loathe each other."

"Nobody could possibly loathe me. I'm just a big Hershey Bar. My daughter says so."

"Well, Mr. Hershey Bar, I wonder if you could do me a favor."

"Name it, Lou."

"I'd like you to go back through the *Times*' morgue and get me all available background on a crime that interests me."

"What sort of crime?"

"Child molestation."

"Ugly."

"Also assault with intent to kill."

"Where did it happen?"

"Somewhere in West Los Angeles. A pretty good neighborhood. The girl lived on a twenty-acre estate that's probably since been subdivided."

"When was this?"

"Twenty-four, maybe twenty-five years ago."

"Who was the victim?"

"This gets touchy."

"How so?"

"Roger, she's a dear friend."

"I see."

"She's also a celebrity of sorts, very much in the public eye."

"I'm intrigued."

"I don't intend to write about this. And I don't want anyone else writing about it."

"If it's twenty-five years old, it's dead material for a newspaper."

"I know that. But someone might be able to use it in a magazine piece. It would hurt her badly if it were all dredged up again."

"If you aren't writing about it, why do you need to know?"

"She's in trouble. Bad trouble. I want to help her."

"Why can't you get the details of this thing from her?"

"She was only six years old when it happened."

"My God."

"She can't possibly remember it all—or remember it correctly."

"And what happened back then has some connection with the bad trouble she's in now?"

"I think it might."

"Okay. I won't send someone else to do the work. There'd be a leak if I did. I'll go down to the morgue and pick through the files myself."

"Thanks, Roger."

"And I'll go as your friend, not as a reporter."

"That's good enough for me."

"What's the victim's name?"

"Mary Bergen. No, wait . . . back then it was Mary Tanner."

"The clairvoyant?"

"That's right."

"We carry her column."

"So do I."

"Who was the assailant?"

"Berton Mitchell. B-E-R-T-O-N. M-I-T-C-H-E-L-L. He was the caretaker for the Tanner estate."

"I'll get the full background. Is there something about it that especially interests you?"

"I want to know if Mitchell ever stood trial. If he had his day in court, I want to know whether he was acquitted and set free, or found guilty."

"You said he was the assailant."

"That doesn't mean he was found guilty. You know what a good attorney can accomplish."

"Anything else?"

"Most of all, if Mitchell *was* found guilty, I want to know if he committed suicide."

"Is that what you've been told?"

"Yes. But I don't know if it's true."

"Lou, if he's still alive, and if he's not in prison, I doubt I could find him through our files."

"I'm not asking you to find him. If Mitchell's alive, then I think I know where he is."

"I'll get back to you this afternoon."

"I'll be at the office."

When he concluded his conversation with Roger Fullet, Lou placed a long-distance telephone call to the home of Dr. Oliver

Railsbeck, an old friend who worked at Stanford University. They talked for fifteen minutes.

At nine-thirty, after he had learned what he could from Ollie Railsbeck, Lou walked down the hall to the guest bath. He had cleaned up the mess the previous night; the broken glass and spilled cough syrup were gone. He stood in the center of the small room and studied the mirror above the washbasin. There was no reflection but his own.

He touched the glass and the mirror frame, touched the faucets and the porcelain sink. The night before, all of these things had been splashed with blood that Mary had conjured up and briefly sustained with her psychic power. Thick wet blood that was real . . . yet not real. Blood that had substance, color, and texture (if only for a few seconds), but which was not of this world.

He wondered whose pain and suffering it had represented. It could be the symbolic blood of the blonde whose death Mary had predicted. Or perhaps it was Mary's blood that had vanished from Max's fingertips.

An omen of her death?

"God help her," Lou said aloud.

14

MARY SAT ON an uncomfortable metal chair, her purse on her lap, her hands on the purse.

Max was on a chair at her left side. He knew she didn't like long conversations with policemen, and that the dreary, cold, atmosphere of police stations unnerved her. Several times during the past quarter hour he had reached out and touched her. Nothing obvious. Little pats and squeezes of affection and reassurance. As always, his presence buoyed her.

To her right Lou had turned another chair around so that he could sit with his arms crossed on the back of it.

The room smelled of stale cigar smoke. The overhead lights were too bright. The only decorations on the walls were photographs of the late J. Edgar Hoover, Chief Patmore's idol, and a military calendar that had a different battle scene for each month.

John Patmore, senior officer of the King's Point police force, hunched over his cluttered desk and spoke earnestly into the telephone to Percy Osterman. Apparently the sheriff was doling out a considerable amount of flattery in order to persuade Patmore to cooperate with Mary. A smile that was almost a smirk played at the corners of Patmore's weak mouth.

He was a surprisingly bland-looking man. Late forties. Round face. Mostly bald. Brown eyes. Plain features. Average height and average weight.

She worried that they hadn't made a strong case in their plea for Patmore's assistance. Lou had advised her not to discuss the more bizarre aspects of her story. She had said nothing about flying glass dogs, deadly sea gulls, or bathroom mirrors that brimmed with blood. All of that, Lou insisted, would confuse Patmore. After Lou explained the nature of Mary's psychic powers, she had told the policeman only that the mass murders of the last few days were the work of one man, that he had killed a young woman in King's Point last night (although the body had not yet been found), and that at seven o'clock this evening he would open fire with a high-powered rifle from one of the three towers that overlooked the harbor.

At last, Patmore said good-bye to Percy Osterman and put down the receiver. He leaned back in his chair. For almost a minute he stared off into space. He was smiling.

"Don't let the chief upset you. He doesn't *mean* to be insulting," Lou said to Max and Mary. "Every once in a while he stops to think and forgets to start again."

Ignoring the newsman, Patmore turned to Mary. "I don't like this—a lunatic killer in my town."

She said, "If we—"

Taking a cigar from the center drawer of his desk, Patmore said, "Not one bit do I like it. I run a very tight little town as chief of police."

"We can—"

"In each of those towers," Patmore said, "because Percy Osterman vouched for you, although I still have my doubts about this psychic stuff, at six o'clock, one hour ahead of schedule if you're right, I'll have the men."

Not certain that she had properly interpreted that convoluted sentence, Mary said, "Then you'll put men in the towers tonight?"

Patmore blinked. He had started to wet the end of his cigar. He took it out of his mouth. "Now, didn't I just say that?"

"You'll have to excuse the chief," Lou said. "He thinks that 'syntax' is the money the church collects from sinners."

Much to Mary's relief, the policeman studiously ignored Lou. He said, "Let's have the details again; your vision from start to finish."

She sighed and relaxed slightly.

She thought: this particular horror is drawing to an end.

Then: Is it? Or is it only just beginning?

"Are you feeling well?" Max asked.

"Yes," she lied.

* * *

On the sidewalk in front of police headquarters, Max turned to Lou and said, "Well, that was a lot easier than you said it would be."

Lou shrugged. "I'm surprised. Ordinarily it takes a surgical procedure to get a new idea into his head."

"Evidently," Mary said, "he's even more impressed by Percy Osterman than you thought."

Lou said, "That's definitely a part of it. But I guess it's also self-preservation. He knows that if he called you a charlatan and threw you out of his office, and then the killer *did* strike from one of those towers, I'd call for his resignation on the front page of my newspaper twice every week until he was out of a job."

Max suggested they leave the cars parked and walk two blocks to the harbor. "We can have drinks and lunch at The Sea Locker while we watch the boats."

She walked between Max and Lou, and gradually her spirits lifted. The breeze scoured Patmore's cigar smoke from her; it sluiced away some of her tension and anxiety as well.

The weather had improved. Although the sky was still overcast, and although rain was forecast for tomorrow, this was one of those widely advertised Southern California winter days. The temperature had risen to seventy degrees. The air was so clean and fresh that it almost wasn't there. This was the kind of day that made all of the transplanted Easterners happy they had moved.

A block from the harbor they came to a pet shop where two spaniel puppies peered out from a window cage.

"Oh, aren't they cute!" Mary said. She slipped from between Max and Lou, went to the window.

The puppies stood with their front paws on the glass and tried to sniff the hand she offered them. Their tails whipped frantically back and forth.

"Never cared for dogs," Lou said. "They're too dependent."

"They're sweet," she said.

"I don't like cats either."

Max said, "Why not?"

"They're too *in*dependent."

"Lou, you're trying too hard," Max said.

Smiling, the newsman said, "Well, in some quarters I'm known as a bitter curmudgeon. I've got to uphold my reputation, don't I?"

Mary spoke to the dogs through the window, and they wiggled and barked ecstatically.

"I know how much you love animals," Max said. "I thought

about getting you a dog for Christmas. Maybe I should have done it."

"Oh, no," she said, still playing with the puppies. "It would have died."

Lou looked at her curiously. "What an odd thing to say."

Memories of mutilated cats and dogs and rabbits and other small creatures flickered in disgusting colors behind her eyes.

She turned away from the spaniels. "Alan had a great many animals when he was a boy. I had a few myself. But all of them were tortured and killed."

"Tortured and killed?" Lou asked. "What in the name of God are you talking about?"

"Berton Mitchell's boy did it," Mary said. "He thought I'd falsely accused his father. So he kept sneaking onto the estate and slaughtering our pets. One by one. Year after year. Until we finally stopped keeping animals."

With a tenderness that touched her, Max said, "So the nightmares didn't end when Mitchell hanged himself in that prison cell."

His gray eyes, so often flat and expressionless, were filled with sympathy and love.

Lou said, "I didn't know that Berton Mitchell had a family."

Mary nodded. "A wife and son. Of course, they moved off the estate after . . . after what happened. But they never left the city. They were always nearby."

She glanced at the spaniels, but they no longer appealed to her. When she looked at them now, she couldn't see anything but Alan's dogs: dead dogs with broken legs and dozens of knife wounds, gutted dogs, beheaded dogs, dogs with their eyes punched out . . .

Lou said, "This Mitchell boy—"

"No more about that," she said shakily. "Let's get to The Sea Locker. I can use a drink."

*   *   *

The men's room at the restaurant reeked of pine-scented disinfectant.

As they washed their hands at the twin sinks (Max being careful to keep his bandaged finger dry), Lou said, "Did I ever mention my friend, Ollie Railsbeck?"

"I don't recall the name," Max said.

"He's in charge of a relatively new research effort at Stanford University. They're investigating all kinds of paranormal things—clairvoyance, precognition, psychometry, telepathy, telekinesis, astral projection, *everything*."

"I think I *do* remember the name," Max said. He turned off the water and jerked a paper towel from the dispenser. "I think they've asked Mary to cooperate in some experiments, but she hasn't found the time yet."

Pulling a towel from the dispenser on the wall, Lou said, "Ever since we learned that the Russians are spending almost a billion dollars a year on research to find military applications for psychic phenomena, the Pentagon's been willing to part with a few bucks to fund general studies in the field. Ollie's department and the one that Dr. Rhine started years ago at Duke University are the best programs of their sort in the country."

"Mary's done some work at Duke."

"This morning I called Ollie Railsbeck and asked his opinion about what happened at the house last night, about the blood that came out of the mirror."

"What did he say?"

"He called it 'ectoplasm.' "

"I'm familiar with the word," Max said. He threw away his paper towel and turned toward the men's room door.

"Wait," Lou said. "I didn't want to bring this up in front of Mary."

Max leaned against the wall. "Go ahead."

"According to Ollie, that kind of experience isn't as unique as I thought it was. He says similar things occur at séances."

Max raised his eyebrows. "Your friend's spending our tax dollars to study séances? Those phony sessions the gypsies run, that dark-room-and-candles bit where people who want to talk to dead relatives get bilked out of their money?"

"There are some highly respected mediums who take their work seriously, who don't want money or notoriety, and who conduct some of the damnedest, scariest séances."

"They talk to ghosts?"

"Maybe. They think they do. They talk to *something* that seems to talk back. Anyway, Ollie says that every now and then the form of a spirit or an object will appear above the séance table or over the medium's head while she's in a trance."

"And it's not done with slide projectors focused on a plastic sheet or anything like that?"

"These apparitions have been seen and studied by researchers in a controlled laboratory environment," Lou said. "Sometimes blood will drip out of thin air. Or what appear to be tears. Whatever the nature of the manifestation, it has substance, just as if it's real."

"But only for a short time. Last night the blood that came out of that mirror faded quickly."

"Right. It usually lasts seconds. Sometimes a full minute. Ollie knows of a case where a child's face floated above the medium for twenty minutes, but that's rare. Temporarily solid apparitions like these are supposedly composed of ectoplasm, a supernatural material that, the mediums say, is able to pass between the dimensions of life and death."

Max said, "This friend of yours believes in ghosts?"

"No. He says most of the genuinely talented mediums have highly developed psychic abilities. They score well on card tests for telepathy. Most of them have well documented records of accurate predictions. Ollie thinks that somehow, by the use of a psychic ability we don't understand, they unconsciously create the ectoplasm."

"He doesn't believe it's material from another world?"

"No. And especially not from the afterlife."

Max thought about that for a moment. He said, "Then in Railsbeck's view ectoplasm is sort of the realized flesh of a psychic's subconscious thoughts."

"Exactly," Lou said.

"So Railsbeck supports what I've been saying."

"That's why I wanted to tell you when we were alone," Lou said. "I didn't want to upset Mary."

"There's no supernatural, demonic force operating here."

Lou sighed and shook his head. "I'm not absolutely convinced of that. You're probably right. But I'm keeping an open mind. However, you *are* convinced, and Ollie sides with you, so I'll keep my mouth shut."

Max made a fist of one hand and pounded it into the other. The sound was sharp; it startled Lou, and it echoed off the tile walls. "*Mary* created the blood that came out of the mirror, like she caused the poltergeist, but she doesn't realize it and refuses to believe it. She's seen something terrible, Lou. To keep from facing it, she's used psychic powers she never knew she had in order to construct a facade of 'supernatural' events to mislead herself. She's seen something she's had to force out of her mind, something she's buried in her subconscious. She's using poltergeists and other supernatural bunk to distract herself from the thing she most fears about this case."

Tense and depressed, Lou said, "We can't help her because we don't know what she's hiding from herself."

Max was grim. "We'll know at seven o'clock tonight." He looked at his watch. "A little more than seven hours to go."

*   *   *

The gray water looked cold and oily. It rolled against the docks; and the prows of boats cleaved it like knives slicing dark gelatin.

They had a window table at The Sea Locker. Initially, while Max and Lou talked politics, Mary sat in silence and studied the sky for sea gulls. But there were no birds today, and gradually she shifted her attention to the traffic on the harbor and to the conversation.

Although there were no gulls to worry her, she wasn't able to relax. She ate too little and drank too much; there were jokes about her trying to drink Lou under the table; but the whiskey didn't steady her hands.

At two o'clock, after Lou had gone to his office and they had returned to the motel, she stretched out on the bed, on her side, intending to take a nap. She would need to be rested and alert for the manhunt tonight.

She closed her eyes and tried to switch off her mind. The wine she had drunk at lunch was of some help. She felt she was drifting in lazy circles on a rubber raft in a gigantic swimming pool. She began some light meditation, repeating the word "one" to herself until it filled her and pushed out all other thoughts.

At the borderland of sleep she heard onrushing wings: *wicka-wicka-wicka!*

She opened her eyes.

Nothing there.

Imagination.

Max was behind her in an armchair, reading the *King's Point Press*. If there had been any unusual sound, he would have spoken.

She closed her eyes and began thinking the word "one" again.

Wicka-wicka-wicka!

She opened her eyes. Still nothing.

She knew the wings had something to do with Berton Mitchell. And they were also part of the case she was working on now. The killer she was stalking was somehow connected to Berton Mitchell. Impossible. Unthinkable. But...

She felt tormented. All she wanted was some peace. All she wanted was to be left alone. All she wanted was to *get through this case!*

She squeezed her eyes shut and tried to stop the tears, but they spilled down her cheeks anyway.

She was frightened. She wanted Max. She wanted him to get up and come to her. She started to roll toward him, was about to say his name, and then she thought: *No, by God! Be strong for once.*

Sooner or later she would have to learn to handle some of her own problems. She was increasingly aware of the fragility of life. She could feel her mortality—and not merely her own but Max's and Lou's and Alan's, too—feel it as surely as if it were fragments of ice melting through her fingers. Someday Max might be gone, and how would she survive if she couldn't deal with adversity on her own?

She would have to face up to what had happened twenty-four years ago. She would have to think, force herself back in time, find the meaning of the wings. She wouldn't be able to uncover the connection between Berton Mitchell and this killer until she remembered all about the wings and what had happened in the caretaker's cottage.

She waited until the tears had dried, then got up from the bed.

"Something wrong?" Max asked.

"Can't sleep."

"Do you want to talk?"

"Go ahead and read the paper. I just want to think."

She picked up the spiral-bound notebook and pen that were on the nightstand. She went to the small desk and sat down.

She would do what she always did when she had a problem

that no one could solve for her: she would write about it. She would write dozens of questions, one on every sixth or seventh line, and search for answers to put on the lines between them. That process always relaxed her. Of course, she sought more than relaxation. She wanted answers. Sometimes she got them.

However, after all these years, she could no longer delude herself. Knowing the solution and being able to act on it were two very different things. She had the wit but not the strength. Although she had performed this ritual with notebook and pen hundreds of times, she had never gotten from it what she most expected: she had yet to reach an important decision entirely on her own; she had yet to handle a serious problem without someone's help.

This time would be different. It *had* to be different. She sensed that if she failed to find a new strength within herself, she wouldn't survive much longer.

She opened the notebook which she had purchased the day before but had not yet used, and she saw writing on the first ruled page.

Mary! Run for your life!

It was written in ballpoint pen. The words appeared to have been put down in haste. And although it was definitely her own handwriting, she had no memory whatsoever of having scribbled it.

* * *

Roger Fullet called at four o'clock and gave Lou a detailed synopsis of the Berton Mitchell story as it had been reported by the *Los Angeles Times*. "... and after only twenty minutes of deliberation, the jury found him guilty of all charges. His lawyer immediately filed an appeal based on technicalities, but Mitchell must have realized there wasn't any chance of a new trial. His sentences on all counts were to be served consecutively and amounted to a minimum of twenty-five years."

"And he hanged himself?" Lou asked.

"Just like you've been told. He did it the day after the sentencing, before he was transferred from the county jail to prison."

"You mentioned his family."

"The wife and one son."

"What was the son's name?"

"Barry. Barry Mitchell."

"How old was he when this happened?"

"I didn't make a note of it. But I seem to remember he was sixteen."

"Was there anything more on him in your files?" Lou asked.

"He visited his father in jail every day. He was convinced Mitchell was innocent like he claimed."

"Anything else?"

"These days the press would badger the hell out of the wife and son. America's gotten more ghoulish in the past couple decades. Every day newspaper readers have a greater interest in peeking into personal tragedies than they had the day before. But twenty-four years ago Americans still had some sense of privacy and propriety. The wife and son were left alone. There's nothing more in our files."

Lou drummed a pencil on the top of his desk. "I wonder what happened to the son."

"Can't help you, I'm afraid."

"You've done more than enough. Thanks, Roger."

After they exchanged another round of holiday greetings, Lou hung up.

As he put down the receiver, his secretary came in to wish him a merry Christmas before going home. The office was quiet after she had gone.

He hadn't turned on any lights when he came back from lunch. Now, as the early darkness gradually descended, he sat alone in lengthening shadows, staring, thinking.

What was it that Mary feared?

What was so special about this case?

One pet theory had been demolished by what Roger Fullet had told him. The psychopathic killer loose in King's Point was not Berton Mitchell.

The son? Barry Mitchell? He would be forty, Max's age. Not much older than his father had been when he attacked Mary. Madness sometimes ran in families, didn't it? Like father, like son. Maybe it would be Barry Mitchell who would climb those tower stairs at seven o'clock tonight.

As the muddy evening light replaced the afternoon, the office grew chilly. Finally, for warmth, Lou got up and poured a double shot of bourbon.

* * *

Determined not to run to Max with the five-word warning in the front of her notebook, Mary wrote down fifty-four questions and half as many answers, seeking understanding and solutions in the only way she knew. As yet she had discovered nothing new about the tortures and outrages that had transpired in that cottage twenty-four years earlier, not the slightest clue to the meaning of the wings, but she was not ready to quit.

Although it interrupted her train of thought and made her increasingly nervous, she repeatedly turned back to the first page and read the two short sentences: *Mary! Run for your life!* She tried to convince herself that it was someone else's work, that some stranger had sneaked into the motel room and had written the warning while she and Max were out. Perhaps the killer had done it. But she knew that wasn't true. It made no sense. Besides, she recognized her penmanship. She must have gotten out of bed in the middle of the night without disturbing Max and, while still sound asleep, scrawled an urgent message to herself. Asleep, she had foreseen great danger. But what knowledge had she possessed in sleep that eluded her now that she was awake?

Getting out of the armchair behind her, Max said, "Do you want to freshen up?"

She turned. "What?"

"It's five-thirty. We're to meet Lou at six. I thought you'd want to freshen up."

"Oh, sure." She closed the notebook. She stood.

"Are you okay?" he asked.

"Yes."

He stared at her, concerned.

"No," she said. "No, I'm not."

He came to her, kissed her cheek.

"I'm scared," she said.

"So am I," he said.

"What's going to happen to me?"

"Nothing bad," he said.

"I don't know."

"I *do* know," he said. "Stay close to me tonight, until they catch the bastard."

She asked, "What if they don't catch him?"

"You said they would."

"No. I just said he'd be in one of the towers."

"If they're waiting for him, they'll catch him," Max said soothingly.

"Maybe."

15

Officer Lyle Winterman parked the squad car out of sight in an alleyway and walked two blocks to St. Luke's Lutheran Church. Even with a streetlight every hundred feet Harbor Avenue seemed dark.

Winterman kept his right hand on the holstered revolver at his hip. The flap of the holster was unsnapped. His palm was on the gun butt. He expected someone to leap out at him. After Patmore's talk at the station, the deputy was jumpy as hell.

Reverend Richard Erdman was waiting in the nave of the church. They shook hands and went to the door that opened on the bell tower stairs.

"What's this all about?" Erdman asked.

"We're working on a tip," Winterman said.

"A tip about what?"

"Chief Patmore would rather I didn't say."

"Is there going to be violence?"

"There might be."

"I don't want violence in my church."

"Neither do I, Reverend."

"This is God's house. It will remain a place of peace."

"I hope so. Just the same, you'd better go back to the rectory and lock your doors."

"I have a Christmas Eve service to prepare for."

"That doesn't start until later, does it?"

"Eleven," Erdman said. "But I begin preparing at ten."

"I'll be gone long before that," Winterman said.

The officer unhooked a flashlight that was clipped to his belt and switched it on. He directed its beam to the tower stairs, hesitated, then began to climb.

Erdman shut the door behind him.

* * *

6:05 P.M.

Officer Rudy Holtzman wasn't supposed to be working on Christmas Eve. It was his night off. All the way up the tower stairs he cursed John Patmore.

Psychics, premonitions, fortunetellers, extrasensory perception—it was all bullshit. The chief was making a fool of himself. Nothing new about that, of course. But a clairvoyant? Too much.

Holtzman reached the top of the tower at Kimball's Games and Snacks. Under him the deserted building was quiet.

He switched off his flashlight and looked out at the harbor for a moment. On a half dozen boats, parties had already gotten underway.

"Damn!" Holtzman said.

He sat down with his back to the waist-high wall around the observation deck. He put his revolver on the floor beside him.

He half hoped that some bastard with a rifle *did* try to come up those stairs. Maybe he would feel better if he could shoot someone.

* * *

6:10 P.M.

A well lighted eighty-foot yacht cruised around the bay end of the harbor and started down the north channel toward the sea. Waves from its wake slapped rhythmically against the sea wall.

The wind from the ocean carried a vague odor of decay.

John Patmore and his assistant—a young, overweight officer named Rollins—used a corner of The Laughing Dolphin Restaurant's parking lot as a command post for the operation. From there they had a view of all three towers.

The Mercedes was parked beside the patrol car. Mary leaned against the fender. Max was at her left side, Lou at her right.

She was hoping for another vision. She still had time to foresee which tower the killer would try to use, time to help the police consolidate their efforts, perhaps even time enough to prevent the slaughter to come. Thus far, however, she had received no new images.

She was shivering uncontrollably, but not because of the cool night air.

At six-fifteen, Officer Teagarten, who was assigned to the Roman Catholic Church of the Holy Trinity, called Patmore on the walkie-talkie to say religious services were in progress. Furthermore, the Knights of Columbus were having a party in the church basement that would last until confessions began prior to midnight Mass. It was Teagarten's opinion that no killer, not even a psychopath, would attempt to use Trinity's bell tower if he had to walk through so many witnesses to get there. Teagarten wanted to go home.

"You," Patmore said over the walkie-talkie, "until I've told you different, stay right the hell where you are."

Officer Rollins divided his attention among the three towers, studying them through binoculars.

Patmore ignored Mary. He hadn't bothered to say hello when she arrived, and he still refused even to look her way.

"If this doesn't work out," Lou said, "the chief will swear he never met you."

* * *

6:30 P.M.

A dozen boat parties were in progress all along the harbor. Within an hour there would be a dozen more. Laughter, the squeals of young women, and music from several stereos drifted across the water.

Most of the craft, from the smallest sailboats to the largest motor yachts, were decorated for the season. Strings of colored lights wound around the deck railings and encircled the ports. A few of the biggest yachts, able to tap the power in their huge engines and banks of batteries, were swathed in layers of light, as if weighed down beneath scores of incandescent Hawaiian leis. There were boats with green lights arranged to form Christmas trees on their masts, boats that used golden lights to transform their masts into gigantic crosses, boats carrying life-size statues of Santa Claus, boats with cardboard and Styrofoam reindeer capering across cabin roofs, boats draped with paper chrysanthemums, evergreen boughs, holly, and fresh flowers. The ships blazed against the night.

In his own way Lou Pasternak was proud of King's Point. He could deliver an hour-long monologue dissecting its many faults, but he never failed to point out that it was, if nothing else, the loveliest beach town in California.

Pretty as it was, however, the harbor could not distract him for more than a few minutes tonight. He finally turned to Mary and said, "Can we talk about Barry Mitchell?"

She jerked as if he'd pinched her.

"Mary?" he said.

"You startled me."

"I'm sorry."

"What about Barry Mitchell?" she asked.

"He was what . . . ten years older than you?"

"About that, I think."

"Do you recall what he looked like?"

"He was tall, a big boy."

"What color was his hair?"

"Dark," she said. "Brown, I suppose."

"His eyes?"

"I don't remember."

"You said he killed Alan's pets."

"And the few I had as well."

"Was he caught at it?"

"Alan saw him killing a squirrel we owned."

"Was he apprehended in the act?"

"No. He was too big for Alan."

"Were charges ever brought?"

"We had no proof," she said.

"You had Alan's testimony."

"The word of one boy against another."

"So you stopped keeping pets," Lou said.

"Yes."

Max put his arm around Mary's shoulders.

"Nothing was done to Barry Mitchell?" Lou asked.

"My father's attorney had a talk with his mother."

"What did he accomplish?"

"Nothing. Barry Mitchell denied killing them."

Max asked, "Why all these questions, Lou?"

Lou hesitated, then decided there was no reason to keep his suspicions a secret. "You've told me there's something very unusual about the killer we're after tonight. Max has told me the same thing. The two of you disagree as to *what* is unusual about him. But suppose ... what if the man we're tracking is Berton Mitchell's son?"

She shook her head. "No."

"Why not?" Lou asked.

"He's dead," she said.

Lou stared in surprise.

"You mean Barry Mitchell's dead?" Max asked.

"His mother, too," Mary said.

"What?"

"His mother died, too. The same night."

Lou asked, "When did this happen?"

"I was eleven at the time."

"Nineteen years ago."

"That's about right."

"They died together?"

"Yeah."

"How?"

"They were killed by an intruder."

"A burglar?" Lou asked.

"I suppose so. I don't remember."

"You don't know the killer's name?"

"Is that important?"

"Did they ever catch anyone?"

"I don't know," she said.

"Who told you about this?" Lou asked.

"Alan."

"Are you certain he knew what he was talking about?"

"Oh, yes," she said. "I think he might have showed me a newspaper clipping about it."

Lou sagged against the Mercedes, disappointed that yet another theory had been demolished.

But if the wife and son had been murdered just five years after Berton Mitchell committed suicide, why hadn't Roger Fullet found that information in the *Los Angeles Times'* files on the case?

Something exceedingly strange was happening. He was not a theatrical man given to bursts of melodrama. Nonetheless, he swore he could *feel* evil in the air that night.

A woman's laughter bounced across the rippled water, high and shrill.

* * *

7:00 P.M.

Mary squeezed Max's hand and waited tensely. Any minute the walkie-talkie would crackle with a report from one of the deputies. Any second there would be news of a man sneaking up the stairs in one of those towers; and when it came, the chase would begin in earnest.

7:03.

Mary repeatedly glanced at her watch in the back glow of the police cruiser's headlights. She shifted restlessly from one foot to the other.

7:04.

For the first time in more than an hour, Chief Patmore looked at her, met her eyes. He wasn't happy.

7:06.

She was beginning to feel that she had been outmaneuvered, outwitted. For the first time in her career she had encountered an adversary who was a match for her. She was tracking a man against whom all of her psychic abilities provided no advantage.

7:09.

She was numb with fear. "Something's wrong," she said.

"What is it?" Max asked.

"The killer's not coming."

Lou said, "But you *saw* him do it."

"And what you see always happens," Max said.

"Not this time," she said. "This one's different. He knows I'm after him. He knows the cops are watching the towers."

Lou said, "If Patmore's men have been too obvious—"

"No," she said. "It's just that the killer's able to anticipate me. He isn't coming."

Lou said, "Don't tell Patmore. We've got to wait a little while. We can't give up yet."

* * *

When there was no sign of a suspect at any of the towers by 7:30, John Patmore began to stride back and forth in front of his patrol car, scowling. As the minutes passed, he paced faster.

At 7:45 he picked up the walkie-talkie from the hood of the car; for fifteen minutes he talked without pause to Winterman, Holtzman, and Teagarten. Twice he lost control and shouted at them.

Finally he put down the walkie-talkie and came to Mary.

"The man isn't coming," she said.

"Was he *ever* really expected?" Patmore asked.

"Yes, of course." She was miserable. She felt she'd hurt Lou by using his influence and then failing to deliver what she promised.

"What made him change his mind?" Patmore asked.

"He knows we're waiting for him," Max said.

"Yeah? Who told him?"

"No one," Mary said. "He senses it."

"Senses it? How?"

"He must . . . he probably . . ."

"Yeah?"

She sighed. "I don't know."

"In my office," Patmore said angrily, "you knew so much this morning. Everything you knew. Now you don't know anything all of a goddamned sudden. Obviously you also don't know that if I want, I can get nasty about someone coming to my office, this false crime report, a thing like that, wasting my time and the time of my men only to have some laughs, all for some sort of a lark!"

"Don't have a stroke," Lou said. "And don't try to give Mary a stroke."

Patmore turned away from her, faced Lou. "You'd share the blame if I pursued this."

"You don't have anything to pursue," Lou said patiently. "You know perfectly well that we didn't file a crime report— let alone one that was false. We simply came to your office to tell you that we had good reason to believe a crime would be committed."

Patmore glared at him. "You set me up."

"John, that is ridiculous."

"And Percy Osterman helped you. Why? Hell, no. You don't have to tell me. I see it, why he did. When people here voted, and Percy was against it from the start, for their own police, he was upset. He doesn't care for me much, does he? He never showed it, but he sure mustn't."

Lou said, "You're all wrong. Be reasonable, John. There's no conspiracy against you. Mary's sincere. Percy was sincere. We all are. We—"

"You want to make me look like a fool." Patmore wagged his finger in Lou's face. "You damned well better not print in your paper anything about this, about me falling for this psychic crap, because I'll sue you if you do for libel. I'll sue you for everything you've got." There was an uncharacteristic fire in his usually dull brown eyes.

Mary took hold of Lou's arm. "I'm wrung out, Lou. I don't want trouble for you or me."

"Yeah," Max said. "Let's drop it. Let's go."

Exasperated with the policeman, Lou said, "John, I'm not going to write about you. I haven't any desire to make you look like a fool in the *Press*. You've got to realize there's a psychopathic killer loose in this town and—"

Still seething, Patmore said, "You've written about me before."

Lou was getting angry. "I've always written tame 'loyal opposition' articles when I've disagreed with you. I've never been unfair to you. In fact, I think I've been too tolerant. It's not my style to do a hatchet job. God knows, if I'd wanted to make you look like an idiot, I could have done it."

Mary squeezed Lou's arm, tugged at him.

Patmore said, "You're a crummy reporter with a stinking two-bit newspaper, and you're lousy drunk to boot."

For an instant she thought Lou was going to hit him. But he only stared hard at Patmore and said, "A drunk can always go on the wagon and sober up. But a stupid man who has a bottom-of-the-bucket IQ has to live with what he has forever."

"Shit," Patmore said. He walked back to the front of the squad car, picked up the walkie-talkie, and called Winterman, Holtzman, and Teagarten out of the towers.

"I'm sorry," Mary said to Lou. "I'm so sorry."

"It's not your fault he's an idiot."

Max opened the car door. "Come on. Let's get out of here."

* * *

When they were settled in Lou Pasternak's book-strewn living room once more, Max asked, "What now?"

"We wait," Mary said.

"For what?" Lou asked.

Wearily, she said, "We wait for him to start killing people again."

Friday,
December 25

16

THE MOTEL ROOM was dark.

She was lying on her side. She turned onto her back.

She felt claustrophobic, as if the ceiling had begun to descend upon her.

"Can't shut off your mind?" Max asked.

"I thought you were asleep."

"I've been waiting for you to doze off first."

"You were so quiet," she said.

"Trying not to disturb you."

"What time is it?"

"Three o'clock."

"Go to sleep, darling. I'll be fine."

"I can't sleep if I know you're worried."

"I keep thinking I hear someone trying the door."

"No one's been at the door. I'd have heard it."

"And I keep thinking someone's at the window."

"Not that either. It's nerves."

"Screaming mimis," she said.

"Maybe you should take a sedative."

"I had a sleeping pill two hours ago."

"So take another."

"What is he, Max?"

"Who?"

"The killer."

"Just a man."

"No."

"Yes, Mary. Yes. Just a man."

Darkness pulsed around her.

"He's something more," she said.

"Take another sleeping pill."

"I guess I should. But I was beginning to cut down. I was beginning to break the habit."

"After this case you can go cold turkey. But right now the

pills aren't an indulgence. You've got good reason to need them."

"Will you get one for me?"

He fetched a glass of water and the sedative, waited while she took it, switched off the light and returned to bed.

"Move close," she said.

Her back was against his chest. Her buttocks against his groin. Two spoons in a drawer.

Several minutes passed in warm silence.

At last she said, "I'm getting sleepy."

"Good." He stroked her hair.

Still later: "Max?"

"Hmmm?"

"Maybe he can't help being bad and doing awful things. Maybe he was born bad. Maybe evil isn't *always* learned. Maybe parents and environment aren't *always* to blame for an evil child. Sometimes maybe it's in the genes."

"Will you hush?"

"Max, am I going to die?"

"Eventually. We all do."

"But soon? Will I die soon?"

"Not soon. I'm here."

"Hold me."

"I'm holding you."

"I want to be strong."

"You are strong."

"I am?"

"You just don't realize it."

In ten minutes she was asleep.

He continued to stroke her hair.

He listened to her breathing.

He didn't want her to die. He hoped she didn't *have* to die. He wished with all of his heart and mind that she would give up on this case. Let the killing be done. She shouldn't feel responsible. Just let the killing be done. Did society feel responsible? No. Did the police feel responsible? They sometimes did their jobs, occasionally made an effort to find the killer, but they had as much contempt for victim as for victimizer; and none of them lost sleep over it. So let the killing be done. Forget it, Mary. Maybe she thought she was something special. Was that it? Unconsciously she might think that because of her psychic powers she couldn't die. Well, she could. Like all the rest of the tender, sweet young girls who thought they, too, would live forever. She would be as vulnerable, as soft against the knife as all the others had been. So she should stop. Go away from this. If she forced the issue, if she pursued the case, she might have to die. She was standing in front of a juggernaut. She was in the path of a force she didn't understand, a force that drew its greatest strength from the past, from an event that was twenty-four years old.

In the darkness, holding her as she slept, he wept at the thought of life without her.

* * *

Although sunrise was not far away, his flashlight was the only relief from inky blackness. His footsteps were the only sounds in the deserted arcade. He crossed the large main room. In summer it was filled with pinball machines and electronic games. Now the floor was bare, the main room empty. He entered the stairwell above which hung a large sign: THIS WAY TO OBSERVATION DECK.

The enclosed stairwell of the tower of Kimball's Games and Snacks was narrow, cold, and dirty. It had not yet been repainted for the next season. His flashlight played off yellow-white walls that bore a thousand stains: children's handprints, streaks of spilled soft drinks, names and messages scrawled in pencil and felt-tip markers.

The wooden steps creaked.

When he reached the walled platform at the top of the winding stairs, he switched off the flashlight. He doubted anyone would be watching at this hour; however, he didn't want to risk drawing attention to himself.

Dawn was nothing but a thin, lustrous purple line on the eastern horizon, as if a razor had been drawn lightly across the skin of the night.

He stared out at the harbor.

He waited.

In a few minutes, from the corner of his eye, he caught movement in the air. He heard the flutter of wings.

Something roosted in the crossbeams of the peaked roof, rustled for a moment, then was silent.

He stared into the crouching shadows above and trembled with pleasure.

Tonight, he thought. Tonight, the blood again.

He could feel death all around him, a thick and tangible current in the air.

To the east, the wound in the sky grew wider, deeper. Morning oozed into the world.

He yawned and wiped the back of one hand across his mouth. He would have to get back to the hotel soon, get some rest. He hadn't slept much in the past few days.

Three times within the next ten minutes, the sound of wings came again. On each occasion there was a temporary commotion in the rafters, and each time silence swiftly returned.

Eventually anemic light filtered through congealed masses of storm clouds and gradually painted the harbor, hills, and houses of King's Point.

He was filled with a deep sense of loss. With light came depression. He functioned best in the blackest hours. Always had. But recently that was increasingly true. He felt at home in the night.

Overhead the highest rafters remained shrouded in shadows. The inside of the roof—a hollow, inverted funnel—was fifteen feet high; and even at noon darkness clung to its upper regions.

Dim as it was, morning had arrived; and now his flashlight wouldn't be noticed by anyone below. He switched it on and pointed it up into the hollow roof.

This was what he had come to see: bats. A dozen bats or more. Clinging to the wooden rafters. Wings folded tightly around them. Some with eyes shut. Some with open eyes that gleamed iridescently in the beam of light.

The sight exhilarated him.

Tonight, the blood again.

* * *

At nine o'clock that morning Lou called Roger Fullet. "I'm sorry to have to bother you on Christmas."

"You're never a bother. Besides, you just saved me from a tedious little chore. The electric train went off the track and all the cars came uncoupled. If I talk to you for a few minutes, I'll get back to the layout after junior's got everything put back together."

"I've learned something very interesting about this Berton Mitchell case."

"Such as?"

"Apparently, Mitchell's wife and son were murdered."

"My God, when?"

"Five years after what he did to Mary."

"You've got to be wrong."

"Did you check to see if there were separate morgue files for the wife and son?"

"No. But even if there are, everything of importance should be duplicated in the Berton Mitchell file."

"Doesn't the *Times* make mistakes?"

"We're loath to admit it. But occasionally things don't get done right. Who killed the Mitchells?"

"Mary doesn't know."

"Nineteen years ago?"

"That's what she says."

"It happened here in L.A.?"

"I gather it did. Do me a favor?"

"I'm not working today, Lou."

"The *Times* doesn't shut down altogether on holidays. There are people working. Can't you call in and have someone check this out for me?"

"It's that important?"

"A matter of life and death."

"What all do you want to know?"

"Everything about the murders . . . if they took place."

"I'll call you back."

"How long will it take?"

"Maybe two hours."

Roger called back in an hour and a half. "There was a separate file on the murders of the wife and son. The story wasn't cross-filed as it should have been."

"It's nice to know even you big city slickers can be wrong."

"This is really a sick one, Lou."

"Tell me about it."

"After Berton Mitchell committed suicide, Virginia Mitchell and her son, Barry Francis Mitchell, rented a small house on the west side of Los Angeles. Judging from the address, I'd say it couldn't have been more than a mile from the Tanner estate. Nineteen years ago, on October 31, Halloween, at two o'clock in the morning, someone used gasoline to start a fire that nearly burned the place to the ground with the mother and son inside."

"Fire. That's the death I fear most."

"This has ruined my appetite for Christmas dinner."

"I'm sorry, Roger. I had to know."

"That's not the worst of it. Although the bodies were badly burned, the medical examiner was later able to deduce that mother and son were stabbed to death in their sleep before the blaze started."

"Stabbed . . ."

"Virginia had been stabbed so often in the throat that she'd been pretty much decapitated."

"Sweet Jesus."

"The son, Barry . . . was stabbed in the throat and chest. Then . . ."

"Then what?"

"His genitals were cut off."

"There goes my dinner, too."

"Before the fire burned it out, that place must have looked like a slaughterhouse. What kind of man could do all of that, Lou? What kind of maniac would be so gruesomely thorough?"

"Did they ever solve the case?"

"Never arrested anyone."

"Did they at least have suspects?"

"Three of them."

"What were their names?"

"I didn't bother jotting them down. Each of them had an alibi, and each alibi eventually checked out."

"So their killer might still be alive and loose. Were the police sure of the bodies?"

"Sure of them in what sense?"

"Identities."

"I guess they weren't burned beyond recognition. Besides, the house was occupied by Virginia and her son."

"The woman's body was probably Virginia's. But isn't it conceivable that the dead man they found was her lover and not her son?"

"They were killed in different bedrooms. Lovers would have been found together. And if Barry was alive, he'd have come forward."

"Not if he was the killer."

"What?"

"It's not impossible."

"Nothing's impossible, but—"

"Barry would have been twenty-one when the house burned that night. Maybe almost twenty-two. Roger, isn't that a bit old for a boy to be living with his mother?"

"Hell, no. Lou, we didn't all rush out to grab our piece of the action at sixteen, like you did. I lived with my folks until I was twenty-three. Why are you so anxious to believe Barry's alive?"

"It would make things easier to understand down here."

"You're too good a newsman to try to reshape facts to fit some preconceived notion."

"Yeah. You're right. I've run into another stone wall."

"What's the story with this Mary Bergen? What are you involved in?"

"I'm afraid it's going to be very messy. I don't want to talk about it yet."

"And maybe I don't want to hear about it either."

"Go play with your train."

"Somehow I'm no longer in the mood for play. Take care of yourself, Lou. Be careful. Be damned careful. And . . . Merry Christmas."

17

THEY SAT IN Lou's living room, listening to music—and waiting for something to happen. Mary couldn't imagine a grimmer Christmas. She and Max weren't even able to exchange gifts. The things he had gotten her were at the stores where he'd left them to be wrapped, and as she'd become preoccupied with this case, she'd had no opportunity to go shopping for him.

Her spirits lifted when Alan called at three o'clock to say he was in San Francisco at his friend's house. He'd tried the number in Bel Air, and the housekeeper had told him to call Lou. He was worried, but she understated the gravity of her situation and calmed him. No sense ruining *his* Christmas, too. When Alan finally hung up, her spirits sank again; she missed him so much.

Because no one had eaten breakfast or lunch, Lou served an early dinner at five o'clock. Chicken Kiev on a bed of rice. Cylinders of grilled zucchini filled with spinach paté. Tomatoes stuffed with hot cheese, bread crumbs, and peppers. There were baked apples for dessert.

No one was hungry. They picked at their food. Mary didn't even taste her wine. By six o'clock they were finished.

Over coffee Mary said, "Lou, do you have a Ouija board?"

He put down his cup. "I have one, but I haven't used it in years."

"Do you know where it is?"

"The spare bedroom closet, I think."

"Would you get it while Max and I clear the table?"

"Sure. What are we going to do with it?"

"I'm tired of waiting for the killer to make the next move," she said. "We're going to try to force the issue."

"I'm all for that. But how?"

Max said, "Sometimes, when Mary can't recall the fine details of a vision, she can prod her memory with a Ouija board. She doesn't get answers from the spirit world, mind you. The things she wants to know are things she's forgotten. They're buried in her subconscious. Not always, but often enough to make it worthwhile when nothing else works, the Ouija board provides her with a pipeline to her subconscious."

Lou nodded with understanding. "The answers the board gives actually come from Mary."

"Right," Max said.

"But I don't consciously guide the trivet," she said. "I let it go where it wants to go."

"Where your subconscious wants it to go," Max said. "You *do* influence the trivet with your fingers, but in a way that you're not aware of."

"I suppose," she said.

Lou put a few more drops of cream in his coffee and said, "So the Ouija board acts like a lens."

"Exactly," she said. "It focuses my attention, my memory, and my psychic abilities."

Lou drank his coffee in three long swallows and stood up. "It sure sounds interesting. Anything's better than sitting around waiting for the ax to fall. I'll be right back." He hurried out of the dining room and down the hall toward the spare bedroom.

Max and Mary stacked the dishes and silverware in the kitchen sink. She finished wiping off the glossy pine dining table just as Lou returned.

"One Ouija board, as requested," he said.

Mary went into the living room to fetch her notebook from the sofa where she'd left it with her purse.

Lou said, "Got to clean out that spare bedroom closet one of these days. The board was literally buried in crap."

"Literally?" Max said, amused.

"Well, it was under at least a hundred issues of *The New York Review of Books*."

"Ouch," Max said. "You set me up for that one."

Lou took a note pad and pencil from the kitchen counter and sat down at the table. He was prepared to record each letter that the Ouija board gave them.

Mary opened the board on one corner of the table. She placed the felt-footed trivet on it.

Max sat down, laced his fingers, and cracked his knuckles.

She opened her spiral-bound notebook to a page filled with her handwriting.

"What's that?" Lou asked.

"Questions I want to ask it," Mary said.

She pulled up her chair and sat down at a ninety-degree angle to Max. She put the tips of her fingertips on one side of the plastic triangle. Max put his fingertips on another side of it; his hands were nearly too large for the game.

"Start easy," Max told her.

She was tense, and that was not good. The trivet wouldn't move an inch if her touch was too heavy. She took several deep breaths. She tried to make her arms limp. She wanted her fingers to feel independent of her—loose, soft, like rags.

Max wasn't as nervous as she was. He didn't appear to need any preparation.

Finally, when she had achieved a relatively relaxed state of mind and body, she stared at the board in front of her and said, "Are you ready to give us answers?"

The indicator didn't move.

"Are you ready to give us answers?"

Nothing.

"Are you ready to give us answers?"

Under their fingers, as if it were suddenly embodied with a life energy of its own, the indicator glided to that part of the board marked YES.

"Good," she said. "We are in pursuit of a man who has killed at least eight people in the last few days. Is he still here in King's Point?"

The indicator swept around the board, returned to YES.

She asked, "Is King's Point this man's hometown?"

NO.

"Where does he come from?"

ALL OUR YESTERDAYS.

"Make sense to anyone?" Lou asked.

Refining the question, trying to be more specific, Mary asked, "Where does the killer *live?*"

Letter by letter: BEAUTIFUL.

"Beautiful?" Lou asked. "Is that in answer to your question, Mary?"

"A town named beautiful?" she asked.

The trivet didn't move.

"Where does the killer live?" she asked again.

The trivet picked out seventeen letters.

Lou wrote them down as they were given, and when the

indicator ceased to move, he said, "It says, 'THE AIR IS BEAU-
TIFUL.' What's that supposed to mean?"

The air at Mary's back seemed suddenly colder, as if an icy
breath had been expelled against the nape of her neck. The
answers the Ouija board gave were less direct and more per-
plexing than usual. Supposedly the Ouija messages came from
her, from deep in her subconscious mind. Ordinarily she believed that was true. But not now. Tonight she felt another
presence, an unseen presence looming over her.

"We're getting sidetracked," Max said impatiently. He looked
at the trivet. "Where is the killer staying in King's Point?"

The indicator slid back and forth, then quickly moved from
one letter to another.

Lou copied them down, but the word was so simple that
Mary didn't need to ask what had been recorded: HOTEL.

"Which hotel?" Max asked.

The indicator didn't move.

"Which hotel?"

Again, it spelled HOTEL.

Lou said, "Try something else."

Mary said, "The man we're after has killed women with a
knife. Where did he get that knife?"

"That's not important," Max said.

The trivet moved: LINGARD.

"*You* made it spell that," Max said.

"I don't believe I did."

"Then why did you ask it such a question? We don't really
have to know where the knife came from."

"I wanted to see what it would say."

Max studied her with piercing gray eyes.

She looked away from him, consulted her notebook and
addressed the board again. "Did I ever know a girl by the name
of Beverly Pulchaski?"

SHE IS DEAD.

"Did I ever know her?"

SHE IS DEAD.

"Did I know a girl named Susan Haven?"

SHE IS DEAD.

Cold breath on the neck again.

She shuddered.

"Did I ever know Linda Proctor?"

SHE IS DEAD.

"Did I know Marie Sanzini?"

SHE IS DEAD.

Mary sighed. The muscles in her arms and shoulders flexed repeatedly, involuntarily. It was a struggle to stay sufficiently relaxed to allow the Ouija indicator to function. Already she was weary.

Lou said, "Who were those women?"

She said, "The nurses who were murdered in Anaheim. When I first foresaw their deaths, I had the notion that I knew or at least had met one of them. But if I ever did, I can't remember where or when it was."

"Probably because you don't *want* to remember," Max said.

"Why wouldn't I?"

"Because maybe if you remembered, we'd know who the killer was. And maybe you don't want to know that."

"Don't be absurd, Max. I want to know very much."

"Even if the killer's connected somehow to Berton Mitchell and the wings? Even if, by finding the killer, you're forced to remember what you've spent your life forgetting?"

She stared at him and licked her lips. "I'm feeling something right now that I never thought I'd feel."

"What's that?"

"I'm scared of you, Max."

There was an unearthly quiet in the house. The three of them seemed suspended in time.

Max spoke softly, but his voice filled the room. "You're scared of me because you think I'm going to force you to face up to what happened twenty-four years ago."

"Is that all it is?"

"What else?"

"I don't know," she said.

Max asked the board another question, but he did not take his wintry gray eyes from her. "Did Mary know Rochelle Drake?"

SHE IS DEAD.

"I know she's dead," Max said irritably, still watching Mary, suffocating her with his attention, pinning her with his gaze. "But did Mary ever know her?"

DEAD.

"Who's Rochelle Drake?" Lou asked.

Mary took the opportunity to look away from Max. Her mouth was dry. Her heart was beating much too fast.

To Lou, Max said, "Rochelle Drake was the girl who was killed in that Santa Ana beauty salon a few days ago. I swear I've heard the name before. Haven't you?"

"Can't say I have," Lou said.

"Well, I'm positive I heard the name before Percy Osterman used it in the morgue. I don't think I ever met the girl. But I heard the name. I can't imagine where."

Mary said, "Well, I *don't* remember her. I would have recognized her at the morgue if I'd ever seen her before."

Suddenly, beneath their hands, the trivet began to move in wide, aimless circles.

"What the hell?" Max said, surprised.

Lou said, "No one asked it a question."

Mary allowed her hands to float freely with the indicator as it moved less erratically and with increasing purpose. Her thoughts were too muddled at the moment, and she was too frightened to have the wit to decipher the chain of letters as it grew. Finally the trivet stopped. She took her hands from it at once; they ached with the strain of forced relaxation.

Lou said, "It's a name." He held up the note pad for them to see.

P-A-T-R-I-C-I-A-S-P-O-O-N-E-R.

Patricia Spooner? Mary thought. She stared at the name in disbelief.

She felt as if a snake of ice lay at the center of her, its crystalline tongue flicking rapidly, its sinuous body radiating cold like the coils of a freezer.

"Who's Patricia Spooner?" Max asked.

"Means nothing to me," Lou said.

"I . . . knew her," Mary said stiffly.

"When?" Max asked.

"Eleven . . . twelve years ago."

"You've never mentioned her."

"She was a good friend at UCLA."

"A college friend?"

"Yes. A very pretty girl."

"Why does her name come up now?"

"I don't have any idea."

"It came from your subconscious."

"No. I'm not controlling the trivet."

"Nonsense," Max said.

"There's someone . . . something here with us."

"Maybe the board just gave us the name of the next victim," Lou said, to avert a quarrel. "Have you kept in touch with this Patricia Spooner? Maybe we should call her and see if she's okay."

Max said, "Should we call Patricia Spooner? Mary?"

"She's dead," Mary said.

Lou said, "Oh, my God. Then the man we're after's already killed her?"

She had difficulty speaking. "Patty . . . Patty's been . . . dead . . . dead almost . . . eleven years."

Although the room was not warm, Lou was perspiring. He wiped his aristocratic face with his broad, thick-fingered, big-knuckled hand. He looked as pale as she felt. "How? Mary, how did Patty Spooner die?"

Mary shivered and closed her eyes. She opened them at once because the memories behind them were too ugly, too brutal. "She was . . . murdered."

The dead, Mary thought, don't stay dead. Not forever. Not even for long. They rise up from their graves. The ground doesn't hold them. Remorse doesn't hold them. Neither grief nor acceptance, neither fear nor forgetfulness holds them. Nothing holds them. They come back. Berton Mitchell. Barry Mitchell. Virginia Mitchell. My mother. My father. And now Patty Spooner. Oh, God, don't let them come back. I've been haunted by the dead most of my life. I've had enough!

"Murdered," Lou said quietly, almost as if in shock.

Mary said, "There was a church. Patty and I sometimes went to Mass together. I was a practicing Catholic then. It was a lovely church. It had a very large, hand-carved wooden altar that was made in Poland and shipped over here in the early nineteen hundreds. The church was open all the time, night and day. Patty liked to go and sit in the front pew when no one else was there. Late at night. Her mother had died of a heart condition a few years before. She was always lighting candles for her mother. Patty was very devout. She . . . she died there."

"In the church?" Lou asked.

Max was watching her intently. He put a hand on her shoulder; vibrations, more emotional than physical, neither good nor bad but powerful, exploded through her from the point of contact.

Max said, "Who killed her?"

"They never found him."

Lou leaned across the table. His eyebrows were drawn together, his face pinched. "She was your good friend. Didn't you use your psychic talent to see the killer's face, his name?"

"I tried," Mary said faintly. "I got a few things. Bits and pieces of images. But it was one of those cases when my power didn't help much. She was strangled with a priest's white silk stole. I got terrible emanations from it. Wicked, evil vibrations. No clear pictures. Just formless images. The church was filled with them. Like . . . invisible clouds of evil. The killer had damaged the altar . . . urinated on it."

Lou got up so abruptly that he knocked over his chair, but he didn't appear to notice it. He stood with one hand on his head as if attempting to force back an unsettling idea. "It's madness. *What are we up against?* Is it possible that the man we're trying to find here in King's Point is the same man who killed your friend?"

"His style is the same, isn't it?" Max said.

"So damned brutal," Lou said. "And with the religious angle. The roots of these recent killings might go back at least eleven years. Perhaps a lot further than that."

Mary saw what he meant, though curiously, until this moment, she had never seen a connection between Patty's death and any other.

Sensing the effect Lou's revelation had upon her, Max squeezed her shoulder reassuringly. Sometimes he didn't seem to know his own strength; his grip was slightly painful.

Agitated as she had never seen him, moving quickly and jerkily, Lou went into the kitchen and got a twelve-ounce tumbler from the cabinet beside the refrigerator. He picked up a bottle of Wild Turkey that was on the counter by the sink, and he poured about four ounces for himself. Glass in hand, he came back and stood in the dining room archway. "It gets more complicated all the time. How many other people has this man killed that we don't even know about? Over the years, how many other unsolved murders was he responsible for?" Lou swallowed some bourbon. "This creature, whoever and whatever he is—and I'm increasingly disposed to think of him as a *thing*—has been prowling about, raping, killing, completely unchecked, unhindered for at least eleven years. It scares the hell out of me."

A peal of thunder punctuated his last few words. It reverberated in the window glass. The Christmas night rainstorm was on the way, as forecast.

Max glanced at the plastic trivet. "Let's ask the board how many victims there have been."

She almost objected. My arms ache, she almost said. Too tired for more of that. Exhausted. Drained.

But she knew that fear was the real reason she didn't want to begin questioning the Ouija board again. She was afraid of what it might tell them.

If she surrendered to her fear so easily, she would never learn to rely on herself. And although she found the possibility disturbing, she had an ever-growing feeling that soon she would find herself in greater danger, against which Max could not or would not offer her protection.

She put her hands on the trivet, and so did Max.

Lou put his overturned chair on its feet. He sat down and picked up his pencil.

She spoke to the Ouija board. "Are you prepared to answer more questions?"

YES.

Thunder rumbled over King's Point. The bulbs in the hanging lamp above the table flickered, nearly went out, then glowed brightly again.

"The man who killed Rochelle Drake has murdered other people, too. How many has he killed?"

35.

Lou said, "My God! He's a regular Jack the Ripper."

"Jack the Ripper didn't kill that many," Max said. "The board's wrong. It has to be. Ask it again, Mary."

Her voice wavered as she repeated the question.

35.

The hanging lamp flickered and went out.

"Power failure," Lou said.

Mary said, "I don't want to sit in the dark."

"If it lasts more than a minute," Lou said, "I'll go get candles from the hall closet."

An incredible barrage of lightning pulsed outside the windows. The sharp bursts of blue-white light created a series of choppy, stroboscopic images: Lou reaching in a half dozen seemingly disconnected movements for his glass of bourbon; Max turning his head toward her as if he were a character on a motion picture screen, with the film slipping and stuttering in the projector.

Then the lightning passed; the darkness was complete; the thunder receded to a distant growl. Rain should have followed that display, but it didn't; the sky held back the deluge.

Less than a minute after the lights went out, they fluttered dimly and came back on full strength.

She sighed with relief.

Max was eager to continue the questioning. "Ask the board when this man will strike again."

Mary repeated the question.

TONIGHT.

"What time tonight?"

7:30.

Lou said, "Little more than an hour from now."

"Where will he strike?" Mary asked the Ouija board.

THE HARBOR PARADE.

"You know what it means," Lou said to Max. He was grim. "For thirty years," he told Mary, "there's been a Christmas night parade of lighted boats on the harbor. Never heard of it?"

"Now that you mention it, yes."

"All those decorated boats you saw last night will be part of it. Plus some that don't use our harbor as home port. Maybe a hundred and fifty or more."

"They have parades like this at Long Beach and Newport Beach in the week before Christmas," Max told Mary. "But the King's Point shindig is more spectacular than any of the others."

Lou said, "There's pretty damned good prize money for the best decorated boats, thanks to a trust fund set up by one of our richer sailors who loved the parade. It's quite a sight. Most of the harbor restaurants open for it. They only serve a limited menu, but they're sold out a week or two in advance."

Mary looked at the Ouija board and asked, "Is the killer after anyone special in the boat parade?"

YES.

"Who?"

HE HAS A RIFLE.

"Who will he shoot?"

HE WANTS TO KILL THE QUEEN.

"The queen?" Mary asked.

"The queen of the parade," Lou said. "She'll make an easy target. She stands on the rear deck of the biggest boat in the lineup, usually midway in the procession. She's in the center of a spotlight. Literally."

"And," Max said, "she makes two complete circuits of the harbor along with the other boats. So if he isn't satisfied with the target he's got on the first circuit, he can wait to see if she presents herself any better the second time around."

Although it had not been asked another question, the plastic trivet moved beneath their fingers, slid through a new series of letters.

KIMBALL'S GAMES AND SNACKS.

"Will he use the tower there?"

YES. KIMBALL'S TOWER.

"One hour to stop him," Max said.

Lou stood up. "I'll call the police."

"Patmore?" Mary asked dubiously.

"He's the man with the authority."

She said, "But will he listen to you after the false alarm last night?"

"He's got to listen!"

Thunder again. And wind.

Mary took her hands from the trivet and hugged herself. She was still cold. "But what if Patmore *does* agree to put a stakeout on the tower?"

"That's what we want, isn't it?"

"Don't you see?" she said. "Won't tonight be a repeat of last night? Last night the killer knew that we were waiting for him. Why won't he know this time, too?"

Lou hesitated, surprised by the question, worried, indecisive. Finally he picked up the tumbler and drank the last of his bourbon. "Maybe he will anticipate us. Maybe we don't have a chance against him. If the Ouija board's right, if he's really killed thirty-five people and never been caught, then he's damned clever. Probably too clever for us. But we've got to try, don't we? We can't just sit here and talk about the weather and the latest books and the newest Paris fashions while he goes on killing!"

"You're right," Max said.

Lou put down his empty glass and went to use the telephone in the entrance foyer.

Mary began to exercise her cramped hands. She closed them into fists, opened them, closed them.

"You look exhausted," Max said.

"I am."

"We'll get to bed early."

"If we get to bed at all."

"We will. Nothing's going to happen to us."

"I've got awful feelings," she said.

"You've had a vision?"

"No. Just feelings."

"Then forget it."

"Tonight will be bloody."

"Don't worry," he said soothingly.

She thought of Patty Spooner.

Rochelle Drake in the morgue drawer.

That feeling again: something behind her, chilly breath on the nape of her neck.

"I don't want to die," she said.

Max said, "You aren't going to. Not tonight."

"You sound so sure of that."

"I am. I won't let you die."

"Are you strong enough to stop it from happening, Max? Are you stronger than destiny?"

Lightning ripped open the sky again: the reflection of light from its blade shone through the windows; and for an instant it turned Max's eyes into icy blanks.

* * *

"King's Point Police."

"Missing persons, please."

"I can help you, sir."

"No. I want to talk to someone in the missing persons' bureau. Didn't you hear me?"

"We don't have a separate department for missing persons' reports."

"You don't?"

"We're a small police force. Can I help you?"

"What's your name?"

"Ms. Newhart."

"I'm Ralph Larsson. Let me talk to a policeman."

"We've only got two on duty tonight."

"One of them will be enough for me."

"They're both in cruisers right now."

"Dammit, my daughter's missing!"

"How old is your daughter, sir?"

"Twenty-six. She was—"

"How long has she been missing?"

"Look, Ms. Newhart, I'm in San Francisco. I live in San Francisco, and my daughter lives in King's Point. I just talked to her a week ago. She was fine then. But now that I think she may no longer be fine, I can't just jump in my car and drive several hundred miles to look in on her. This could be an emergency. She was supposed to call me on Christmas Eve, but she never did."

"Maybe she went to a party or something."

"I thought for sure she'd call sometime today, but she hasn't. I've tried calling her, but there's no answer. Now, dammit, it's not like her to do something like this! It's not like her to forget her family on Christmas."

"Have you tried calling her friends? They might know something."

"I don't know Erika's friends."

"Maybe her neighbors—"

"She hasn't got neighbors. She—"

"Everyone has neighbors."

"She lives in one of those three cottages on the South Bluff, at the end of the paved road. She's the only one who lives there year 'round."

"You know what? I'll bet your daughter's trying to call you right now. Why don't you hang up and see? If she doesn't call tonight, then ring us back tomorrow."

"Are you serious?"

"Well, we can't do anything anyway."

"What do you mean?"

"It is a policy of this department, and of most police departments, not to enter a missing person's case if the report involves an adult who's been gone less than forty-eight hours."

"She has to be missing more than two days before you're interested?"

"That's our policy."

"Well, how do I know she didn't disappear the day after she last called me, six days ago?"

"You said she was supposed to call last night."

"And didn't."

"So officially, she's only been missing since last night."

"Jesus!"

"I'm sorry. That's policy."

"If my daughter was ten years old instead of twenty-six—"

"That's different. Children are different. But your daughter isn't a child."

"So your officers can't become involved until tomorrow night?"

"That's right. But, sir, I'm certain your daughter will call you long before then."

"Ms. Newhart, my name is Ralph Larsson. I told you once before, but I want you to remember it. Ralph Larsson. I'm an attorney. A very successful attorney. I was also the governor's college roommate. Now, Ms. Newhart, if your officers don't take a drive out to my daughter's house to check on her right away, tonight, within the next half an hour, and if later we should discover that something happened to my daughter between this moment and tomorrow night, I will come down there to King's Point and find a reputable cooperating attorney. I will devote the next few years of my life to breaking you and your idiotic superiors. I will sue your fucking goddamned police department, and I will sue your chief for his stupid arbitrary policies. And by God, Ms. Newhart, I will also sue you for every nickel you now have or ever hope to earn. And even if I don't win the case, Ms. Newhart, you will go broke paying for your own lawyers. Do you read me clearly?"

* * *

Lou Pasternak was angry. Furious. The chief of police had hung up on him *twice!* The third time, his wife answered the phone and said he wasn't at home.

"A demitasse would fit Patmore's head like a sombrero!"

"I gather," Max said, "that he wouldn't put a stakeout on Kimball's tower."

Lou snatched his empty glass from the table, went into the kitchen, and picked up the bottle of Wild Turkey. "If the bastard had a little more sense, he'd be a half-wit."

From the dining room Mary asked, "Shouldn't we call the sheriff?"

"Remember, Percy Osterman can't step into King's Point police business unless Patmore asks him to."

"But when a man's killed people all over the country, isn't there an exception? Something called 'hot pursuit'?"

Lou said, "If a guy robs a bank that's in the county's jurisdiction, hops into a car, and flees into a city with its own cops, the sheriff's men can chase and arrest him. *That's* hot pursuit. This isn't."

Max said, "Maybe Osterman can persuade Patmore to cooperate again."

"Not a chance. Not after last night." Lou returned to the table with a fresh glass of bourbon.

"So what now?" Max asked.

Mary said, "We'll have to stop him ourselves. We'll have to go down to the tower."

Lou stared at her in amazement. "Are you serious?"

"It's absolutely out of the question," Max said.

She said, "What would you prefer to do? We can't just sit here and talk about the weather and the latest books and the newest Paris fashions while he goes on killing."

Lou recognized his own words, and he had no effective argument against them.

"If we just sit here," she said, "he'll kill the queen of the boat parade. And most likely a lot of other people, too."

"The rain might force the queen and her court inside, off the open deck," Max said. "Then she wouldn't be a target."

"It isn't raining," Mary said.

"It'll start soon."

"Do you want to bet their lives on that?" she asked. "Lou, we have to stop this man. We haven't any choice."

"I don't want him to kill again," Max said. "But he isn't our responsibility."

"If not ours, whose?" she asked.

Lou saw an uncommon determination in her lovely face. Unshakable resolve in those big blue eyes. He suspected that neither he nor Max could change her mind about this. Might as well argue with a post. He could see that. But he was frightened for her. And as her friend, he felt he should at least try to make her reconsider. "Mary, we're no match for this man."

"Why not?" she asked. "Isn't it just one of him against the three of us?"

"But he's a killer," Max said.

"And we're not killers," she said.

"Exactly."

"Knowing what he's done," she said, "and what he'd do to you if he had the chance, couldn't you shoot him if he came at you with a gun?"

Max said, "Of course, in self-defense—"

"That's just what this is," she said. "Self-defense."

"But this psychopath will have a rifle," Lou said. "And probably a knife. What would we have? Our hands?"

"There's a pistol in the dashboard of the Mercedes," Mary said. "Max is licensed to carry it."

He looked at Max and raised his eyebrows. "You're allowed to carry a concealed weapon?"

Getting up from his chair, heading toward the kitchen, Max said, "Yeah."

"How'd you manage to wrangle the permit? They usually reserve those for people in businesses where they've got to carry around diamonds or a lot of cash."

In the kitchen Max poured himself a double shot of Wild Turkey. "We worked on a couple of cases with the L.A. County sheriff's office. The sheriff saw what dangerous situations Mary can find herself in. He knew I collected guns. He knew I was a marksman, and he figured I wasn't the type to get excited and accidentally blow someone apart." Max drank his bourbon neat and quick: a nervous thirst that briefly exposed the tension that lay beneath his studied composure. "So the sheriff got me the permit." He rinsed out his glass under the kitchen faucet, came back to the dining room, and stood over Mary. "But I'm not going to load that pistol and go out hunting someone to shoot."

"You wouldn't be hunting just anyone," she said. "You'd be hunting a man who has—"

"Forget it," Max said. "I won't do it."

"Let's talk about it," she said.

"No use. It's decided."

Lou saw a spark of anger in her eyes. Max's resistance would do nothing but harden her resolve.

She said, "Okay, Max. Stay here. I'll take the gun and go by myself."

"Mary, for God's sake, you don't know how to handle a pistol!"

She stared up at him without blinking and said, "You take

off the safeties and jack a bullet into the chamber, point, pull the trigger—and the son of a bitch falls down."

Lou knew how stubborn Max could be sometimes. He saw the set of the man's jaw, the drawing up of his shoulders, and he wanted to warn him off. Max was accustomed to playing father-lover to her, accustomed to saying what would be done and what wouldn't. But tonight she wasn't the easygoing Mary they both knew. Even now changes were occurring in her. Conflicting emotions played across her face, but the primary expression was always determination. She was going to make her own decision, and she wasn't going to heed anyone's advice. He had never seen such strength in her before, such purpose. It was exciting, attractive. He sat mute, wanting to advise Max against an authoritarian approach but unable to interfere.

"This is absurd," Max said. "Mary, I won't let you have the pistol."

"Then I'll go without it."

He glared down at her. "You aren't going anywhere."

She stood up, faced him. She met his eyes and held them, as if to prove, through the directness of her gaze, the depth of her commitment. She spoke with quiet intensity and with a foreboding tone that chilled Lou to the bone. "I'm up against something so big, so evil that I can only guess at the dimensions like a blind child feeling an elephant's leg. These past few days have been a living hell for me, Max."

"I know. And—"

"You can't know. No one can know."

"If you—"

"Don't interrupt," she said. "I want you to understand. So you've just got to listen. Max, I'm afraid to go to sleep, and I'm afraid to wake up in the morning. I'm afraid to open every door I come to, afraid to turn around. I'm afraid of the dark. I'm afraid of what might happen—and of what might *not* happen. Dammit, I'm even afraid to go to the bathroom alone! I cannot live like this. I refuse to live like this. There's something about this case that makes it different from all others, something that's working inside of me like acid, eating me alive. This case touched my life like nothing else I've worked on, but I don't know why. Max, I sense, I feel, I *know* that if I don't pursue this man with every ounce of energy I have and in every way I know how, then he'll come after me."

The trivet on the Ouija board moved, but Lou was the only one to see it. It slid to the spot marked YES, as if in agreement with Mary's prediction.

"If I don't take the initiative," she said, "I'll lose what little advantage I might now have. I can't walk away. If I try to run, I won't get far. I'll die."

Max said, "And if you pursue this man, if you insist on going down to that tower tonight, then you'll probably die sooner."

"I might," she said. "But if I do, at least I'll have taken responsibility for my own life and death. All my life, I've been scared of everything, and I've let someone else deal with my bogeymen for me. Not anymore. Because this time no one else *can* help me. The answer is inside of me, and if I don't find it soon, I'm finished. It's past time I stopped hiding behind strong men. I've got to take chances. When I risk something and fail, I've got to suffer the consequences like anybody else. If I'm always pampered, cuddled, and cushioned from shock, then my successes in life are meaningless. I've decided that no one—not Alan, not you, Max, and especially not that part of me that's still a dependent six-year-old—*no one* is going to stop me from living a full life."

They stood in silence for a while.

The grandfather clock chimed the quarter hour.

Lou said, "Forty-five minutes until he takes a shot at the queen of the boat parade."

Mary said, "Well, Max?"

Finally he nodded. "We better get moving."

* * *

Blood. Blood like ribbons tangled in her hair. Blood spotting her punctured breasts. Blood on her hands, her arms, her belly, her thighs. Blood on the sofa and chair. Blood on the draperies, on the wall. Bloody little footprints of a cat all across the light tan carpet.

Trying to hold down the taste of vomit, Officer Rudy Holtzman stepped carefully around the mutilated body of Erika Larsson, went into the dark kitchen, and turned on the lights. He used the wall phone to dial headquarters.

When the night girl, Wendy Newhart, answered, Holtzman said, "I'm out here at the Larsson place." His voice was strained and hoarse; it cracked on a couple of words. He cleared his throat. "The lights were on when I got here. Nobody answered the bell, but the door was ajar. She's dead."

"Oh, my *God!* Well, I'm not going to tell her father. That's out of the question. Someone else will have to tell him."

"Better get Charlie over here with the other squad car," Holtzman said. "Call the medical examiner right away. And Patmore, of course. Tell Charlie to move his ass; I don't like being here alone."

Wendy Newhart asked, "When was she killed?"

"How should I know? The medical examiner will know."

"I mean, did it just happen before you got there? Within the past half hour?"

"What's it matter?" Holtzman asked.

"Rudy, tell me! Did it just happen?"

"The blood's mostly caked and dry. I can't pinpoint the time of death, but it must surely have been a good many hours ago."

"Thank the Lord for small miracles," she said.

"What?"

She had hung up.

Holtzman put down the receiver and turned to see a black cat standing in the doorway between the kitchen and the front room, no more than five feet from him. Its fuzzy white muzzle had been tinted red-brown with blood. Holtzman took one step, kicked out at the cat, missed.

It squealed and ran.

* * *

They arrived at the harbor at five minutes past seven.

Max parked the Mercedes in a corner of the lot that, in season, served both a restaurant called Italian Villa and Kimball's Arcade. Tonight the restaurant's side of the lot was nearly full, while the other side was nearly empty.

The three of them got out of the car.

Lou drew up his shoulders against the cold. As the storm air had moved in from the Pacific, the temperature had dropped rapidly from a one o'clock high of seventy degrees to a current low of forty-four. The wind had increased, too; it whipped in from the harbor, lashed King's Point, made the night seem even cooler than it was.

Lou said, "I still think I should go with Max, and you should stay here, where it's safe."

"It's not safe anywhere for me," Mary said.

"At least if you stayed here in the car—"

She waved one hand impatiently, interrupted him. "We've got two weapons we can use against this man we're after: one is Max's handiness with guns, and the other is my psychic talent. The two of us shouldn't split up."

The sea wind lifted her long hair, made it flap like a banner behind her.

Max put one hand on Lou's shoulder. "I don't want her in the thick of the action any more than you do. But maybe she's right. She's probably not in any greater danger there than here. Besides, neither of us is going to change her mind."

"I feel so useless," Lou said.

"We need someone here in the car," Max said. "You're our early-warning system."

"We're wasting time," Mary said.

Lou nodded glumly. He kissed her cheek and told Max to take good care of her.

They hurried into the wind, across the parking lot toward the huge, deserted barnlike building that housed the array of souvenir stands, trinket stores, amusements, and coffee shops known collectively as Kimball's Games and Snacks.

He got behind the wheel of the Mercedes and closed the door. Through the windshield he could barely see Max and Mary as they drew farther away and blended into the darkness around the clapboard and cedar-shingled pavilion.

A fierce gust of wind rocked the car. Forks of lightning stabbed through the sky, but still there was no rain.

Lou settled back, resigned to his role as a sentinel. If the killer didn't anticipate Mary tonight, as he had last night, he would probably approach Kimball's openly, brazenly. If Lou spotted a man moving toward the building, he would switch on the Mercedes' ignition and alert Max with two short blasts of the horn. The pavilion and tower stood only sixty yards farther along the boardwalk that connected seven or eight businesses on this section of the harbor. The sound of the horn would travel that far undiminished, but it wasn't likely the killer would recognize it as a signal. Even if Mary was able to foresee the exact time and direction of the man's approach, the horn would be a welcome confirmation of her vision.

Of course, the psychopath might have anticipated them again and already be at the pavilion.

Lou shifted uneasily behind the wheel.

He thought of Patty Spooner, strangled to death with a priest's stole. He thought of Barry Mitchell, hideously mutilated.

He looked left and right, peered into the rearview mirror. No one. He squinted at the deep shadows along the side of the pavilion. All was still.

* * *

The black cat crouched on the top of a seven-foot-high set of bookshelves, no more than eight or ten inches from the ceiling in the front room of the cottage. Its forepaws hung over the edge of the shelf; it was motionless, staring down at Rudy Holtzman with suspicion and contempt.

Filthy damned thing. He hated cats. Always had. And it gave him the creeps just to think about this one eagerly lapping up the murdered woman's blood.

It made a deep, throaty sound, as if daring him to approach it.

He didn't want to wait with the cat and the corpse, not even for the few minutes Charlie would need to get here in the other cruiser. He walked down the short hallway to inspect the part of the house he'd not yet seen.

In the bedroom he found an open window, where the wind played havoc with a pair of flimsy curtains and an oilcloth blind that was drawn down only halfway. The recent storms had soaked and badly stained the carpet.

Holtzman was suddenly excited. He studied the room, recreating in his mind those first few seconds when the sanctity of the house had been violated. He knew that more than rain had come in through that window. He was certain that he'd found the killer's entrance. And as his glance traveled over the floor, he could hardly believe what he saw. It was one of those lucky breaks you seldom get in police work. Apparently the pistol had fallen unnoticed from a coat pocket as the killer climbed through the window.

Holtzman knelt on the damp carpet to get a closer look at

the weapon. He was careful not to spoil any fingerprints that might be on it. If this killer was the same man who had slaughtered those nurses and the people in that beauty salon—and the style sure seemed the same to Holtzman—then the Anaheim and Santa Ana police already had more than enough good prints. So far prints had been of no use in cracking the case because the killer evidently had never had his taken by any police organization in the country. Nevertheless, because he prided himself on being more professional than anyone with whom he worked, Holtzman didn't grasp the pistol and smear the evidence. He took a ball-point pen from his shirt pocket, slipped it through the trigger guard, lifted the gun off the floor, and held it in front of his eyes.

It was an unusual piece—a .45 Auto Colt. But nothing off the shelf. Something special. A collector's item. The metal was engraved with delicate leaves and vines. There were also a number of animals—rabbits, deer, pheasants, foxes—etched in positions of flight beginning at the forward sight on the barrel, all of them incredibly detailed, beautifully rendered, all racing toward the butt.

He saw what appeared to be printing on the steel, where it met the wooden handgrip. The bedroom light was poor. The letters were tiny, between a quarter and a half inch high, inscribed with a spidery flourish of the engraver's tool. Holtzman couldn't read them.

He stood up and, carrying the Colt on the pen, went to the nearest lamp.

by W. Thorben
Seattle 1975

A collector's piece like this one often passed through the hands of many owners who purchased and resold it at gun shows without bothering to register it with authorities. Nevertheless, with the engraver's name (and providing the gun had not been stolen from a collection), they should be able to find the man who had commissioned it from Thorben. From him they had a chance of tracing it to the man who'd dropped it while coming through the window.

Still manipulating the weapon with his ball-point pen, Holtzman looked at the opposite side. Again, where the steel met the wooden handgrip, there was writing. Not the same words. He squinted. He read it. Then read it again. "Well, I'll be damned."

A siren rose in the distance and grew rapidly nearer.

Holtzman went down the hall to the side of the house that faced the dead-end macadam road. He stood in the open doorway he'd first found ajar.

Another police car, emergency beacons blazing, roared up the long hill from town. Patmore's station wagon wasn't far behind it.

Beneath the hall light Holtzman held up the Colt and read the second legend again.

commissioned by
Max Bergen

18

THE DARKNESS AROUND the pavilion was lumpy, velvety, and deep. It offered dozens of hiding places.

Mary carried the flashlight, hooding it with one hand. Every time she made a sudden move in response to imagined noises, shadows danced.

She stayed close to Max as they circled the building, looking for a place where the killer might have gotten inside. Last night the police had entered with a key provided by the owners. That was a convenience denied both them and their quarry. The killer would have to break something to get in and reach the tower; he would have to leave a trail.

She was impatient. Twice she urged Max to hurry.

Already the parade of lighted boats had begun its first circuit of the harbor, entering from the staging area at sea, still far down the channel but approaching fast. By seven-thirty the queen of the parade might well have begun her first pass of the tower.

On the west side of the pavilion, which faced the harbor and was flanked with a railed boardwalk, they found a shattered pane of glass in one of the mullioned windows that looked in on the lightless, deserted coffee shop.

"Did the killer do this?" Max asked.

She directed the flashlight at the ground, and in the soft glow of its backwash, she studied the damaged window. With the fingertips of her left hand she traced the wooden ribs that framed the missing pane. The night was already chilly, but the air got suddenly colder as she concentrated on the psychic impressions that the window held for her.

Wicka-wicka-wicka!

She shuddered, squeezed the flashlight as hard as she could, gritted her teeth but refused to panic.

"Something?" Max asked.

"Yes. He did this."

"Is he inside now?"

"No. He was here . . . late yesterday . . . after the police left . . . I can see . . . many hours after the police left . . . early this morning . . . at dawn . . . up in the tower." She took her hand from the window, and an invisible connection snapped. "But he hasn't returned yet tonight."

"You're positive about that?"

"Absolutely."

"But he'll be here any minute?"

"Yes. So hurry."

Wicka-wicka-wicka!

Ignore it, she told herself. It's not real. Max doesn't hear it, does he? Only you hear it. Psychic impressions. Nothing is really overhead. No wings. No danger. No wings at all.

"We don't want to make this any more of a spectacle than we have to," Max said. "Some of these restaurants farther around the harbor might have a pretty good view of us. Better shut off the flashlight."

She did as he said.

The night closed around her.

Max put one hand through the missing pane, reached up, and fumbled for the latch on the vertical, metal center post. "Do you realize this is breaking and entering?"

"I suppose it is," she said.

"Doesn't that bother you?"

"Max, will you *hurry?*"

He swung the tall halves of the window outward without making a sound.

She climbed onto the sill, which was only three feet above the boardwalk, stepped down into the coffee shop. She glanced around the room, but she couldn't see anything.

Max looked both ways along the boardwalk, then followed her, closed and latched the window.

"It's even darker in here than it was out there," she said. "We'll be tripping over something every other step if I don't use the flash."

"Just be sure you don't point it at a window," he said. "Keep it hooded."

She switched on the light, shielding half the lens with her left hand.

The restaurant contained approximately thirty tables, all of

them bolted to the floor. Apparently because the chairs couldn't
be bolted down as well, they had been removed and put in
storage until Kimball's reopened in the spring.

The only public entrance to the coffee shop—a pair of
many-paned glass doors that matched the big mullioned windows—was from inside of the pavilion, of which this restaurant
was but one small part. The killer had smashed the lock. When
Max pushed open the doors, they moved stiffly and grated on
their unlubricated hinges.

He stood still for a moment, listening to the settling sounds
of the building. Finally he said, "You're really sure he's not
here already?"

"Positive."

Although the psychic impressions were not always complete, they'd never deceived her. She hoped her talent hadn't
failed this time; because if it had, if the killer *was* already here
and waiting, she was as good as dead.

From the coffee shop they entered a corridor that curved
out of sight in both directions. It was lined with small gift
shops: Silly T-Shirts, The Ceramic Factory, The House of Glass
Miniatures, and a dozen more, all empty and dark.

Max and Mary turned left and quickly discovered that the
long corridor was a semicircle leading, at both ends, into the
cavernous main hall of the arcade. That huge room was bare
now, but in season it would be filled with a variety of pinball
machines, shuffleboard bowling, shooting galleries, electronic
games, and carnival booths where you could get your fortune
told or where a boy could spend ten dollars in quarters to win
a three-dollar toy animal for his best girl.

They walked to the center of the room. Their footsteps
echoed hollowly from wall to wall and from curve to curve of
the high domed ceiling.

Mary stopped and pointed the flashlight where Lou had said
to look. She saw an archway at the rear of the room, steps
beyond it. Above the arch was a sign: THIS WAY TO OBSERVATION
DECK.

*Screams, the sound of wings, a body hurtling off the bottom
steps and through the archway, wings, a body writhing on the
wooden arcade floor, wings, strangled cries for help . . .*

She swayed under the impact of the psychic images.

"What's the matter?" Max asked.

"I see . . ." She tried to hold on to the vision, but it rapidly faded and would not be coaxed to return. "Someone's going to die tonight at the foot of those stairs."

"One of us?"

"I don't know."

"The killer?"

"I hope."

"It'll be him," Max said. "Not us. We'll live. We've got to. I know it."

Not as certain as he was, reluctant to think about it for fear her courage would vanish, she asked, "Where should we wait for him?"

"I'll wait at the bottom of the steps. You'll wait at the top of the tower."

"At the top of . . . oh, no!"

"Oh, yes."

"I'm staying with you," she said.

"Look, if Lou uses the car horn to warn us, we probably won't hear it in here. But you'd be certain to hear it if you were in the tower—"

"Forget it."

"—on the open deck."

"Max, I'm staying here."

"No, dammit!"

She took a step back from him.

His face was dark with anger. *"I'm* the one who's an expert with guns. If it comes down to a shooting match, you'll be in my way. If I have to move fast, I don't want to have to stop and worry whether you're in the line of fire."

"I'm not a hopeless idiot," she said. "I can stay out of your way."

He glared at her and said nothing.

She said, "But what if I have a vision while I'm up there, something important? How will I let you know what's going to happen?"

"I'll be here at the bottom of the steps—not more than sixty feet from you. You can reach me quickly if it's necessary."

"I don't know . . ."

"I'll put it more bluntly," Max said. "Either do what I say and go to the observation deck, or so help me God, I'm going to take a punch at you, lightly as I can, but hard enough to knock you out. Then I'll carry you back to the Mercedes and call this whole thing off."

"You wouldn't."

"Wouldn't I?"

She knew he wasn't making idle threats.

"I'll do it because I love you," he said. "I don't want you to get killed."

"And I don't want *you* killed," she said.

"Good. Then you'll listen to me. We've both got a better chance of living through this if you're not here to distract me when and if the shooting starts."

She was filled with conflicting emotions. "Will you kill him?"

"If he forces me to."

"Don't hesitate to do it," she said. "Don't give him a chance. He's too clever. Shoot him the second you see him."

"The police might have something to say about that."

"To hell with the police."

"Mary, *are* you going upstairs? There's not much time. Do we stay or do I carry you out of here? It's entirely your decision, but you've got to make your mind up fast."

Partly because she saw a glimmer of truth in his argument, but mainly because she had no choice, she said, "All right."

They walked quickly to the archway. At the foot of the stairs he put his hands on her shoulders, and she raised her face to him. They kissed.

"When you get to the top," he said, "don't stand around looking at the sights. Even at night someone on the ground might be able to see you. If the killer spots you, he might back off. You say we'll have to have a showdown with him sooner or later. So we may as well do what we can to end it tonight."

"Who gets the flashlight?" she asked.

"You keep it."

She was relieved, but she said, "You'll be in the dark down here . . . with him."

"If I switched on a flashlight when I heard him coming," Max said, "I'd only be making a target of myself. Besides, if he isn't aware I'm waiting for him, he's not going to enter a pitch-black building and try to navigate through it without a flash. I'll be able to see him by his own light."

She kissed him again, turned away, and climbed the eight flights of stairs alone.

At the top she doused the flashlight and stood for a moment in the fierce wind, looking out at the parade of lighted boats on the harbor. Then she heeded Max's advice and sat down with her back to the waist-high wall that bordered the deck.

Darkness. Some light. Not much.

Alone now. All alone.

No. Not alone. Where did a thought like that come from? Max was nearby.

The wind raced through the belfry, moaned like a human voice.

She huddled in her leather coat and wished for a sweater.

It would rain soon. She could smell it in the air.

She pushed the read-out button on her digital wristwatch, and lighted numerals glowed blood-red in the dark.

The eyes.

She suddenly remembered the luminous, reddish eyes that she had seen in Berton Mitchell's cottage. She could not conjure up a face to go with them. Just the eyes . . . and the sound of wings . . . and the feel of wings all over her . . . and still the eyes, wild, inhuman.

She remembered something else, too; remembered it with a jolt—a small voice at the back of her mind, whispery but intense: *"I'm a demon and a vampire. I like the taste of blood."*

Someone had spoken those very words to her in Mitchell's cottage twenty-four years ago.

Who? Berton Mitchell himself? Who else could it have been?

Although she tried to use her psychic talent to transform the vivid memory into a clairvoyant vision, she was not able to bring much light to the gloomy, penumbral images that swam and pulsed malignantly. The mysterious face of the creature that spoke to her remained just out of sight.

But the inner voice grew louder. Somehow it swelled and thundered and overwhelmed her, yet remained a whisper. The harsh words came faster, even faster, and she was shaken by them. *"I'm a demon and a vampire. I like the taste of blood. I'm a demon and a vampire, I like the taste of blood, I'm a demon and a vampire—"*

"Stop it!" she said.

She put her hands to her ears and willed the voice from her mind. Gradually it faded. When it was gone, she slumped forward, dizzy.

"I'll be all right," she said softly, urgently. "It'll be all right.

No one will die. It'll be all right. Tonight it ends. It'll be fine after tonight."

Slowly the realities of the night impressed themselves upon her once more: wind, cold, darkness.

Distracted by the memory of those luminous eyes, she hadn't noticed the time when she pressed the button on her watch. She pressed it again.

7:24

Six minutes to go.

*   *   *

Heavy ebony clouds, vaguely phosphorescent at their bearded edges, sailed soundlessly toward the east. The sky was silent for long minutes, a muffling blanket tented over the earth; but now it crashed and flared again.

The wind lifted a scrap of paper from the pavement, pasted it to the windshield of the Mercedes for a few seconds, then tore it away.

Lou shifted uneasily, leaned into the steering wheel, squinted at the purple-black shadows that flanked the pavilion. The longer he stared, the more the darkness seemed to shimmer as if it were alive. He kept seeing movement where there was none; his eyes played a hundred tricks on him. He didn't have the proper temperament for a sentinel. He had no patience.

He looked at his watch.

7:29.

Someone rapped three times, hard, on the window to his left, inches from his head.

He jerked around.

A familiar face peered in at him, smiled.

Confused and somewhat embarrassed by the terror that must have been visible on his face, Lou said, "Hey! You startled me." He felt for the latch, opened the door, and got out of the car. "What are you doing here?"

Too late, he saw the butcher knife.

*   *   *

Lights were on in most of the downstairs rooms at 440 Ocean Hill Lane, but when Rudy Holtzman rang the bell, no one answered.

Patmore tried the door and found it wasn't locked. He pushed it open. Wind rushed past him and swept a stack of unopened mail off the small table in the foyer.

Patmore couldn't see anyone in the entranceway or in the living room beyond. He leaned through the door and shouted, "Pasternak! You in there?"

No one answered.

"Maybe he's dead," Holtzman said.

Because he was wearing civilian clothes, Patmore took a silvery badge from the pocket of his overcoat and pinned it to his lapel. He drew his service revolver from the outer coat pocket, and, holding it with the barrel pointed at the ceiling, he stepped into the house.

Behind him, Holtzman cleared his throat and said, "We don't have a warrant."

Patmore stopped, looked back at him, and said, "Rudy, your ass, get it in here."

*   *   *

Syrupy darkness. A coppery odor. Barbed wire twisting inside him.

His tongue hurt. He'd bitten it. A coppery taste.

He was lying on his stomach. On the macadam parking lot. Near the Mercedes. His arms flung out in supplication. Head to one side. Ear against the ground as if listening for the approach of an enemy.

He opened his eyes but just barely. A pair of shoes were in front of his face. Inches from him. Gucci loafers. They turned and walked away. Toward the pavilion. In seconds they were out of sight, but he could still hear footsteps.

He tried to raise his head. Couldn't.

He tried to remember how many times he'd been stabbed in the stomach. Three, maybe four times. Could have been worse. But it was surely bad enough. He was dying. He had no strength at all; and now even his weakness was draining out of him.

I'm such an idiot, he thought bitterly. How could I have been so careless? A damned fool. The closest I'll ever come to a brainstorm is a light drizzle.

Should have known who the killer was. Should have known

the moment the Ouija board said the target was the queen of the boat parade. She was one of his old girl friends. Seemed to get along with a woman for only a few months. So now he was going to kill one of his old girl friends. Probably had killed others. Why? No matter why. Should have known.

He felt as if thousands of insects were crawling inside of him, stinging and biting his guts.

He closed his eyes and thought, I don't want to die. I *won't!*

Then: You fool. Do you think you have a choice?

A coppery odor. Syrupy darkness.

It didn't look bad.

Inviting, actually.

He floated in the inviting darkness. He sank down and down, away from the pain, away from everything.

* * *

Curious, John Patmore paged through the spiralbound notebook that lay open beside the Ouija board on the dining room table. The ruled pages were filled with neat, feminine handwriting that he supposed belonged to Mary Bergen.

Mostly she had recorded questions and answers that appeared to be connected with the case she claimed to be investigating. In the middle of the notebook, however, there was a page that contained only five hastily scrawled words: *Mary! Run for your life!*

The same message was repeated in the center of the following page. And then on a third.

Under the third warning there were more questions and answers:

> *When did I write these warnings?*
> *Don't know.*
> *What do I mean by them?*
> *Don't know.*
> *Who am I afraid of?*
> *Don't know, don't know, don't know!*
> *Am I going crazy?*
> *Maybe.*
> *Where can I run to?*
> *Nowhere.*

Strange.

It made him nervous.

There was a note pad at the other side of the Ouija board. Patmore began leafing through it.

> A-L-L-O-U-R-Y-E-S-T-E-R-D-A-Y-S
> ALL OUR YESTERDAYS
> B-E-A-U-T-I-F-U-L
> BEAUTIFUL
> T-H-E-A-I-R-I-S-B-E-A-U-T-I-F-U-L
> THE AIR IS BEAUTIFUL

He glanced at the Ouija board, at the trivet, then down at the note pad again. He remembered working a board with his mother when he was a boy. He began to read every other line of the transcript.

When he finished, he thought of Erika Larsson and realized she matched the description of the girl whose death Mary Bergen had predicted. Reluctantly, he admitted to himself that perhaps the clairvoyant was not a fake after all. "Holtzman!"

Rudy Holtzman returned from the far end of the house. "No one's here."

"Max Bergen intends to kill the queen of the boat parade."

Blinking in surprise, Holtzman said, *"What?* Jenny Canning?"

"Apparently Mary Bergen doesn't realize her husband's the man she's after." Patmore looked at his watch. "We might be too late." He ran through the cluttered living room, out the front door.

*   *   *

Marie Sanzini.

Unbidden, the name came to Mary.

Marie Sanzini.

Marie Sanzini was one of the nurses killed in Anaheim—and suddenly her name was familiar. Mary knew it, but she didn't know where she'd heard it before. Marie. Marie Sanzini. It teased her.

She closed her eyes, tried to see the woman's face, but it eluded her.

She thumbed the button on her watch.

7:33.

No signal from Lou.

Was tonight just another wild-goose chase?

* * *

Standing in absolute blackness, Max began to feel that he was closed inside a coffin. Then he heard the coffee shop doors grating noisily on their hinges, and his claustrophobia was replaced by an even more elemental fear. Quietly, he stepped out of the archway into the arcade, the gun in his right hand.

A hundred feet away a man with a flashlight came out of the curved corridor that served the restaurant and gift shops. He kept the beam pointed at the floor ahead of him; behind it he, too, was in darkness.

Mustn't have come across the parking lot, Max thought. Lou hadn't blown the car horn. Must have sneaked between two buildings farther north along the harbor, and then down the boardwalk.

Max intended to wait until they were only fifty feet apart before ordering the killer to stop. Fifty feet would give him safety, room to maneuver. And if he's fifty feet from the corridor, Max thought, I'll have time to pull off a few good shots if the bastard tries to dodge out of sight.

Seventy feet now.

Sixty.

Fifty.

The killer spoke first, a hoarse, whispered: *"Max?"*

Shocked at being called by name, Max took one step into the darkness and asked, "Who's there?"

The man kept walking, hidden behind the light.

Forty feet.

"Who's there?" Max demanded.

Again, a forced whisper: *"It's me. Lou."*

Thirty feet.

Max lowered his gun. "Lou? For God's sake, it's only a few minutes past seven-thirty. We can't quit yet."

Lou said, still whispering, *"Trouble."*

Twenty feet.

"What trouble?" Max asked. "What do you mean?"

Ten feet.

Suddenly Max knew it wasn't Lou Pasternak.

The killer jerked the flashlight up, in the direction of Max's voice, temporarily blinding him.

Although for an instant he could see nothing, Max raised the gun and pulled the trigger. Once. Twice. The shots crashed like cannon fire in the huge, high-ceilinged room.

Simultaneous with the explosion, perhaps even a fraction of a second prior to it, the flashlight spun up and up, out to the right.

I hit him! Max thought.

Even before he completed the thought, the knife ripped into him, rammed out of the darkness and into him, felt like the blade of a shovel, enormous, devastating, so devastating that he dropped the gun, feeling pain like nothing he'd ever known, and he realized that the killer had pitched the flashlight aside as a diversion, hadn't really been hit at all, and the knife was withdrawn from him, and then shoved hard into him again, deep into his stomach, and he thought of Mary and his love for Mary and about how he was letting her down, and he grappled with the killer's head in the dark, got handfuls of short hair, but the bandage came off his finger and the cut was wrenched open again and he felt that pain separate from all the others, and he cursed the sharp edge on the car's jack, and the flashlight hit the floor ten feet away, spun around, cast lunatic shadows, and the knife ripped loose from him again, and he reached for the hand that held it, but he missed, and the blade got him a third time, explosive pain, and he staggered back, the man all over him, the blade plunging again, high this time, into his chest, and he realized that the only way he could hope to survive now was to play dead, so he fell, fell hard, and the man stumbled over him, and he heard the man's rapid breathing, and he lay very still, and the man went for the flashlight and came back and looked down at him, stood over him, kicked him in the ribs, and he wanted to cry out but didn't, didn't move and didn't breathe, even though he was screaming inside for breath, so the man turned away and went toward the arch, and then there were footsteps on the tower stairs, and, hearing them, he felt like such a useless ass, outsmarted, and he knew he wasn't going to be able to recover his gun and climb those stairs and rescue Mary because stuff like that was for the movies, pain was pulverizing him, he was leaking all over the floor, dripping like a squeezed fruit, but he told himself he had to try to help her and that he wasn't going to die, wasn't going to die, wasn't going to die, even though that was exactly what he seemed to be doing.

* * *

She stood up when the shots were fired. She went to the head of the tower stairs, and within a minute she heard footsteps.

"Max?"

No answer.

"Max?"

Just footsteps coming up.

She backed away from the stairs, across the observation deck, until her buttocks encountered the low wall.

Wicka-wicka-wicka!

Marie Sanzini.

She saw Marie's face, and she knew it.

Rochelle Drake. She knew Rochelle, too.

Erika Larsson. That was the name of the fuzzy-haired blonde—the delicate, ethereal woman who had been in the vision in the mirror at Lou's place.

Mary had known them all along, but she had forced the knowledge into her subconscious. If she cared to pursue it, the answer was there now, waiting. But she still didn't want to face the truth. *Couldn't* face it.

She reminded herself of her announced determination to find her own strength, her own solutions to the problems of life. Defeated already? But she couldn't shame herself; right now, she would accept perpetual weakness and dependence and continued ignorance of the past for a chance to get out of here.

From the stairwell: the slow ascent of footsteps.

"No," she said desperately. She pressed back against the low wall, eyes fixed on the entrance to the stairs. "I don't want to know." Her voice was high, tremulous. "Oh, God. No. Please!"

Lightning slashed the sky, sharp and bright. Thunder cracked. At last the storm broke: scattered pellets of rain testing the earth; then a sudden downpour; stinging, eroding sheets of water slanting in from the ocean.

The wind drove the rain under the overhang of the belfry roof. Fat droplets pummeled the back of her leather coat, soak-

ing her long black hair. But she didn't care if she got wet. The
only thing that worried her now was the past, for it kept coming
back to her against her will:

*The living room of Berton Mitchell's cottage. Windows with
paper blinds drawn almost to the sills. Lacy curtains. The only
light, gray light, filtering in from a cloudy afternoon. Shadowy
corners. Pale yellow walls. A dark brown davenport with a
pair of matching, overstuffed chairs. Pine floor, rag-twist rugs.*

*A six-year-old girl lying on the floor. Long dark hair tied
into two ponytails with orange ribbons. Beige dress with Kelly-
green piping and buttons. Me. The little girl is me. On my
back. Dazed. Confused. The side of my face hurts real bad.
And the back of my head. What did he do to me? My legs are
spread. I can't move them. Each of my ankles is tied securely
to a different foot of a bulky armchair. My arms are stretched
out behind me. My wrists are tied to the feet of another chair.
Can't move. Try to raise my head to look around. Can't.*

*Maybe Mrs. Mitchell will come untie me. No. She's gone
away. Visiting relatives with Barry. Mr. Mitchell is off someplace trimming hedges.*

Scared. So scared.

*Footsteps . . . Just him. Nothing frightening. Just him. But
what's he want? What's he doing?*

*He kneels beside me. He has a pillow in his hands . . . big
feather pillow . . . he shoves it . . . in my face . . . presses down
on it. This isn't a good game . . . not good at all. This is wrong
. . . scary. No light . . . no air . . . I scream . . . but the pillow muffles
my voice. Try to breathe . . . can't draw in anything but linen.
I thrash in my bonds. Daddy, help me! And then he pulls the
pillow away. He's giggling. I gulp air and start to cry. He rams
the pillow into my face again. I twist my head, can't get out
from under. I bite and chew the pillow. Spinning. Dizzy. Weightless. Dying. Hollering in my mind for Daddy, thinking oh-so-
hard of him, knowing he can't hear me. And then the pillow
is taken away again; cool, delicious air rushes over my face,
into my hot lungs. And the pillow is jammed onto me again.
And in the final moment before I faint it's removed. Repeatedly
reprieved on the verge of suffocation, I reach the thin red line
between sanity and madness. And he's giggling as he tortures
me. But finally he lifts the pillow and tosses it aside, finished
with the game.*

But there are worse games to come:

He takes my head in both hands . . . his fingers like iron claws. The ache at the back of my skull is getting infinitely worse . . . unbearable. He forces my head to one side . . . descends upon me . . . breathes across my face . . . hissing like a snake . . . moves toward my exposed neck . . . lips on my neck now . . . he takes a pinch of my skin between his teeth, bites hard, bites it off, swallows. I cry out at the sharp little pain . . . struggle . . . the cords bind. He puts his mouth to the tiny wound in my neck . . . sucks . . . draws blood. And when he finally raises his head and lets go of me . . . and I turn . . . I see him grinning, blood smeared around his mouth and streaks of blood on his teeth.

He is only nine years old, three years older than me, but his face is carved with a very adult hatred.

Weeping, choking, I say, "What are you doing?"

He leans even closer, inches from my face. His breath is fetid, corrupted by my own blood.

"I am a demon and a vampire," Alan says. There is a childish tone of make-believe in his voice. Yet he is also serious. "I like the taste of blood."

Mary said, "Ahhhh," as if she had opened an enormous heavy door after many hours of strenuous effort.

And a flashlight beam swung back and forth at the head of the tower stairs.

And Alan walked onto the observation deck.

And he centered the light on her, but not in her eyes.

And they stared at each other.

And finally he grinned and said, "Hello, Sis."

I am still spread-eagled on the floor.

Alan returns . . . wearing gloves . . . carrying a wooden box with a wire lid. He reaches through a spring trap in the lid . . . clutches something, withdraws it . . . a small dark creature, its head thrust out of the top of his fist . . . eyes luminous . . . a bat . . . a brown bat . . . one of those he found in the attic of the manor house. It doesn't appear to be scared of him . . . seems almost tame, not wild at all.

He isn't allowed to keep the bats as pets. They're dirty. Daddy told him to get rid of them.

He changes his grip on the beast, which flutters but is more docile than not . . . holds it with both hands . . . but lets the wings free. Wicka-wicka-wicka! *He holds the bat above my head . . . six or eight inches from me . . . then slowly lowers it until the luminous eyes are staring directly into my eyes . . . until I beg to be released . . . beg him to take the bat away, put it in the box . . . until the membranous wings lightly brush me . . . until the wings strike my face with increasing force, with leathery flapping sounds,* Wicka-wicka-wicka!

When peals of thunder tolled over the harbor, Mary felt as if they were waves of some tangible substance passing through her; for deep within she shook sympathetically with each crash.

The past and present were two bottomless caverns of terror between which and above which she walked on a fine thread of self-control. She needed all of her attention and will-power to maintain her equilibrium as the memories swooped over her; she wasn't even able to speak to Alan; she couldn't find the strength to form words.

Without switching it off, Alan put his flashlight on the belfry floor, snug against the wall, where the rain hadn't dampened the boards. A rifle was slung from his left shoulder; he slipped the strap off his arm and put the gun down, too.

He still held the butcher knife.

He picked up the flashlight and pointed it toward the ceiling, into the hollow, cone-shaped roof. "Look, Mary. Look up. Go ahead. You should see this. Look!"

She looked—and tried to draw back from the sight. She was already pressed against the low wall; there was nowhere to run.

"They're not all here at the moment," Alan said. "Some have gone hunting, of course. But most of them stayed in tonight. They sensed the coming rain. See them, Mary? See the bats?"

I am only six years old, and I am tied up, on the floor, my legs spread. Alan holds the bat with both hands. He moves it between my legs, under my dress. It squeals. I am sobbing, gasping for breath, pleading with him. Alan pushes my dress up immodestly. He's sweating. His face is pale. His lips quiver. He doesn't look like a nine-year-old boy; he is truly demonic.

The tips of the bat's wings tickle my bare thighs.

Tickle . . . then scratch painfully.

Although I am much too young to understand the more mysterious functions of my body, too young to imagine what pleasure and pain it will one day give me, I am engulfed by primal fear, overwhelmed by terror at the thought of the bat shoved against the exposed center of me. I find this much harder to bear than having the creature on my face, and I squirm and kick uselessly at Alan, and the wings beat in the cramped space between my spread legs, and then I feel what I most dread, for Alan has forced the bat against me, and the thing writhes and nips and claws and screeches shrilly against me, and Alan is trying to ram it inside of me, and I scream at the thought, spit, cry, and the bat is screeching, too, so Alan has great difficulty merely holding on to the thing, but he forces it against me with all of his strength, and suddenly a pain, a monstrous pain, shoots up through me—

The memories were physical as well as mental agony. She had refused to face them for twenty-four years; and in that time they had acquired incredible power. They struck her as if they were a man's fists. She ached. She resisted the urge to vomit. Her legs were weak. She wept.

Alan put the flashlight on the floor again and shifted the knife from his left to his right hand.

Richard Lingard's knife.

Max had been right about that: no ghost had picked it up. She had refused to confront the truth, had been incapable of dealing with it; therefore, she'd convinced herself that the missing knife could be explained only as the work of supernatural forces.

"I killed Max," Alan said.

She knew that must be true, but she didn't want to consider it. The tears for that, the shattering grief would have to come later—if she lived long enough to grieve.

The observation deck was fifteen feet across. Less than three yards of wet pine flooring separated her from him.

He spoke softly, not much louder than the monotonous hiss of the rain. "I'm glad you came. It's time I finished what I started twenty-four years ago."

When asked where the killer was from, the Ouija board had said, THE AIR IS BEAUTIFUL. That wasn't a literal translation of "Bel Air," but it was close enough.

Why hadn't she seen that?

She hadn't wanted to see it.

At their feet the beam of the flashlight was diffused and cast back by the glossy paint on the deck wall, highlighting his chin and cheeks and nose. Because the rising light created odd shadows on his face, he was not handsome now; instead, he resembled one of the fright masks worn by a witch doctor in some savage ceremony. He held the knife in front of him, but he didn't come any closer.

"I *knew* you'd come tonight. We're so close, Mary. As close as two people can ever be. We share blood, but more than that, we share pain. I've dealt it out, and you've endured it. Pain binds us. Pain makes a far stronger cement than love does. Love is an abstract human concept, meaningless, nonexistent. But pain is real. I knew we were so close that I could communicate with you at a distance, without words. I knew I could make you come after me. Each day since Monday night I've meditated, put myself in a light trance. When my mind was clear, when I was relaxed, I tried to send thoughts to you, images of murders I intended to commit. I wanted to trigger your clairvoyant vision. And it worked, didn't it?"

He was a raving lunatic—and yet he had such a calm demeanor, spoke in such measured tones.

"Didn't it work, Mary?"

"Yes."

He was pleased. "I kept a watch on Lou's house, and when you showed up there, I knew you were after me."

An especially fierce gust of wind buffeted her, drove deafening blasts of torrential rain against the hollow roof.

He took one step toward her.

"Stop right there!" she said frantically.

He obeyed her. He hadn't decided suddenly to be merciful. And certainly he wasn't afraid of her. He stopped because he was willing, even eager, to see her cower before him and to kill her slowly.

If she played along with him, she would gain minutes of life, might even find a way to escape. "If you wanted to kill me, you could have done it Monday night at the motel, before Max returned."

"That was too easy. By making you pursue me, I had more fun."

"Fun? Killing is fun?"

"There's nothing like it."

"You're insane."

"No," he said serenely. "I'm just a hunter. And everybody else is a game animal. I was born to kill. It's my purpose. I've no doubt about that. I've been killing all my life. It started with the bugs."

She remembered: she was about four years old and Alan was seven; there was a praying mantis in a big glass jar; and Alan unscrewed the lid, squirted lighter fluid on the mantis, dropped a match into the jar. For years he had gathered insects for the sole purpose of torturing them to death with chemicals, razor blades, pins, and fire.

She said, "*You* were the one who killed our cats and dogs."

"And all the other pets."

"Barry Mitchell had nothing to do with that."

He shrugged. "I got tired of the damned bugs."

He took a step toward her.

"Stop!"

He stopped, grinned.

That morning she had suggested to Max that evil was not always acquired, not always learned by example. Most educated people were convinced that, without exception, the motivations behind the antisocial acts of violent people had their roots in poverty, broken homes, childhood traumas, parental neglect or parental ineptitude. Sociologists insisted criminals were spawned primarily by social systems founded on injustice. Most psychologists appeared secure in the belief that any neurosis or psychosis could be explained in terms of Freudian or Jungian theory. But was it possible that some people were rotten from the start, hopelessly corrupt before environment had an opportunity to affect them? Was that a reactionary, medieval thought? She'd read a great deal about the XYY-man, the genetically ordained criminal type that had inspired so much scientific research over the past few years. Some people might be born less civilized than most—for chemical or genetic reasons that no one fully understood.

That was a dangerous theory. It could be misinterpreted. Every racist group would point to every hated minority as evidence of genetic inferiority. In fact, if there *were* people who were born to do evil, they were evenly distributed among all races, religions, sexes, and nationalities.

Born evil . . .

A bad seed . . .

She looked at Alan and knew that's what he was: a very special creature, both more and less than human.

A bat darted in from the rain, swooped into the hollow roof with a leathery flutter of wings that made her gasp and cringe. *Wicka-wicka-wicka!*

"I wanted to meet you here at Kimball's," Alan said, "because neither of the other towers had bats in them. I thought they'd help you remember what happened twenty-four years ago."

—and Alan takes the bat from between her legs, and it is dead, its neck is broken, soaked with her blood as well as its own, and she hurts so bad, and Alan tosses the dead bat into the box from which he got it, and he turns back to her, and she is unable to scream anymore, unable to resist, drained of strength and will, and he begins to pound her with his fists, blows landing on her stomach and chest and neck and face, a flurry of small fists driving her down into darkness . . . and when she comes to a short while later, he is standing over her with a knife he's gotten from the Mitchells' kitchen, and he brings it down, into her arm, then her side, the knife, Oh, God, the knife!

* * *

Clean thrusts. In and right out again. Clean, quick thrusts. No ripping. No tearing. No long, ugly gashes.

Max explored the dimensions of the bleeding holes with his hands and figured there wasn't any danger of his intestines sliding out of him through an enormous jagged rent in his flesh.

He supposed he should be thankful for that.

He was losing a lot of blood. His clothes were gluey, his hands sticky, the floor stained with a warm and spreading puddle. But in the dark it probably felt like a lot more blood than it really was. It felt like *quarts!*

After resting only a few seconds, before the sound of footsteps ascending the tower stairs faded away, he got up on his hands and knees.

The four punctures in his chest and stomach throbbed wildly, incessantly. He choked on the pain. He felt as if a knife still protruded from each wound.

There was no special agony when he drew his breath. Neither of his lungs had been damaged.

Another small blessing.

He crawled to the left, then to the right, dripping on the floor, groping in the perfect blackness for the gun he had dropped. He found it sooner than he'd expected.

He located the nearest wall, pressed one hand against it to steady himself, and got to his feet in spite of the pain that slammed through him like an endless series of electric shocks.

He couldn't possibly climb the tower stairs. He was barely able to walk on level ground; the steep stairs would kill him. And if by some miracle he *did* reach the observation deck, he would make so much noise in the ascent that the killer would be waiting for him; he'd be blown away the instant he achieved the top step.

The only thing he could do was go for help. Back to the parking lot. To the Mercedes. Fast as he could move. Let Lou know what had happened.

Aware that every second wasted might count against Mary, he pushed away from the wall. He staggered into the vast, dark room. Although he was dizzy and slightly disoriented, he thought he knew which way to go to find the corridor that served the coffee shop; but in any event, he could do nothing but trust his instinct. Each step caused new bubbles of pain to burst in his guts. He felt as if he were walking miles, and he wondered if he were going in circles.

Just as despair began to grip him, he stumbled around a corner into a corridor that was less dark than the main hall of the arcade. Vague grayish light, the next thing to nonexistent, shimmered farther down the hall: light from the harbor boat parade, light shining through the coffee shop's exterior windows, bouncing around, then leaking thinly through the mullioned doors.

He walked down the corridor with his right hand on his stomach, as if trying to squeeze shut his wounds. He went through the coffee shop doors, between the tables, and fell to his knees at the window that looked out on the boardwalk and harbor. It was closed, and he didn't think he had the strength to lift it.

Love is strength, he told himself. Find strength in your love for Mary. What would you have or be without her? Nothing.

Outside, lightning ripped open the sky again. The reflections of light from its electric blade shone through the window; and for an instant it seemed to turn to ice the rain that streamed down the glass.

* * *

In the cold rain Chief John Patmore stooped beside Lou Pasternak and turned him onto his back, used the flashlight to study his face and then his blood-sodden clothes. "Bergen got to him. He's been stabbed."

Holtzman said, "Is he dead?"

The chief felt for a pulse in one of the cool, limp wrists. "I think he is. But you'd better call an ambulance anyway. There might be others."

Holtzman ran back to the patrol car.

* * *

Only seven or eight feet of rain-slicked planks separated her from Alan.

She had to keep him talking. The moment he lost interest in the conversation, he'd use the butcher knife. Besides, even if she were going to die, there were things she still had to know.

"So Berton Mitchell never touched me," she said.

"Not even once."

"I sent an innocent man to prison."

Alan nodded, smiled, as if she'd merely told him that he was wearing a pretty shirt.

"I caused him to commit suicide," she said.

"Wish I could have seen him swinging."

"I disgraced his family."

Alan laughed.

"Why would I do that?" she asked. "Why would I tell them that he attacked me when it was actually you?"

Alan said, "You were in the intensive care unit at the hospital for four days. When the crisis passed and you no longer needed the support machines, they transferred you to a private room."

"I remember."

"Father and I virtually lived there for two weeks. Even Mother crawled out of her bottle to visit every couple days. I played the concerned big brother, oh-so-attentive for a nine-year-old boy."

"The nurses thought you were cute," she said.

"There were lots of times when I was alone with you in that hospital room. Sometimes just for minutes, sometimes for as much as an hour."

Another bat flew in from the storm and settled in the rafters overhead.

Alan said, "Your lips and gums were so badly swollen and full of stitches that you couldn't talk for eight days—but you could *listen*. You were conscious most of the time. And when I was alone with you, I told you over and over again what I would do to you if you dared to expose me. I told you I'd come after you with the bats again . . . let them tear you apart." He was leering at her. "I told you I'd force you to eat the bats alive, that I'd make you bite off their heads and swallow if you told on me. I warned you that you'd better put all the blame on Berton Mitchell—or else."

She was shaking. She had to get control of herself, had to be prepared to move fast if she was given an opportunity to escape. However, the tremors continued, no matter how hard she tried to still them.

Alan said, "Then a funny thing happened. You told them it was Mitchell who did it to you—but you *believed* it. I'd achieved more than I thought. I'd gotten way down in you, way down where it counts, and I'd worked a little magic. You actually came to believe it *was* Berton Mitchell. You couldn't accept the truth, couldn't tolerate living in the same house with me after what I'd done to you, so you convinced yourself that I hadn't done anything at all, that I was your friend and that the bogeyman was someone else."

"Why?" she asked weakly. "Why did you hurt me?"

"I meant to kill you. I thought you were dead when I left the cottage."

"Why did you want to kill me?"

"It was fun."

"That's all? Just because it was 'fun'?"

"I hated you," he said.

"What had I done?"

"Nothing."

"Then why did you hate me?"

"I hate everyone."

Lightning.

A gust of wind.

"You killed Mitchell's family."

"Seemed like a good idea, wiping out an entire family."

"Why? Was that 'fun,' too?"

"You should have seen the house burn."

"God Almighty, you were only fourteen then."

"That's old enough to kill," he said. "Don't forget, I tried to kill you five years before that. And when I thought you were dead . . . when I pulled the knife out of you for the last time . . . oh, Mary, you can't know how that felt! So natural. Like it wasn't my first kill at all. Like I'd stabbed people to death a thousand times before. And I was only nine!"

He stepped closer.

His shoes squished on the wet floor.

Desperately she said, "You killed Patty Spooner, too. Didn't you, Alan?"

"She was a bitch."

"No. She was sweet."

"A rotten bitch."

"Why did you defile the altar?"

The question clearly intrigued him. "Killing Patty in that church . . . was so different . . . so special. I knew that night that I truly *was* a demon and a vampire. I realized I was meant to destroy anything holy, anything good."

"You killed Marie Sanzini."

"And her three roommates."

"At one time, you loved Marie."

"No. I only dated her."

"Why would you want to kill her?"

"Why not?" he asked.

"You murdered Rochelle Drake."

"Don't tell me I loved her, too."

"You once said you did."

"I lied. I love no one."

"Why did you kill the beautician and his wife?"

"They were in my way."

A ship's horn blared across the water.

"You murdered Erika Larsson . . . and now you're going to kill the queen of the Christmas boat parade."

He glanced at the lighted vessels cruising slowly through the winter rain. "The storm will have driven her off the deck. I'll have to take her some other time."

"But what is she to you?"

"Don't you know who's queen? Jenny Canning."

"Ah, not her. She's good. So gentle. She mustn't die."

"She's just the most recent of my bitches. She's game like all the others." He was getting weary; he looked at the blade in his hand and licked his lips.

"Your women always leave you," Mary said.

"Or I leave them."

"Why can't you hold one?"

"Sex," he said. "Tenderness is a bore. They all want me to be tender. I can only manage it for a few weeks or months."

"What do you mean?"

"I like sex rough," he said, his voice almost a growl. "The rougher the better. After a while, when the novelty of a new body . . . a new girl . . . wears off, then the only way I can come is when I hurt them. And that turns them off . . . that and the other thing."

"What other thing?" she asked.

"They won't let me drink their blood."

She stared, shocked.

He said, "Now and then I like to have sex . . . and drink their blood."

"You cut them?"

"No, no. Menstrual blood."

Shocked, she closed her eyes.

Heard him move.

Opened her eyes!

He took two quick steps and was less than the length of the knife from her.

* * *

Max rolled from the yard-high windowsill onto the boardwalk, and the short fall seemed like twenty miles. In his mind, at least, he tumbled over and over. For a long moment after he fell, floating in a sea of pain, he considered the appealing, beckoning emptiness that welled up inside of him. Then he thought about Mary and about transforming love into physical strength. Somehow he smothered the pain and clambered to his feet.

The pistol was still in his left hand. It felt impossibly heavy. He tried to drop it, but he wasn't able to let go. His paralytic fingers were hooked tightly, immovably around the butt.

He swayed and looked at the line of decorated boats gliding through the rain and thought how pretty they were—and suddenly realized that he wasn't here to watch the parade. Silently cursing himself, he lumbered along the boardwalk. Each shaky step he took was an adventure ten times greater than the one before it; and each yard of ground he covered was a triumph.

On all sides of him, the night pumped in and out, in and out like the muscles of a heart.

He turned the corner of the pavilion and saw that no more than a hundred feet away two men were coming behind flashlights.

Lou and who else?

He tried to shout.

He had no voice.

* * *

Alan's eyes seemed to have light *behind* them. They were blue eyes like hers, but a peculiar and piercing blue. Eyes like the blade of the knife in his hand—sharp, cold, deadly.

"How many people have you killed?"

He didn't answer.

He raised his left hand. He put his icy fingertips against her temple, felt the pulse thumping there. He slid his fingers down, traced the delicate line of her jaw, then raised them and touched her lips.

Trembling, she said, "You've killed more than thirty-five, haven't you?"

"How'd you know that?"

"If you killed so many over the years," she said, "why didn't I go after you before this?"

"You were asked to work on some of the murders I committed," Alan said, "but you refused. I advised you to turn down all of those cases, and you listened to me. I think you suspected the truth, but you hid it from yourself."

"You tried to murder me when I was six years old. So why have you waited twenty-four years to try again?"

"Oh, I originally intended to get you a few months after you were released from the hospital. I figured I'd have to wait that long to allay suspicions. But then I was going to knock you off in a carefully planned accident."

His fingertips gently stroked her brows.

He said, "I thought of throwing you down a long flight of stairs and then saying you tripped and fell. But I finally settled on drowning you in the swimming pool."

"Why didn't you?"

"By the time I could safely go after you again, you'd begun to exhibit psychic powers. You fascinated me. I wanted to see what would happen to you next."

She said, "If Max is dead, I'll need your help again. I'll need you to guide me through the visions."

He laughed. "Darling, I'm not naïve."

"Do you think I'd turn you in to the police? I haven't told them about you for twenty-four years. Why would I now?"

"Then, you didn't know," he said. "But now you do."

He put his hand on her breast.

She flinched.

"My lovely little sister," he said.

"Don't."

* * *

Carrying a flashlight in his left hand and a revolver in his right, his shoulders drawn up in an unsuccessful attempt to keep the cold rain off the back of his neck, Rudy Holtzman accompanied the chief along the side of the pavilion.

Patmore stopped suddenly.

"What's the matter?" Holtzman asked nervously. He was very keyed up.

"There's a man ahead."

Holtzman raised his flashlight.

A man was approaching them, no more than fifty feet away.

"It's Bergen," Patmore said.

Bergen was staggering like a drunk.

"He's got a gun!" Patmore said.

Remembering Erika Larsson's viciously mutilated body, remembering the blood splashed everywhere inside her house, remembering Lou Pasternak on the macadam parking lot, Holtzman raised his service revolver and fired.

Max Bergen was flung backward by the impact of the bullet.

* * *

Alan pressed against her. He put his left hand around her throat.

She told herself to resist, to fight back. She was strong, not weak. A weak person would have sought escape in madness twenty-four years ago. But she was strong; she had hung on to her sanity and had developed psychic abilities as a way to keep herself alive. She should be able to find the will to fight him now.

He held the blade to her cheek as if branding her, the point below her right eye.

"I wonder," he said, "if you were blind, could you still see your clairvoyant visions?"

She snapped. Abruptly, violently, her fear vanished in an explosion of anger and hatred far more intense than any emotion she'd ever known. Twenty-four years of hidden, festering hatred went off like a bomb in her subconscious. She despised him. Loathed him. He wasn't fit to live. Never had been. Never would be. All she wanted was a chance to hurt him as badly as he had hurt her. She didn't even care any longer whether she lived or died. She wanted only to get him down, tie him down, torture him, hurt him, cut him, choke him, beat him, see him cry. She wanted most of all to put the bats on him, to rub them in his face, make them claw and bite, force them into his mouth while they were squirming and still alive—

Overhead two dozen bats began to scream in the darkness: a shrill chorus of tiny voices.

Startled, Alan looked up.

A single bat swept down, hooked its claws into Alan's coat collar. It fluttered wildly at his neck.

She couldn't believe what she had done.

Alan let go of her, reached behind him, grabbed the animal. He struggled with it, finally tore it loose and pitched it away from him.

His hand was bleeding.

In the past few days, every time she'd had a vision in which the killer's face began to be revealed as Alan's, she had chased away the truth by distracting herself with poltergeists. She had been responsible for the glass dogs careening around Dr. Cauvel's office; the pistol floating in air; the sea gulls at The Laughing Dolphin Restaurant; inanimate objects flying this way and that in Lou's bathroom. Max had been right.

Now she would use the bats.

Another one flew down and clung to Alan's face.

He screamed. Ripped it away. Dropped the knife.

Blood streamed from his forehead into his eyes.

Chittering, beating the air furiously with their wings, three more bats attacked him. One tangled in his hair. The other two fixed themselves to his throat.

"Kill him," she said.

Flailing at himself, Alan turned away from her. He weaved across the platform toward the stairs.

Every bat in the rafters descended upon him. They tore at his head and face and neck, clawed his hands, bit his fingers and hung on and wouldn't be shaken loose. When he screamed, one of them got into his mouth.

He stumbled down the tower stairs, bouncing from wall to wall.

She picked up the flashlight and followed him.

The bats stayed with Alan. If anything, their cries grew louder, angrier.

Five steps down he fell, rolled to the next landing, got up, went on, plucked a bat from his nose, tried to shield his eyes with one arm, fell again, couldn't keep from screaming, had to bite another bat that crawled from his chin into his mouth, had to spit out part of it, gagged, choked, stumbled, leaped from the final flight of stairs into the dark arcade and collapsed.

She walked out of the archway and stood over him.

He was very still.

One by one the bats rose from the body, circled, and flew back up the stairwell to the belfry.

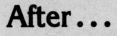

AT NOON THE December sun fell straight down on the cemetery, leaving virtually no shadows on the grass. There was a chill in the air that didn't come from the sea wind; it radiated from the tombstones and the silent mourners and, most of all, from the plain dark casket suspended above the open grave.

As the winch motor began to purr and the coffin lowered out of sight, Mary turned away. She walked between the small granite and marble monuments toward the open wrought-iron gate, walked by herself, unassisted, alone, because that was what she wanted.

She sat for a while behind the wheel of the Mercedes and stared down the hills to the sea. She was waiting for her hands to stop shaking.

Yesterday, she had buried Alan; and in spite of what he had been and done, she had grieved for him. But this final ceremony was far sadder than yesterday's. She felt as if a piece of her own flesh had been torn from her.

She needed to cry and wash some of the pain from her system, but she choked the sobs before they could start and squeezed back the tears. She had one more duty to perform before she could allow herself to break down.

She started the Mercedes and drove away from the cemetery.

* * *

Sunlight streamed through the venetian blinds and banded the private hospital room with shadow and light.

Max was sitting up in bed, one shoulder heavily bandaged, one arm in a sling. He was drawn, sallow, sunken-eyed; but he had a gentle smile for Mary when she came through the door.

She kissed him and sat in the chair beside his bed. They

held hands in silence for perhaps a minute; then she began to tell him about Lou's funeral. When she had nothing more to say, she leaned away from her chair, rested her forehead on the edge of the mattress and finally began to weep. He murmured soothingly, massaged her neck, stroked her hair. She broke down completely. She cried out loud for Lou, but for herself as well; his death left a hole in her life. However, her despair couldn't last forever; eventually, gradually, her sobbing subsided.

For a while they listened to classical music on the radio, neither of them able to speak.

Later, over dinner in the hospital room, her eyes grew heavy, and she couldn't stifle her yawns. "Sorry. I didn't get much sleep."

"Nightmares?" Max asked, concerned.

"No. In fact, I had lovely dreams—the first pleasant dreams I've ever had in my life. I woke up about four-thirty in the morning, exhilarated, full of energy. I even went for a nice long walk."

"You? A walk? Alone at night?"

She smiled. "I don't mind being alone as much as I used to," she said. "And I'm not afraid of the dark anymore."